Z2136

Z2134

Book 3

SEAN PLATT

DAVID W. WRIGHT

STERLING & STONE

To YOU, the reader.
Thank you for your support.
Thank you for the wonderful emails.
Thank you for the thoughtful reviews.
Thank you for reading and loving our stories.

ONE

Anastasia Lovecraft

JANUARY 2136
  A half mile from the Halo …

ANA PEERED THROUGH THE SCOPE, focusing her rifle on the veering road below, watching and waiting for the transport vans to pass, trigger-ready to free her brother.

There were three roads leading to the Halo, where the Darwin Games would detonate in a bloodbath known as the Opening Rush — always with host Kirk Kirkman's untethered glee. Only City 6 came in from the west, and in the months that Ana had been spying on their routes, the State always sent two vans. She assumed one transported prisoners while the other carried City Watchers as backup in case the trip turned sour.

She adjusted her position, still chilly on the fresh-fallen snow despite her insulated jacket and pants; the all-black outfit had been scavenged from a group of bandits two months ago. The jacket kept her relatively warm, and more importantly, allowed Ana to blend into the line of trees where she'd been ordered by Liam and Katrina to hide. She held her stare down the hill on a perfect view of the stretch where the vans were scheduled to pass at any moment.

Ana tried to ignore the rolls and roars in her stomach. There had been no time to eat — not that she could have soaked more than a morsel of bread in the stewing acid in her gut.

"How ya doing, baby?" Liam chirped in her earpiece, as if he could sense her unease from his spot on the road's north side, where the tree line crept closer to the old, cracked concrete. He and Katrina were waiting downhill from Ana.

"Scared as hell."

"We've gone over this a dozen times," Liam reminded her. "You've nothing to worry about. Two vans, like always."

"I know," Ana said, though she couldn't quite shake the gnawing sensation that plans meant little and things wouldn't be simple at all.

She flashed back nearly seven months to the caravan robbery gone wrong and the ambush that had claimed most of their party. "What if this is a trap?"

Katrina, with the most years of experience fighting the State, answered for Liam. "If it's a trap, we deal with it. We've not come this far to abandon Adam on the off chance that it *might* be a trap." A beat, then, "Have we?"

Ana paused, waiting — *wanting* — for Liam to back her up. Instead he said nothing, and Ana took it for the invisible nod to Katrina that it was.

Lately it seemed that he and Katrina were on the same page more often than not. Nothing official, but if the trio chopping their way through the Barrens ever stopped to cast ballots, the vote would've gone 2–1 with Ana on the losing end, almost always.

She tried not to let her past annoyance poison her present thinking around Adam's reality. Emotions weren't part of the mission. Katrina was right. They had to get him *now*. It would be nearly impossible to find him in the chaos following the Opening Rush.

Ana sighed. "You're right. Just getting butterflies is all."

"It would be odd if you weren't, Ana." She imagined Katrina's smile, not quite maternal but supportive in its own uncomfortable way. "Don't worry. We'll be fine, and we *will* get your brother."

"Damned right," Liam chirped with a gusto that reminded Ana why she loved him so much.

"Okay, I'm good."

Black dots in the distance shut her up.

She raised her rifle and narrowed her eye through the scope. "They're coming."

"Copy," Katrina and Liam said together.

They too were likely watching — Liam through his scope and Katrina through a pair of fancy binoculars she'd stolen from Hydrangea before their flight from Sutherland's insanity six months before.

Ana turned her scope to see Liam and Katrina rushing toward the road to place the spike strips about ten feet apart. They were painted the same dull gray as the cracked concrete, but Ana didn't think the difference in color was enough to keep a sharp eye from seeing the strips, which was why she was tasked to shoot at the drivers. She'd become an excellent shot since shedding her old life in City 6, though she still couldn't match Liam's or Katrina's sniper eyes.

The real reason they'd put Ana up on the hill was to keep her from danger — in case things went south. She was the only known person who had contracted the virus and come out the other side. Oswald had placed an incredible burden on her when he claimed that she might be humanity's last and only hope. He believed her blood was the final piece in finding a cure.

Of course, that was assuming the zombie-cyborg doctor ever got away from Sutherland, where he'd stayed behind to work in a lab filled with samples of Ana's blood. Even if Oswald *could* develop the cure, it would do the world no good in the hands of a psycho like Sutherland — the madman who had forced her father to unleash a strain of the zombie virus inside City 1.

Ana, Liam, and Katrina might have to liberate Oswald and work for that cure. Until then, Liam and Katrina treated Ana like an Old Nation porcelain doll.

Ana stared at Liam through the scope. The past seven months had been cruel. He was thin, though his gauntness was cloaked by oversized clothes and a thick, dark beard that made him look more like a bandit than she cared to admit.

She turned her scope back toward the approaching vans, now 300 yards away: large dusty transports with tinted windows driving side by side like those that had ferried her to the Games.

"Three hundred yards away."

"Copy," they said, assuming position in clustered shadows along the tree-lined road.

Ana inched her finger toward the trigger, barely breathing as she waited for her moment.

She had to wait until the vans were close enough to the strips that a sharp turn would be deadly and a full stop impossible. Hitting a pair of moving targets in rapid succession had seemed improbable while she'd been waiting in her perch, but now felt nearly impossible.

She closed her eyes, breathed deeply, and tried to shove her fear as low as it would go.

Focus. For Adam.

As the vehicles drew nearer, she could see two men through the front window of the left van — wearing City Watch dark-visored helmets, though they worked for the State-run network and weren't really Watchers at all.

Focus.

She lined up her first shot, anticipating where the van would be by estimating its speed and accounting for the slight breeze and the angle of her shot — skills Katrina had taught her during the long months leading up to their mission.

She squeezed the trigger and, without waiting to see if she hit her target, quickly turned the rifle toward the second van.

But it raced by in a blur through her line of sight before she could shoot.

She took her eyes from the rifle and looked down as the tires of the second van ripped into the strips. The van she'd shot at screeched to a stop — she probably hadn't killed the driver, or the passenger was quick-thinking and reached over to slam on the brakes.

The second van kept going before sliding to a stop on the right, putting about forty yards of road between the vehicles, making it impossible for Ana to see both vans through her scope.

Her heartbeat somehow found a way to pound harder. Ana wished she could get closer to the road, where she might be able to do something useful.

Instead, she raised the rifle and trained it back and forth between the vans, watching and waiting for doors to open, men to emerge.

Liam and Katrina burst forth from the trees. Ana

hoped they'd reach the drivers before either had the notion to harm Adam or any of the other passengers.

"Get out!" Katrina fired her blaster at the first van. The window and driver disintegrated into a bright shock of dust.

Ana scowled from the top of the hill, hating that someone else was doing her job.

The helmeted passenger got out of the van with raised hands, likely begging for his life.

Liam approached the second van, with his rifle aimed. "Get out!"

Ana noticed how much darker the windows were on the second van — dark enough that both driver and passenger were barely suggestions.

The gnawing in her gut tightened.

She flashed back on the zombies pouring from the transport truck during last year's failed mission …

"Something's wrong," she said into the radio.

"What?" Katrina asked.

"The windows of the other van. I'm having trouble seeing through them."

Liam stepped closer to the van, rifle raised. "Get the fuck out!"

Ana turned her scope back to the first van's passenger, frozen behind Katrina's aim. His gloved right hand trembled above his head.

Maybe nervous hands were shaking her view.

But then she zoomed in and saw that his hand held something — a small black square with a blinking red light.

She remembered the driver they'd pulled over, opening the doors to unleash a horde of zombies.

"THERE'S SOMETHING IN HIS HAND!"

The passenger turned to her spot on the hill.

Time crawled as his fingers curled around the device — one pressing down on the flashing red light.

For a moment Ana could only hear the rapid pulse throbbing in her ear.

Then the suspicious van exploded.

TWO

Adam Lovecraft

ADAM WAS DEAD.

At least he wanted to be. His father, Jonah, had been murdered in front of any citizen who cared to watch the cruel display on the ample widescreen monitors plastered across all the cities, murdered by a man whom Adam had looked up to almost as much as his father — Chief Keller.

Since that moment every breath had felt harder to draw. Yet strangely, Adam had not cried.

Prison had withered his tears. Time felt borrowed but was a debt he didn't care to repay. His strongest recurring thought was the aching certainty that Ana was still alive somewhere, pursued closely by a bruised and ever-swelling need for revenge.

The Darwins were coming. Adam didn't know why he hadn't been cast outside the Walls with an army of cameras already, but the trip was inevitable. What happened to his father was all the more powerful because of its rarity. Death seemed pervasive to Adam now that his eyes had finally been opened to what was happening inside the cities, but public executions still weren't a regular thing inside the Walls. Outside, among the charred and rotten hands of the undead, it happened all the time. Adam would one day blink into the bright light outside the City, but the thin sliver of hope that he *might* one day see Ana kept him hanging on, like a cupped palm to a wind-flickered flame.

Adam's back was pressed to the cold metal of a pitch-black van, on its way to the Halo. He hoped they would return to asphalt soon. The dirt, snow, or whatever they were driving through was doing terrible things to his already tangled gut.

Soon, the door would open and he'd be yanked from the van into blinding light. A cannon blast would herald the chaos of a mad dash by contestants, all willing to kill for supplies, murdering to live through the Opening Rush.

The chaos Adam was pretty sure he wouldn't survive.

In this, the beginning of Adam's end, darkness was his blanket. The van's only light bled from lights on a black metal cuff glowing blue around his wrist. A small gray screen sat atop the cuff, with blue lights running around the top and bottom of the cuff, with tiny holes running beneath the screen.

Though Adam had theories, he didn't know what the bracelet was. The man who had fastened it to his wrist grunted as he did so, but his coward's face stayed hidden behind a black visor, stripping Adam's chance to search for the truth in his eyes. It felt cold, as if the bracelet could not absorb warmth from his body. After a while on his wrist, it made Adam feel colder than he was, and despite more than six months spent mostly in isolation, the new frost in his body made him feel twice as alone.

In every game Adam had ever seen, vans usually carried more than one passenger. He didn't want to wonder why he was the only one in this van, because the truth was likely as ugly as every other truth he'd come to know since his father was first accused of murdering a mother whom Adam still missed every day.

But he couldn't help dwelling on his solitary transport, remembering how much he used to enjoy this part of the Darwins: the Pre-Game. He loved getting to know the players and picking his favorites before the cannon was shot. That was always his favorite part, because there was never any killing, and often there were jokes.

Now he was in the dark alone, save for small cameras in all four corners, offering a bird's-eye view of his death ride. He wondered how many people were watching him, as he'd watched so many in the past. And what kind of contestant did he appear to be? Was anyone voting on him as a potential winner?

Some contestants were quiet, most tried to seem braver than they were, keeping quivers from speech and flinches from eyes. A few always cried. Some picked fights. Adam's favorites pretended that being in a van on its way to the Halo, and the promise of spending their final few days on the run — gasping and hoping for bullets instead of a death by feasting undead — wasn't so awful at all.

He wanted to be strong enough to pretend and bury his fear behind jokes like those men and women. But there was no one else to joke with, and that absence made everything worse.

Something was wrong, because things were so different. Every Game he'd ever seen had *at least* two players from each City, yet Adam hadn't heard a second van rolling ahead or behind them.

I can't be the only one from City 6, can I?

Adam had been on a fairly fixed schedule for his long months in prison, moved from his cell to the yard for an hour each weekday, two on the weekends. The consistent routine made it easy to tick off the time — which was important when trying to preserve a sense of normalcy. It also helped him cling to his sanity, knowing there were others around him. Others *like* him.

Adam had done his best to track prisoners as they came and went, but the block's population stayed in constant flux, with guards ushering ever larger groups around the prison. Adam could mostly only stare through a large window in his cell overlooking the yard, a view designed for his torment, trapping him in the dark even as he was bathed in the day's brightest light.

Like his glowing blue bracelet, the sun never quite warmed his body as Adam sat for long hours alone in his cell.

On his ninth weekend, the other prisoners disappeared and never returned — and he realized they *weren't* like him at all. Adam was led to another part of the prison that he had never known about, even as a Junior Watcher. The second cell was smaller, colder, and — impossibly — even lonelier. He found himself surprised to miss his horrible view.

He started hearing the whispers, from a few guards in this new area. They all wanted him to hear, and to be afraid, because fear in isolation rotted the body. There were whispers among the Watchers of a special edition of the Darwins brewing, with additional (or fewer) players, perhaps an extended play length. Different rules. New weapons.

Harsher environments would also make sense, but Adam was only guessing from the few snippets he was allowed to hear. It turned out that, for him, guessing without knowing made him sicker, as he waited to see what Keller — a vengeful man, moving his diseased breed of justice from father to son — was planning.

Adam saw no one except his daily interrogators after the move. Each day he stayed strong, giving them nothing and hoping to make his murdered father proud — a sentiment he would have sneered at just a few months ago. They came in at different times, usually in the morning when he was still blurry-eyed. Each time they ordered him to rat out members of the Underground. Beyond the interrogations, they only came in to bring Adam rancid food or drag him out of his cell for the occasional shower. He always trembled as the door cracked open, certain that this time he'd see Keller instead of the guard and finally suffer the ugly man's wrath.

Now, in the back of the van and Halo bound, Adam wondered if he'd ever see Keller again. The chief could be watching him right now. Bile rose in his throat as the van came to a grinding halt and jostled the thought from his head.

His heart started to race. Even though he'd been numb for months, the Halo's "promise" poured fresh life into his body. The rear door swung open after what felt like eternity. The bracelet finally felt warm as it hummed, then shone a brighter blue.

A speaker blared from the guard's helmet. "Exit the van, Lovecraft! Stand in line and wait for the cannon." He pointed a gun in Adam's face. "Now."

He stepped into the snow, boots sinking as he shivered and rubbed warmth into his arms.

He looked around, wondering where in the hell he was. Somewhere he'd never seen: the center of a giant stadium, surrounded by ancient and mostly rotten seats.

Games were usually confined to wilderness areas. It made for better shows to see contestants fleeing through forest to escape the swarming hordes of undead. Adam couldn't remember ever having seen anything in an arena like this one.

The guard spun him around and shoved him toward what looked like a hundred or so contestants — the most Adam had ever seen waiting for the Games. Four oversized hunter orbs buzzed overhead, hovering a few feet above the line. A pair of men — behemoths in black suits and mirrored helmets — stood at the line's rear, rifles ready. Many more guards (they seemed more militant than those usually assigned to the Games) were scattered through the snow, black on white like a sickness on flesh.

Everything seemed larger: the stadium, contestants, guards, and weapons — *the Games.*

He swallowed hard, looking up and down the line at all the soon-to-be-dead. Contestants were outfitted in the same blue jumpsuits that he'd been wearing for months. Each City usually had an assigned color — that made it easier for viewers to identify and root for their favorites. The hundred or so contestants in the same blue didn't make sense.

The line started on the far side of the field from where Adam was standing, and wrapped the perimeter spooling back toward him. In the center of the field there were mountains of crates stacked four high and many more deep. All except the smallest were wide and tall enough to hold many humans ... or creatures that used to be.

Adam saw four exits and, rising above the stadium walls, a crumbled city with old buildings like diseased fingers raking into the sky. After months of solitary confinement, he had hardened himself for this reality, preparing himself to be the killer he would need to become. But as the moment raced toward him, Adam wondered if he'd be able to be as ruthless as he needed to be.

He looked down the row, dividing contestants into two halves: those Adam thought he could kill, and those he knew to run from. He searched for familiar faces, not really expecting to find one. About twenty people down, he actually did.

A stout, dark-skinned man in his forties, with thick hair, a scruffy beard, and a pair of piercing green eyes that Adam would recognize anywhere: Derek Colton, a friend of his father's from City Watch.

He hadn't seen Derek in forever, let alone thought of him. He had no clue why the man was waiting to be zombie food now. His dad had always spoken fondly of his friend. Adam wondered if he was an ally, as he watched the man trying not to shiver, fifty feet away. Was he Underground? A traitor like Michael — and now Adam? Or something else? Something worse? Maybe a murderer from the Dark Quarter?

A dark thought crept in: *Better to be killed by a friend than an enemy.*

Derek Colton must have thought something similar. He barely turned but gave Adam a mostly imperceptible smile. Like a ray of sunlight on his face, it flickered and faded before he looked ahead and left Adam to wonder if he had seen what he thought — and whether he could trust what he thought he saw.

All four orbs crackled to life with a loud shriek. Screens lit with Kirk Kirkman's weaselly face. Adam's bracelet glowed brighter and buzzed, clearly in response to the orbs. A familiar crescendo of the State's National Song swelled the air with the usual fanfare as the screens showed fireworks erupting over City 6. Adam saw the usual rowdy — yet still somehow orderly — crowds of people watching from a large studio in City 6, waving plenty of flags, swaying in time with the orchestra.

Adding to his confusion, the cameras never cut to another city. The Games showed all the cities. Now cameras panned through the many varied pockets of City 6, catching swarms of rapt citizens staring up into the lenses so Adam could see them onscreen.

Cameras seemed to crawl into every corner of City 6, but there was no footage from 5 or 4, or anywhere else, for that matter.

Finally, the broadcast cut back to Kirkman. Cheery as ever, he chirped, "Welcome to a special edition of the Darwin Games!"

He waited as the audience erupted with pent-up excitement, then boomed:

"We welcome you to this very special edition of the Darwin Games, our first ever *All-Traitor Edition*. The men and women standing before you are Underground scum, *each and every one!* These are the people who threaten our safety. These are the people who endanger our lives. These are the people who have turned on their neighbors and conspired to weaken our State. Who conspired against *you*. And since the heart of this dark cancer was thriving most *in* City 6, we've decided to host the show here this time *for* City 6. Now, who's ready to watch these traitors pay?"

Kirkman paused for applause — no shortage from the overly enthusiastic crowd. Cameras continued to flicker from pocket to pocket showing just how invested the entire City was to witness its enemies' punishment.

"The All-Traitor Edition has a record number of contestants. There are exactly 104 traitors who had direct ties to the terrorist attack on City 1. Killing these people isn't just our duty, but our obligation for a healthy, prosperous State. And to be clear: there will be no glory for anyone. This time, for the first time in Darwin Games history, there will be no winner. In the All-Traitor Edition, *no one* will get to see City 7."

Another beat for applause, then the camera cut to Adam, standing surprised in the snow. "After all, we wouldn't want to chance the Games being won by Adam Lovecraft, now would we? *Of course not!* Just look at what his father did with *his* second chance. I hope you're ready for the best Games we've ever had, knowing that when they end — however they end — we will have justice for what happened to our fine citizens in City 1."

Another pause for the crowd, the longest so far. Adam imagined the many months of advertisement preceding this *special edition* of the Games. The State would have had every citizen drooling by the time the contestants were being marched out onto the snowy field. He thought of all the commemorative wrappers with the special edition's colorful logo that would cover the arcade food. An ugly thing to admit, but as Adam stared up at the screen, steeling his gaze at the view, he couldn't help admiring it: the logo was pretty amazing — the City Watch eye surrounded by flames like a blazing star.

Adam thought back through most of his life and knew that in a different present where his father was still a decorated Watcher, he would have loved seeing traitors like himself getting shredded to pieces.

"We brought our contestants to the Outback, a four-square-mile city from the Old Nation, teeming with thousands of zombies, bandits, and ..." Kirkman dropped his voice to a whisper, "God only knows what else."

The orb screens showed an overview of the crumbling buildings, streets filled with zombies, and bandits driving through the city with their victims' heads on pikes.

His voice back to a fever pitch, Kirkman continued. "For your enjoyment, we've outfitted our contestants with some very special Darwin Games Special Edition bracelets. Aren't they pretty, folks?"

The screen cut to a half-dozen bracelets like Adam's, glowing bright blue on a swath of ivory velvet, then to a tall man wearing one, seemingly panicked as he raced through the woods. He clomped through the snow, dodging thin and barren branches. Adam wasn't sure if the screen was showing Games footage or something else, but the background music, like the image, held a steady beat of terror. The fleeing man was armed, running with his pistol in front of him, ready to fire at the slightest movement.

A scream, shrill and sudden, pierced the air onscreen, yelping from the man's bracelet. Zombies exploded all around him, pouring through the trees, arms outstretched. The man fumbled through the snow, occasionally firing at pursuers until his blaster had fully lost its charge. No chance to reload, or anything else. Zombies swallowed the view in a wave that rolled so fast that the man never stood a chance. The camera hovered above the fury until the swarm receded to piles of bloody flesh, scattered around a still-glowing ring of bright blue.

"These bracelets cannot be taken off, and to make things even more fun for you at home, they are programmed to go off at random. A contestant's bracelet might go off never, just once, or once a day." As if confiding in a friend, Kirkman smirked, "Watch out, Adam!"

The host continued. "These fancy bracelets emit a loud alarm, along with a strong chemical scent specially designed to attract zombies. Zombie Alerts, as we call them, will last anywhere from a minute to an hour. *Why the bracelets,* you ask? Because they'll keep the Underground scum from sticking together like rats ... and because we think you'll love them!"

The cheers were deafening. There wouldn't be a person of age in City 6, or anywhere else, who wasn't watching the Games and rooting for the traitors' downfall.

"Though this is a new location, rules for the Opening Rush are the same. In the field's center we've stacked an abundance of weapons and much-needed supplies. Of course — as promised — we also have boxes of zombies."

Kirkman turned his address to the contestants.

"Test your luck and load up on supplies and weapons now, or flee to one of the four exits and take your chances in the Outback."

His face took on a devilish look. "Just one thing you should know ... we've *bombarded* the Outback with flyers announcing rewards for anyone who captures and kills Darwin players. *Be careful who you trust.*

"And, oh, one more thing. Before any of you start getting ideas of trying to leave the Outback, know that if you do so, your bracelets will go off. And if you think you can avoid both zombies *and* our hundreds of hunter orbs circling the Outback, THINK AGAIN!"

The screen showed orbs swarming the Outback. With no winner or chance of escaping, Adam wondered how he would ever survive. He wondered how many people would even attempt to just outlast the Games.

If there's no Mesa to battle in, why not just hide and wait things out?

But then he understood the network's genius. No player in the Games could ever expect to live in the Outback for any amount of time. Someone or something — other players, bandits, zombies, or hunter orbs — would find and kill them.

There was no escape.

The State surely planned to rob the players of hope, to further weaken them, but so long as he stayed alive, Adam would continue to search for a way out — of the Games and the Outback, bracelet be damned.

Kirkman's voice went into its familiar singsong as he wound up the audience. "And nooooooow … let the Darwin Games BEGIN!"

Fireworks exploded in the sky. Even with the noise, Adam could hear zombies jostling boxes.

And then it began.

The line of contestants broke like a wave crashing onto the field in every direction, most toward the weapons and zombies.

But Adam spun in the other direction, toward the tunnel ahead and to his left, out into the broken city toward the only hope he barely had.

THREE

Anastasia Lovecraft

ANA STARED down at the exploded van in open-mouthed horror. Chunks of truck littered the road. Fire crackled out from the billowing clouds, marring her view of Liam and Katrina as well as the trigger man from City 6.

"Liam!" she cried out, digging into the snow to shove herself up.

She grabbed the rifle and started down the incline, eyes searching for signs of life, friend or foe.

Please, please, please be okay.

Nearing the road she heard coughing, then saw Katrina trying to stand. The man from City 6 was moving toward her, blaster drawn.

Ana raised her rifle, looked down the sight, and fired twice.

Her first bullet missed, but the second pierced the side of the man's black helmet and sent him to the ground.

Katrina stood, looking around, dazed but seemingly in one piece.

"Liam!" Ana cried out again.

No response as she rounded the first van and found

him face down on the edge of the road. She couldn't tell if he'd turned and run at her warning, or if the blast's impact had thrown him.

Heart in her throat, she raced over and dropped to her knees beside him in the snow.

At first glance she saw no blood, though his back was filthy from the explosion. "Liam," she said, reaching to feel his pulse. She pulled his long hair aside and saw the blood spilling out of his left eye socket.

His body jerked at her touch. He spun onto his back, hands clenched, good eye wild, as if under attack. He finally focused on Ana and tried to relax, but he seemed to notice that something was very wrong.

He reached up, felt the ridge just below his damaged eye, and with a confused expression pulled away blood-tipped fingers.

"There was a bomb in the truck," she explained.

"What?"

Ana repeated herself, pained to see realization color his face.

"I can't hear," he said. "I can't hear."

She reached out for his hands, "You'll be okay." Ana mouthed her words carefully so that Liam could use the skill learned while spying for the Underground and read her lips. She could only hope his damaged eye didn't hamper this ability too much.

Katrina stepped toward them. "Is he okay?"

Her face had a few bloody scratches, but her eyes (and ears) seemed fine.

Ana gestured toward Liam. "The explosion got his eye. I don't know if it's really bad or just really bloody. He can't hear me, though. Don't react too much, until we know more. How are your ears?"

Katrina made a conscious effort not to meet Liam's

eyes — or, specifically, his eye. "Aside from the ringing, they're good. I just checked the other van. Your brother's not there."

"Do you think he was in—?" Ana looked back at the bombed truck's burning remains.

"No." Katrina shook her head. "I don't think so. You were right. It was a fucking trap."

Ana turned toward a mechanical sound behind her. A hunter orb hovered above them, cannon muzzle surrounded by crackling bright blue light.

"Enemies of the State, lay down your arms and surrender at once."

This was it. No way they could take out an armed hunter orb without one — or all three — of them dying.

Ana lowered her weapon. Katrina followed. Liam's rifle lay on the road, lost when he was knocked back by the blast.

The orb descended, crackles and hums escalating in volume and menace the closer it came. The monitor showed a City Watcher's visored helmet in a command station somewhere. The orb went to Ana's right, then left.

"Ana Lovecraft," the man onscreen said. Then, "Liam Harrow." He studied Katrina. "Citizen, state your name."

"My name is … Fuck You!" Katrina spit at the orb.

The orb pulled back, darted up about five feet above them, then took aim at Katrina, cannon belching with a whistling cry as it prepared to fire.

Ana expected Katrina to make a move, to grab her blaster, or something. But she stood defiant, seemingly ready to die — or perhaps *give up*.

Ana was braced for death from above, when the orb's screen went suddenly dark.

Then it fell silent and plunged to the snow with a crash but nary a dent.

"What the hell was that?" Ana reached down for her rifle.

Katrina retrieved her blaster, capitalizing on the moment without seeming to care about how or why the machine had stopped working. She was about to finish off the orb when a girl's voice cried out from behind them.

"Don't!"

Katrina turned along with Ana, then Liam, and saw five figures emerging from the woods, all wrapped in thick layers of winter clothing, faces concealed by wraps and masks. They were dirty and armed with blasters and swords. One held something that looked like a small box with a glowing red ball at the end.

Ana thought *bandits*, but as the group moved closer and out of the shadows, she realized that all but one were children. The closest child removed the wrap from her face, revealing a girl with bright blue eyes and short brown hair, surely no older than twelve.

"Ana Lovecraft?"

Ana, not quite sure if the girl was friend or foe, didn't know how to answer. But if these kids were responsible for bringing down the hunter orb, she wanted them on her side.

She nodded.

The girl removed her glove and extended her hand to Ana.

"My name is Calla Egan." She made a small curtsy. "And it is a pleasure to meet the daughter of Jonah."

FOUR

Adam Lovecraft

Adam stepped over no less than a thousand dirty and wet red flyers that had fallen across the city like confetti, each one announcing prizes for killing a Games contestant. He saw the hard lines of their art only in flashes, never daring to stop long enough to read one.

It might have been an hour, or twice that since his flight from the field. He'd split at the cannon shot, away from the boxes of zombies, but also away from the weapons, food, and supplies. Away from the few things that might keep him alive for more than a night.

But the risks were too great, and Adam would find a way to survive without supplies.

The city was old but not empty. He saw no people or zombies — yet — but could hear plenty of rustling from people (or things) seeking refuge in frigid shadows and icy hollows. He saw (or imagined) proof in flickers he spied through cracked alleyways and crooked corridors.

Adam wondered if those flickers were friend or foe, people or zombies — or all of the above.

Extra players, a broken city, and the added element of

wild bandits made these Games different from the zombie-centric versions he was used to watching. Adam wasn't sure if he was better or worse off. Part of him dared to hope and believe that maybe the sprawling city might make it easier to wait out his opponents. Wait for what, though? Who knew? But fewer contestants meant he had longer to live.

That's what he kept telling himself, over and over as he crept from one crumbled exterior to another, darting from shadow to shadow as he slowly sneaked down overgrown streets toward the city's long-forgotten heart.

Adam peeked into the hollowed shells of several old buildings before leaving them behind. None seemed quite right, though he couldn't say why — just trusting his instincts and training with the City Watch — so he kept trudging forward until he finally found what looked like an old office building, charred on the sides from flames and covered in graffiti.

The paint said something he'd only seen in the Dark Quarter a few times before, something he assumed was in relation to the Underground:

Blind the eyes of the oppressor with the fire of truth.

Adam entered through a rear door and drifted from room to room, then floor to floor, unsure of what he was searching for, other than something to hopefully keep him alive. The place smelled damp and, for lack of a better description, *old*. After visiting several floors he'd found nothing of use. There were plenty of broken things — desks, tables, office equipment from another era — plus plenty of boxes filled with things he couldn't define, all wearing a thick sweater of dust.

Hallways were patches of murky fog, dark shadows pierced by beams of bright light. Walls of dust poured through shattered windows to fleck scattered light through every room.

Adam surrendered his search on the building's seventh floor. He was standing on the landing, one hand on the knob and about to head back downstairs, when he heard something move from somewhere above him.

He swallowed, trying not to let fear short-circuit his deliberate pace.

Adam wrapped his hand around the thin metal railing and looked up into the light-peppered darkness. He'd run from so much in his life. Avoided bullies, failed to trust Michael when he should have, and taken the easier route every time instead of facing what had to be done.

He was in the Games. He would have to fight to survive, and he couldn't let the first strange sounds scare him away. He would adapt to his surroundings and play the cards he was dealt.

A few more steps — just see what waited. If it was too dangerous, he could still turn back around. But he couldn't allow his fear to scare him off, not before he saw what he was dealing with. He inched the stairs, turned the corner once he reached the top, then stepped into the first definite signs of life he'd seen since fleeing the arena.

Adam saw no survivors but did see signs of their recent presence: discarded ration packs, broken bottles, and a portable, solar-powered space heater with coils rigged in what looked like hands in a prayer. There was a soiled bedroll that looked awful to sleep on, though still better than the littered floor. Adam stepped deeper into the room, wondering who had been there before and how long ago they had left it.

Lost in his observations, it took him a moment to remember, with a sudden chill, the sound from just moments before.

Adam crossed the first room, then went into another. The second room looked more lived-in than the first. Almost immediately he found a pile of old clothes shoved into a corner. As he did each day — despite his daily desire to stop it — Adam thought of his many hours in City Watch cadet training, watching videos that taught him the basics of reading a crime scene. He remembered every lesson: interrogation, autopsy, trace, ballistics, forensics, and DNA.

Unfortunately, none of those lessons would help him now.

Adam wasn't sure if it was something in the building or his rattled nerves, but his instincts were screaming, ordering him to run and obscuring his focus.

But he couldn't run. Not without gathering any useful supplies that could be in the room, abandoned by whatever might be hiding in the shadows. He ignored the humming buzz in his head and sifted through the room, searching for food, a weapon, *anything*.

After a lot of nothing, Adam found an empty backpack and an old rusty hammer.

He slung the empty pack over his shoulder, tightened the hammer in his grip, and made his way toward the door. There was one more flight in the nine-story building.

Just one more flight. I can do this.

He climbed.

Beads of sweat on his brow continued to thicken. The hammer felt loose in his hand, the wooden stock slick from his sweaty palm. He just had to see what was ahead. He just hoped that he wasn't trading fear for stupidity.

Adam stopped cold, his foot an inch above the stair. He fell back a step and tightened his grip, both on the railing and on his hammer. There was laughter above, but it wasn't friendly.

It held the edges of menace, the sort of laughter he'd heard all his life, mostly from guys like Tommy, Morgan, Daniel, and all the other bullies that had been tormenting him since forever.

The part of Adam that had spent months in City Watch under Keller's care, training hard to follow in his father's footsteps and become a City Watcher, wanted to charge the stairs with only his hammer and confront the waiting danger. The rest of him, the part that cried when City Watchers took his books as a child, wanted to flee — down the stairs, out of the building, and into the street as fast as he could.

Adam finally listened to the coward inside him. He slowly turned, then took a step. He followed with a second, slower step; then his heel landed on the back of a bottle and sent him tumbling down the stairs.

Adam could feel himself flying through his life's longest second, then his back crashed onto the concrete and his head smacked the wall hard enough to burst a melon. He bit his lip to keep from crying out, but even the sudden metallic taste of blood couldn't stop his yelp.

The upstairs fell silent.

A few seconds later, shadows fell on his body from above as he lay trembling and hurt on the landing. He forced himself to stand and face the strangers.

A group of men stood on the flight above. A half dozen it seemed, but with so many shadows he couldn't be sure. The one in front, the shortest, must be the leader. He cocked an eyebrow, looked back to his group, grinned, then turned to Adam as he took a step down.

"Ay, are you one of dem Darwin players?"

Before the stranger had finished the question, he'd drawn a pistol from his coat and had it aimed between Adam's unblinking eyes. An old-fashioned gun, the kind that shot lead. It took everything inside him not to turn or flinch or show his weakness.

Gun on Adam, the leader said, "Ooh, we got ourselves a reward, folks!"

Adam cleared his throat as he stood, one fist balled, the other tight on the hammer. He'd rather die like a man than run like a dog. That didn't mean he needed to charge heedlessly into his own death, though. He could use his words and maybe convince the men above to spare him.

Maybe they weren't looking for blood.

Maybe he had a chance.

Adam opened his mouth to speak, then saw how much the stranger's smile reminded him of Tommy, and all hope was lost. So instead he spun around and leapt to the landing below.

He ignored the shock as it tore through his body, turned the corner, ran down another six stairs, then jumped the remainder. At the next landing, he ducked into the corridor and ran down the long hallway without looking back.

He kept running, racing down the hall as footsteps echoed behind him. He had no idea if the door at the end was locked, or what he would do if it were. He didn't really have a choice. He could hear his pursuers rounding the corner behind him.

He reached the door. Grabbed the handle and gave it a twist.

No luck. So while frantically searching for something to smash the lock with, he spied a hallway to his left that he hadn't seen before.

He ran harder. He had only seconds. When they rounded the corner this time they'd send a bullet into his back.

The doors on either side of the hall were all closed,

and he couldn't take a chance to try any of them. He only had the window ahead.

Just forty feet from the window, Adam had already made up his mind to jump. Death would be too immediate for pain. A leap from above would be better than whatever was running behind him. He wouldn't see Ana again or taste his revenge against Keller, but his rotten life would finally be over. Maybe he'd be reunited with his parents.

Heavy breath harmonized with victorious laughter behind him as his pursuers realized they had him cornered. He pictured the leader raising his gun and tried not to imagine lead ripping into his flesh.

Now just ten feet from the window, he steeled himself. Maybe his bold decision would be rewarded by a soft fall. God knew there was enough trash littering every corner of the Outback. Maybe he'd get lucky this time.

Maybe.

But a few feet from the window his feet found something wet and sticky.

With his second fall in only minutes, he slipped in what smelled like blood and fell hard on his face. On the ground, Adam was shocked to realize he still had his hammer. He tightened his grip, got to his knees, and held it up in the air, turning to face his attackers.

"What are you gonna do with that?" one of the men chortled. "Build a wall?"

The leader laughed loudly, waited for the chorus of echoes behind him, then took a step forward, raising his gun. "Think it can stop a—"

The man's head burst into gore. The first shot was followed by many, until his attackers were painting the wooden floor with their bodies and Adam heard a series of clicks.

He flinched. Adam had been prepared for death and now feared facing something worse.

The two men standing before him were garbed in City 6 blue. One was a giant of a man with a thick brown beard and long curly hair.

And the other was … the dark-skinned, green-eyed man from his youth.

Colton reached down and held out his hand. Adam hesitated, so his father's old friend reached down farther, grabbed Adam gently by the arm, and lifted the boy to his feet.

"Come with us, son. We're getting you out of these Games."

FIVE

Anastasia Lovecraft

"DID YOU KNOW MY FATHER?" Ana asked the young girl.

"Yes, he stayed with us when he was left for dead after the Games." She spoke with an unrecognizable accent, slight but noticeable. Her speech was slow, as if trying to get her words right. Ana couldn't tell if she was nervous or normally spoke another language. She had never met someone who spoke anything other than English. Ana had heard of people speaking Spanish, French, and even Chinese at home, but no other languages were allowed in school.

With a bull's diplomacy, Katrina said, "Jonah stayed with you? Where?"

Calla looked back at the eldest boy, a tall, skinny kid still in his mask.

He nodded and she said, "We're fifteen minutes away in an old train station."

"How many of you are there?" Katrina asked.

"Enough," said the boy.

Ana met Katrina's eyes: *Don't scare them away.*

Katrina shut up, reached into her backpack, and pulled

out some gauze, tending to Liam's still-bleeding socket. Ana cringed as he winced.

She turned to Calla and her crew. "You did this? To the orb?"

"Yes," said the boy. "But please don't destroy it. We can take it back home and tinker with it. Use the State's tech against them. We picked up on a City 6 transmission, instructions to draw you out. They suspected that you might try to save your brother."

"So you came to save us?" Ana asked. "Why?"

Calla met her eyes. "Because I owe your father."

Ana was about to ask for details, but she had more pressing questions, like: "Have you heard anything else … about my brother?"

The boy shook his head. "They didn't say anything, but we can check back home to see if Egan's heard more."

Calla looked at Liam, who hadn't spoken. He seemed like he was having trouble standing.

"How badly is he hurt?" Calla asked.

"Besides his eye, I think his eardrums might have burst. Can you help him?"

"I think so, if you come with us."

Ana turned to Katrina and whispered. "What should we do? Do you think we should continue to the Halo? Or get Liam some help first?"

"We need to regroup. The State was expecting us to make a move for Adam. We need to figure out what's happening and avoid more traps. Plus, Liam does need to rest and heal."

"Come," Calla said, impatient. "We've got a skidder waiting."

"A skidder?" Katrina asked. "How the hell did you manage to get one of those?"

The boy laughed as he went over to the orb and leaned

down to pick it up with both hands. He stood there, the orb concealing most of his chest and torso. "You think you're the only ones causing trouble for the State? We stole it from 'em."

This made Katrina laugh too, and supporting Liam between them, she and Ana entered the woods and climbed into the back of the large floating war truck.

THEY ARRIVED at the underground train station without incident and stepped from the truck into a cavernous bay, oddly stacked with parts from seemingly every sort of vehicle, orb, and robot from the present to what looked like the ancient past.

Bright lights hummed above as they made their way toward a set of red double doors where a young man in gray coveralls stood guard with a blaster rifle.

The man, who couldn't have been older than twenty-four, looked Ana and Katrina up and down like a dog eying a roast. Ana looked back at Liam to see that, yes, he had noticed despite holding rags over his left eye, and no, he wasn't pleased.

Calla ignored the guard, though, and led them through the doors. She took them on a tour of the Station, which was what they called their home, explaining that it had been an underground train station built before the Plague. She said the tunnels stretched for miles, though Station residents had sealed most of them to prevent bandits from raiding their home.

The tunnels were mostly industrial gray, some blue, and plastered with old posters announcing the MagLive Train with travel photos showing wide-open vistas — brilliant swaths of green beckoning the adventurous to lands lost long before. Most of the halls were dimly lit by wide squares of light, which only flickered on as they entered.

The place felt claustrophobic and lifeless, save for their echoing footsteps and voices as they walked.

After turning another corner in an endless series of the Station's maze, Ana smelled something that both pulled her back to her childhood and got her stomach growling.

"Is someone baking … *bread?*"

"Yes," Calla replied with a smile. "And through these doors ahead, we are home."

Two more guards stood at a set of blue double doors, one a young woman of about twenty, the other an older, heavyset man. Both wore City Watch uniforms, though they'd patched over the insignia with skulls, and neither wore the visors, likely useless without the associated tech. A shock stick dangled from each guard's belt.

"Hello, Calla," said the woman with a smile. "And hello, newcomers."

The older man, while not smiling, wasn't unpleasant. "Welcome."

Then they opened the doors to what Calla called home.

Ana stared, wanting to believe her eyes, hard as it was. There was a large central space with people talking to one another, children playing, the area surrounded by what looked to be former offices turned into homes.

The walls were alive with earth tones: warm terra cotta that swirled into an almost chocolate brown. Up top, maybe to mimic the sky, there was a line of icy blue that smeared into a smudgy sunset of yellow and orange at the edges. Two walls were covered with curtains, one deep green and the other a rich burgundy. Neither really matched the rest of the room but both were somehow warm. Ana felt suddenly safe, seemingly inhaling their color.

In addition to the vibrant colors of the walls, children's paintings lined them and decorated the windows of the homes. Much of the glass was covered with curtains, and there were wooden doors with numbers like addresses, like many homes in City 6. Strings of colored lights ran along the ceiling and lined the place in a beauty that could only come from somewhere called *home*.

People congregated in the halls, conversing. Children played, many smiling at Ana, Katrina, and Liam.

Ana asked how many people called the Station home.

Calla ignored the firm look from the boy who'd helped rescue them and said, "Sixty-four." Then, after a moment, as if realizing she'd slipped with such a dangerous confession, added, "But we're all very well trained. So don't think of trying anything."

Ana tried not to laugh at Calla's attempt to carry a swagger she couldn't quite manage. As the girl led them down a wide hallway, they were greeted by numerous people. Many seemed to recognize her. She assumed they'd somehow watched the Games down here, though she had yet to see a screen besides the Orb's.

Katrina and Liam looked uncomfortable as they smiled and waved. Ana reached for Liam's hand and squeezed it. She smiled and mouthed, *I love you.*

He mouthed the words back and seemed to relax — though not entirely. Old habits died hard.

They turned with the hallway and reached a single black door at the end.

"This is my father's office. He's the Station's leader."

Ana noticed that the girl had said "office," not "home," but didn't question her.

"He would like to talk to you first, Ana. If you two don't mind waiting."

Katrina turned to Ana, her lips pursed, looking like she minded quite a lot.

Ana spoke up before the other woman could voice her concerns, though. "Okay."

"And I'll take you both to see Father Truth so he may help you look better, mister," Calla said.

Ana couldn't tell if Liam understood the girl's mouthed words or not. But he didn't resist when Katrina took his hand, and he nodded along as Calla led them back the way they'd come.

Liam waved goodbye.

Ana turned and stepped into the office.

A man stood to greet her. "Happy to meet you, Miss Lovecraft. My name is Charles Egan, but everyone just calls me Egan." He extended his hand.

"Pleased," she said, shaking his warm palm.

He was a short man in his forties with dark, wild hair and tired eyes. He wore a dark-brown coat, black shirt, beige pants — and a relaxed look, as opposed to the more formal clothing she'd seen other leaders wearing.

"Please, have a seat." He waved to the chair opposite his own, behind a large wooden desk piled with a small mountain of papers. She sat, noticing that there wasn't much in the office to indicate what sort of man Egan might be. No photos, paintings, or even old books like Ana had seen in the few offices she'd ever been in. She wondered how much time the man spent in the room. Maybe he was more of a people's leader, spending community time in the living area rather than tucked away in his own space all day like those who ruled the Cities.

"I hope your journey here wasn't too eventful," Egan said.

"Not after your daughter and the others took out the hunter orb. How did you all know we'd be there?"

"I intercepted a State transmission. They were planning on you trying to get your brother. They want you and Liam dead … for real this time."

"Yeah, I'll bet. Thanks for saving us."

"You're most welcome. But I must admit that my motives weren't entirely altruistic."

"Oh?" A nervousness stirred in her stomach.

"I understand that you may hold a cure to this zombie plague."

She shifted in her seat, suddenly wishing that either Liam or Katrina were in the room with her. This situation might get out of control fast.

"What do you mean?"

"Your secret is safe with me, Miss Lovecraft. I know you were infected, and that you were also cured. That makes you the only known person to come back from the infection."

"What makes you say that?" Had that also been overheard in transmission? And if so, how did the State find out?

"Relax, Ana." He smiled at her hedging. "We have a mutual friend. Dr. Oswald has been staying here since he fled Hydrangea."

"Oswald is here?" Ana said, more at ease, and eager to see him.

"I'll bring him in a bit. But I wanted to ask you a favor first." A beat and then, "I need you to help the doctor work on his cure."

"I'm not a doctor or a scientist."

"I need you to stay here until he finds the cure. We believe we're close, but he's run out of your blood and needs more to continue his experiments."

Ana shook her head. "I'm sorry, Mr. Egan, but I need to leave here as soon as possible. My brother is in the Games. I need to save him. He'll never make it out on his own."

"I know, and I'm sorry to ask you, but I can't just let you leave."

"What do you mean you can't *let* me leave? I am *not* staying here."

He swallowed, ran his hands through his hair, and blinked back tears. "Believe me, Miss Lovecraft, I would not ask if it weren't so important for us."

"Why?" Something in his tone gave her pause. "Are you infected?"

"No. But my daughter is. And you're her only hope."

SIX

Keller

CITY 1

PROVISIONAL LEADER of the State Keller knew he was dreaming: life hadn't been so kind in a while.

The sky was too blue for reality, the clouds too white, and the air too sweet. The music was loud and bright but in no way grating to his ears.

He wanted more. Here, the music made him happy and filled his son with joy. He planted his hand on Joshua's shoulder and let it rest, lightly squeezing, telling himself it was okay to inhale the dream. He would wake to it missing — the sky, the clouds, the too-sweet air — but he wouldn't leave before savoring as much of it as possible.

"Are you enjoying the parade?"

The boy nodded without looking up at his father. "It's my favorite."

"Which part?" Though he already knew because Joshua's answer was always the same.

"All of it."

"Pick one," Keller insisted, not because he wanted to know so much as that he hoped knowing might prolong the illusion.

"I like the drums best, but I also like the horns."

"Why do you like the drums?"

"Because songs don't sound right without them. Drums make everything better. Sometimes I like to close my eyes and see if I can hear the different kinds. You can't do that with a regular song, but the parade always has so many."

"Are you doing that now?"

"Yes." Joshua turned and met his father's eye, not wanting to keep his wide grin to himself.

"How many do you hear?"

"I think I hear seven."

There are six.

Keller said nothing, just squeezed his son's shoulders and stared at the parade, watching the band marching by.

"There are six drummers! I was wrong."

His son smiled wider. As he did, the sun grew hotter and brighter. The sky turned the blue of a fully bloomed iris and the clouds collapsed into a powder of white.

Keller had been inside the dream so many times in the years since he'd lost Joshua. Now it was as if he could control the hues in his dream's waning moments.

He smiled back at his boy ... then everything was gone.

The explosion was deafening wrapped in sleep's infinity.

The sky withered to black and clouds turned into coal.

The sun went bright white, then started to scream.

Keller woke in his office, tears streaking both sides of his face.

He wasn't surprised to wake up in his ugly world — he'd been doing so since long before he woke in City 1. He was half startled to find himself behind his desk with a puddle of drool soaking his cheek. He should be hugging his pillow or pressed to his wife, like he usually was upon waking.

Keller picked up his tumbler, swallowed the scotch, and winced at the burn in his throat. He glanced at the half-empty bottle, thought about a refill of liquid sorrow, then wiped his mouth and pushed the glass toward the edge of the desk, slightly out of reach.

It was only noon, and he was already plastered and falling asleep at his desk. He needed to get something to eat and freshen up.

He had planted his palms to the wood, ready to push himself to standing, when there was a slight knock on the door — three raps without waiting for an answer. The door opened a crack. His wife poked her head through the wedge.

"Hi, sweetie. Would you like to watch the replay of the Opening Rush? I've seen it but would love to watch it together."

"No, thank you."

He couldn't meet her eyes, knowing his were guilty, and likely bloodshot.

She opened the door and entered his office. Her eyes flitted to the open bottle, then to the empty tumbler, and finally back into his soaking wet — and likely red — eyes.

Her pity filled him with hate.

"How long are you going to be like this?"

"Please. I'm busy. I don't have time for this conversation. I have Cities to run. Evil to root out."

"I know that—"

"You don't *know* anything, Jacquelyn. And be grateful you don't. Now I have work to finish before I can leave my office, and I'd appreciate it if—"

"I'm sorry." She nodded, slipping back a step and shutting the door on his tirade.

Keller stared at his wall, the monitor set to *Off* and showing nothing but black. He kept flinching with the idea of flicking it on. After five minutes he was certain he wouldn't.

He should apologize to his wife.

Get something to eat.

Maybe step outside and get some fresh air.

Again he planted his palms to the wood, ready to stand. And again he was interrupted, this time by a call. He looked at his phone: *Kern.*

"What is it?" he barked.

Kern's breathing sounded nervous. "We failed to get Ana and Liam, sir." Before Keller could explode, Kern added, "We're confident this is controlled."

"Do you have any leads?" he asked through gritted teeth.

"We're working on it." Kern, an unflinching man, was clearly trying to keep the quiver out of his voice. He cleared his throat. "Freedy wants to know if you'd like to activate Adam's bracelet."

"No," Keller said. "We continue as planned."

SEVEN

Adam Lovecraft

"WE'RE NOT GONNA HURT YA," Derek Colton assured him, reaching out to help Adam up. The man hefted him to his feet, eyeing Adam toe to nose along the way. "You remember me, son?"

Colton drilled his deep green eyes into Adam's, hard enough that he forced the boy to blink.

"You were a friend of my dad's, right?"

"Yeah." Colton grinned, just like Adam remembered from ages ago. "Man, last time I saw you, you were what? Six? Seven?"

"I dunno," Adam shrugged. "It's been a long time. Where have you been?"

"I moved to City 5 about ten years ago to head up the City Watch unit when they had some corruption issues. They needed an outsider to come in and help clean things up."

"So," Adam asked, "if you were doing that, why are you here in the Games now?"

"Let's just say I learned that the real corruption was coming from the people I worked for."

"Come on," said the giant bearded man who had been standing behind Colton as he and Adam caught up with each other. "We need to move."

"This is Hooper." Colton jabbed his thumb at the man. "He's good people."

Hooper reached out a massive paw. Adam expected the man's grip to swallow his — like Commander "Trunk" Avery at City Watch — but it was surprisingly soft, a lot like his smile. Adam noticed a leather strap across his chest and a sword's hilt sticking up over his left shoulder. He wondered how they'd landed such excellent weapons so quickly in the Games. It didn't take a ton of imagination to guess: both men's coveralls were spattered in crimson, evidence of what they'd had to endure in the Opening Rush.

"Hi," Adam said to Hooper, before turning back to Colton. "What do you mean you're going to get me out of here?"

Hooper answered for Colton as he turned and started toward the stairwell. His voice was soft and raspy. "We're with the Underground. We got ourselves put into the Games on purpose."

"But … *why?*" Adam said, hesitantly following the two men back down the corridor, watching them creep into the dim stairwell with their drawn blasters.

Colton nodded back, letting Adam know the path was safe.

He followed the men down the first flight feeling safer by the step. He had been vulnerable without a weapon other than his puny hammer; now he saw himself as having two weapons — both walking in front of him and each one capable of pulling its own trigger. That gave him enough confidence to at least keep putting one foot in front of the other.

But once the silence became too much, he broke it.

"Why would you get yourselves put into the Games on purpose?"

Colton paused, one landing up from the lobby. He turned back toward Adam, looking at the boy a half flight up. "After your father's execution, the State mandated that the Cities crack down on the Underground. Watchers weren't just grabbing 'traitors' — they were taking spouses and children, torturing and executing entire families. Never saw anything like it. They were looking for something and willing to do anything to find it. The Underground had always been good about keeping its own secrets, but once the Watchers started going after families, people began talking, betraying their comrades. Who knew the State could stoop that low?"

Adam thought of his own betrayals and his own place in the State. Feeling awful enough that he barely knew what to say, he managed, "So, is the Underground gone?"

Colton licked his lips, looking like he was in a hurry to get going. But he answered anyway. "It might as well be. It's broken for sure. A few members left, and the rest of 'em are too terrified to come out of hiding. The State will do anything to 'get the rest of the roaches' as they say."

Colton turned from Adam and headed down the final flight.

"The Underground will fight." Adam stopped his father's old friend after only a step. "They'll come back."

Adam's confidence grew as he spoke — until Colton brought him back down to earth.

"Not this time, kid. Not with Keller in control. No one's seen Jack Geralt since what happened with your dad. We're assuming the leader is dead. And like I said, the State's never been more aggressive. They aren't just rooting out the threat in order to till the soil, they're salting the earth so nothing can grow."

Colton looked as angry as he did beaten, like Hooper beside him. He kept on talking, nostrils now flaring. "They started in City 6, since that's where the resistance was strongest. They got to my sister's son ..." His face flashed with a pain so wrenching Adam was sorry to witness it. But Colton carried on. "They also took another girl from City 6, a girl named Zelle."

"Zelle?" Adam asked, the name uncommon enough that it had to be the same girl he'd known. "Zelle Howes? She lived two doors down from us."

"Yes, they grabbed her and her parents. They were trying to get her father to spill his guts about the Gardens. When he refused, they killed his wife. Then they threatened to kill the girl. Way I heard it, he died during questioning, and they threw her in the Games."

"What are the Gardens?"

Hooper cut in. "A home far away from the State's reach: a place where they can't touch us."

"Sounds like a good place to be right about now."

"Which is why you're going to help us find the girl," Colton replied.

"She's in *these* Games? Now?"

"Oh yeah," Colton said. "And she knows where the Gardens are."

"How do you know that? She's like ten, isn't she?"

"Yes," Colton nodded. "but she's got one of those photographic memories. There's no way her old man didn't tell her how to get there."

"That's a pretty big assumption," Adam said. "My father never told me any of his secrets ..." *And he never will.*

"It's a hunch, but word is that Zelle and her dad were

very close. It's risky, looking for her, but it's a risk we're willing to take."

"Okay." Adam swallowed. "So we're just going to find her, and hope she trusts us?"

"Exactly. Unless you've got a better idea."

Adam didn't.

Nor did he have a reason not to join them. For one thing, Adam liked the girl. He had played with her a few times when Ana was asked to babysit. And though she was six years younger than he was, Zelle was smarter than any kid he'd ever met — probably smarter than most adults.

No child deserved to be in the Games. If there were a way to save her, he'd do his best. "I'm in."

"Good," Colton said. "Let's get going."

They had just started on down to the lobby, when Hooper hissed and reached out an arm to stop them. He put a finger to his lips, then pointed down to the lobby where a trio of zombies were milling about in the threshold.

They made their way down, slowly. A few steps up from the lobby, Hooper turned back to Adam and handed him a blaster. "You ever fired one of these before?"

"A bunch of times," Adam said with a nod, loving the cool touch of the smooth black steel and nylon polymer. Hooper handed him two energy cartridges with twelve rounds each, which Adam slipped into his coverall pocket.

"Good." Hooper nodded as he drew the sword from its sheath on his back. Without another word, he left Adam and Colton and glided silently into the lobby, then ran up to the closest zombie and swung his blade in a heaving arc that sliced through its neck like scissors through string.

The zombie's head flew from his body and landed with a sickening thud. Adam managed not to gasp. Colton smiled and lifted his rifle, balanced it with his left hand, then lined up his shot and pulled the trigger twice.

THWAP! … THWAP!

The two remaining zombies dropped to the floor.

Hooper stood back, sword at the ready, giving Colton the first shot while staying on standby in case things spiraled out of control.

"Your gun has a silencer." Adam said in awe, pointing at the muzzle he'd not noticed until the pair of muffled pops.

"Yeah," Colton nodded, eyes full of pride. "This was worth the Rush." He petted the rifle's stock and turned back to Adam. "You okay back there?"

"Great," Adam nodded. "You're a really good shot."

"Thanks," Colton said, still holding his grin. "I was the best City 5 had to offer, but that was only because I'd left City 6 and your old man behind. No one shot like Jonah."

Hooper dragged his sword across his pants, cleaning the blood from the blade before sheathing it. "We'll roast marshmallows and jaw later. We need to *go*."

Colton clapped Adam on the shoulder and led him down the few remaining stairs. Hooper was already waiting by the outside door as they hit the center of the lobby. "Ready, kid?" Hooper asked, looking out through shattered glass at the broken city.

Adam followed the man's stare past the windows to the long steel fingers of the obliterated city. Even early, the sun was high and blinding on the snow. During the last several months of nights alone, Adam had believed that anything would be better than his cell. Now, with the living waiting to kill him and the already dead starving to feast on him, he almost missed the loneliness of prison. Outside this lobby, shadows whispered a promise of death. He could only keep moving forward at all thanks to Hooper and Colton doing it ahead of him.

He shrugged off his shuddering hesitance and stepped out into the city behind them.

He stayed silent as the three of them cautiously walked the snow-covered streets. Only after Colton and Hooper began to trade mumbles did Adam finally think it safe to speak up.

"How are we going to find Zelle? And how do you know she's not already dead?"

"Because you can't trust the network to tell the truth, but you can always trust 'em to do what's best for themselves," Hooper said.

"I don't understand. What's best for them in keeping Zelle alive?"

Colton answered. "Because the network likes a good story they can sell the people to keep 'em watching. You, son, are the star of these Games. But Zelle: she's young, scared, and everyone likes to root for — and bet on — an underdog. I guarantee that the network is trying to keep her alive as long as possible. They'll find ways to manipulate the Games — have her 'find' some supplies, or maybe an orb will take out some zombies if they get too close to her."

"Not that the folks back home will ever see that," Hooper chimed in.

Colton nodded, but the doubt must have shown on Adam's face.

"When's the last time you remember a kid dying this early?" Hooper asked.

"Never," Adam admitted, then without a breath between thoughts added, "But like Colton said, things have never been like this. I still don't get why they put her in the Games in the first place. Just to get even because her dad wouldn't tell them where the Gardens are? Seems extreme."

Colton said, "You're right. Zelle's never done nothin' to no one. But her daddy, Daniel Howes, was one of the most notorious Underground leaders. The kind even Hooper and I thought went too far ... the kind responsible for at least four bombings."

"That ain't her fault," Hooper cut in.

"Didn't say it was," Colton finished. "But fact is fact. Her daddy did what they said, and when he refused to give up the Gardens, you knew they'd make an example of the family."

"That's so cruel to go after his daughter. She's just a little girl, not a threat to anyone."

"You spent months with Keller," Colton sighed. "You should know all about sins of the father by now."

~

"BUT WHY HERE?" Adam repeated, though his first three times asking had yielded no answers. "What makes you think she's in this apartment?"

Colton finally looked up. "We're not looking for her in here."

"Then what are we looking for?"

From behind Adam in the room's far corner, Hooper said, "This."

Adam turned and saw the giant fiddling with a long black monitor. It looked like it might have carried a signal a century before. He didn't bother to ask. He knew he only had to stand back and see for himself what the black screen was for.

Sure enough, Colton was by Hooper's side a moment later, kneeling down and pulling a small, cobalt-blue metal cylinder from a pouch on his belt. It looked like a blunted flashlight. He handed it to Hooper and the man did something to the rod's side. Several prongs jutted from the rod's base. Hooper eyed the rod, then something on the back of the monitor. Whatever it was made him smile — Colton too. Then he seemingly inserted Tab A into Slot B — Adam had to guess because he couldn't see — and the screen brightened with the Games.

Hooper then handed Colton a small blue circle that looked like it had come from the tip of the blue device.

"Wow," Adam said. "Cool."

"Yeah," the grown men agreed. "Cool."

Hooper leaned the large screen against the far wall. The two men sat on the floor, palms to the wood, with Adam in front and between them.

Colton pressed a button on the blue thing, flipping through several different feeds.

"What is this?" Adam asked.

"It's a network receiver. It allows us to bypass what the Games shows the citizens. We can see the raw feeds — the same ones the producers are seeing back at the network.

"Where did you get this? Was it in the Opening Rush?"

"No," Colton told him. "The network wouldn't put something like this in the Rush. I smuggled it into the Games."

"How did you manage that?" Adam had been thoroughly searched several times.

"Let's just say I had some help on the inside. Being a former City Watcher has its perks. As for getting it in here, well, I had to hide it in a place I'm not too proud to talk about."

"Oh, man," Hooper said. "I wish you'd told me that *before* you handed it to me."

"Please. That's probably the cleanest thing you've had in your grimy hands this week."

Hooper laughed as he wiped his hands on Colton's coveralls.

"That her?" Colton asked when Zelle appeared onscreen, standing on a rooftop in a long black coat, with straggly blonde hair hanging over her face.

Adam could see enough to recognize the mousy girl as she walked out from between two tall air towers, dragging a large chair. "Yeah, it's her. What's she doing?"

As the orb filming her pulled away, Adam saw her location: the large spired building he'd spotted piercing the skyline while searching for a place to hide. "That's the tallest building in the city."

"Fortunately half its height is that spire," Hooper added. "Let's get going. I figure it's gonna take at least a day to get there from here."

"Wait." Colton pointed at the screen as the orb circled the girl, revealing a fort made of furniture she must've dragged up the stairs. There was a small fire in front of it. "Looks like she's settling down."

Zelle had somehow managed to start a fire, likely for warmth since it wasn't yet dark. Just seeing it reminded him of the cold. His coveralls were mercilessly thin against the bitter wind that was brewing itself into something worse. Adam was both surprised and impressed at how quickly the girl had managed to get a coat, climb to the rooftop, and build a fort of furniture and a fire to warm herself.

She'd already proved more resourceful than he had — he would've jumped out a window to his death if not for Colton and Hooper.

Zelle dragged the chair and set it in front of her home-made hideout. They couldn't see what was inside the fort because the orb's angle was wrong, and it seemed the entrance was just large enough for the girl.

She sat, retrieved her gun from inside her coat, laid it in her lap, then looked up and glared at the orb.

It zoomed in on her face and her defiant hazel eyes.

Adam felt the distance between them melt.

Her eyes were hard, exposing the ghost of the happy girl he'd lived next to for so many years. Haunted but hard. As if she were daring whoever was watching to come try and get her. She would use that gun, he had no doubt. But even with a weapon, she was only a child, ill-prepared to fight zombies, bandits, and — perhaps worst of all — other players.

The orb pulled back and descended who-knew-how-many stories to the street, where a horde of more than a dozen zombies milled about as if waiting for something.

"Jesus," Hooper said. "How long you think she can last up there?"

"Well, they don't seem to know she's up there yet," Colton replied. "But come nightfall, that fire may give her location away. If not to the zombies, then definitely to other players."

"We need to hustle." Hooper looked up and tried to find the sun in the hazy gray sky. "Looks to be around two, and that building's at least a mile and a half away."

"A mile and a half through hell," Colton corrected.

"Like I said: probably take a whole day to get there." Hopper grabbed the blue receiver from the back of the monitor, handed it to his buddy, then stared down at the city.

"Let's go get Zelle," Colton said.

For the first time in a long while, Adam felt like he had a purpose other than drawing breath.

And it was always best to have a purpose.

EIGHT

Anastasia Lovecraft

ANA SAT in the chair staring down at her hands, unable to meet Egan's eyes.

How could she look into the stare of a distraught father desperate to save his baby girl from becoming a zombie and tell him *no* because she had to leave and save her *own* kin — especially after his daughter had saved Liam, and Katrina and her?

She looked up and met his gaze. "You can't know I'm the only cure. That's only a theory."

Egan asked Ana to hold that thought, then left the room, leaving her to stare at the piles of papers on his desk. Part of her wanted to peek and see what was written on them, but then the door opened behind her and it was too late to snoop.

She turned to see a welcome sight — Oswald. Ana had worried and wondered about the doctor ever since he risked everything to help them. She constantly imagined his betrayal being discovered by the madman, Sutherland.

Ana stood and hugged him, thankful that he was fully dressed in a long, dark shirt and pants, because as fond as she was of the man, she didn't want to touch his decayed skin or metal chest and arms.

"How are you?" Oswald asked.

"Good."

The doctor looked her over. "No further signs of the virus?"

"I haven't felt anything since Hydrangea."

"Amazing!" Human skin stretched awkwardly up his face to greet alloy in a smile. "Please, have a seat."

Ana sat, as did Egan opposite her. Oswald stayed on his feet, standing to her left at the end of the desk so the three of them formed a loose triangle.

"I was just telling Ana about your work," Egan said. "Can you fill her in?"

"I've been continuing Dr. Goelle's research as promised. Using your blood samples, I've managed to degrade the virus and temporarily arrest the effects within the host. However, I've not yet been able to kill the virus outright without harming the host's blood cells, nor have I managed to replicate your reversal. But I feel close to a breakthrough. We have a few subjects in another part of the Station responding positively to my latest course of treatment, though it's still too early to tell."

"And is Calla one of those subjects?"

"Not exactly. I'm using a variant of the treatment Dr. Goelle prescribed for your old friend, Duncan. In other words, we're holding the virus at bay, but there's no telling how long these treatments will stay successful. The antidotes I'm working on are unstable, so we can't use them to dose the child. I'm hoping with your help to further Dr. Goelle's plans for a true cure."

Ana turned to Egan, unable to hold her question. "Why isn't Calla with the other subjects, away from the population?"

Egan nodded, as if expecting her question. He'd probably heard it plenty from his own people. "Because I'll not have my daughter locked up like a dangerous animal."

"You *do realize* you're putting people at risk, don't you?" She felt herself getting angry. "I watched my friend turn and it only took seconds. One moment Duncan was feeling a little off, then the next, we were dinner."

Oswald intervened. "While I do understand your concern, Ana — especially since you yourself were quarantined — I believe this is best for the child."

"How's that?"

"We believe that patients who are locked away from others degrade at a faster rate than those allowed managed interactions. Calla is supervised at all times by one of her elders, who has been instructed on what to do in the event of her turning."

Kill her?

"She's had a hard life. If these *are* her last days, I want her with loved ones. Of course, it is our hope that these *aren't* her last days, and that you will help find a cure for my daughter."

"Can't you just take my blood and let me go? I have to save my brother. There's no way in hell that Keller would ever allow him to walk away, even if he were to somehow win the Games.

"I understand, and I agree with your assessment." He met her eyes. "But you must see beyond your brother. Your blood is a gift for the *world*."

Her cheeks flushed. "And tell me, Mr. Egan, would you not do the same in my place? If it were Calla in the Games, and you held the cure in your blood, would you be so generous?"

Ana knew his answer, though the man said nothing.

"As far as I'm concerned, Adam *is* my world. I'm fine

with that making me selfish. I never pretended to be anything other than what I am."

"The Lovecraft streak." His words were as sour as his smile. "Always so charming."

"I'm done here." She stood. "Thank you for your hospitality and for saving us from the hunter orb. But I need to find my brother."

She turned, ignoring Oswald's gaze, and headed toward the door.

"Wait!" Egan called out, his tone like daggers in her back, goosebumps rippling up her spine as she turned.

"Yes?"

"Leave, and you will never find your brother."

"Is that a threat?"

"Not at all. Learn to distinguish, Miss Lovecraft. I'm simply stating a fact. The Games have changed, both their rules and location. Head to the Halo, and you'll find it empty."

"Where is he?"

"It seems we both want something, Miss Lovecraft. You wish to save your brother and I wish to save my daughter. Whatever shall we do?"

NINE

Adam Lovecraft

ADAM COULDN'T BELIEVE it was taking so long to reach the tallest building. They'd been walking forever, changing routes several times to avoid other players, zombies, and bandits. What would have taken an hour to walk in any other city had become an epic trek in the Outback.

"I'm starving," Hooper said.

"Don't look at me, I'm too skinny," said Adam to the big man, daring to joke.

Hooper surprised him with laughter.

"We'll eat in an hour if we've not yet reached the building." Then Colton smiled and joined in the joke. "But please, try not to eat us."

"I'll try to contain myself," Hooper said.

As the sky darkened to a bruised violet, the light snow stopped, along with the howling wind. The world would have been silent, if not for the horrifying noises echoing off of the concrete and glass jungle around them.

The scraping of metal, the crunching of glass, the ragged breath and grunting of zombies mingled with the rushing hushes of men, same as when he'd first entered the streets from the arena, except now it was dark and somehow worse, despite the two large men by his side.

After a few more blocks, Colton stopped cold, Hooper a tick after that. Adam was last to halt, and found himself a few full steps ahead. He turned back toward them as the two men traded a look.

"Exactly," Hooper said.

"What?" Half of him wanted to know what they were talking about, the other half wanted to hide.

"When's the last time you heard a zombie?" Colton asked.

"A few blocks back."

Hooper said, "I'm wondering if they're swarming somewhere or maybe something's got their attention. Could be a trap set by one of the players, or more likely a group of them. Maybe bandits. Could be the network. No way to know."

There was an awful crash from somewhere far off, chased by a horrible grunting — first from the undead, then immediately followed by a human female scream.

"In there!" Colton nodded toward an old storefront without a face.

Hooper grabbed Adam, flung him over his shoulder, and followed Colton into the hollow before Adam could think to move on his own.

He didn't dare to ask what it was as they huddled behind a shallow dusty counter. He peeked around the side, through the shadows of what was left of the store, and into the wide street draped in snow and littered with debris — cars, lumber, and fallen metal poles — as first one, then two, and finally a moaning mass of zombies swarmed by in a wave through the street.

A group of men trailed the last of them, all wearing

blue. They had to be contestants. Outside the hollowed storefront, close enough that Adam could see it as he peered around the counter, a half dozen contestants attacked the lagging zombies, hacking them to bits with hatchets and swords. Blood sprayed from the falling bodies in red rain, looking black against the shadow-covered snow. The men dispatched the horde with their blades, keeping things quiet, not one of them so much as brushing their blasters.

Though Adam couldn't see the zombies ahead, he assumed that whatever was calling them to the swarm was more enticing than the possible dinner behind them.

Colton slipped from his spot behind the counter to a position behind a shelf and out of Adam's sight.

Adam started to follow.

"Don't move," Hooper growled a whisper into his ear and held him in place. "They'll kill us for sure. We couldn't stand before we'd be dead."

Hooper surely wanted to say more and was probably biting his lip as he fell into silence.

It was almost too much to bear. Adam had so many questions and couldn't ask one. Hooper and Colton wouldn't know the answers.

The men outside carried giant guns. One held something that looked almost like a cannon. Adam could see why even a brave man like Hooper would be frightened. Colton was out of sight from where they were huddled, but the same was surely true for him.

If his two protectors were scared, he didn't stand a chance.

Why was it taking the men outside forever to leave? Every moment felt like the second ahead of his death. His heart was pounding; surely they could hear it.

He held his blaster, tight in his grip, ready to leap up

and empty it into the bad guys outside, knowing that even his best attempt would be futile.

"It's okay," Hooper whispered, now softer in his ear, as if reading his mind. "They'll be gone soon. They're just assholes, celebrating kills."

"How much longer?" The whisper felt dangerous as it slipped through his lips.

"Not long."

But not long was *too* long.

Black seemed blacker, every sound now a boom. Adam couldn't help but picture Zelle on the rooftop and wonder how she was doing — trying not to think about how she was probably dead.

As crunching glass grew faint enough to promise the men's departure, Adam suddenly realized why the special edition offered so many guns.

"They need to get rid of more people," he said, louder than he intended to. "So they gave more guns to the players!"

From outside: "What was that?"

Adam heard Hooper swallow.

A long three minutes of silence followed, then the counter exploded in chunks as bullets ripped it to pieces.

"Come on!" Colton cried out, crawling across the floor toward the rear exit.

The door had no handle but gave way as Colton slammed his body against it. He stood on the other side, away from the line of fire, holding the door open for Hooper and Adam. Once through, all three ran as bullets flew into the building.

Colton kicked the kitchen's back door hard. It splintered at the knob and swung out into the alley. They ran as fast as they could, rounding the corner before the other players made it through the store, buying seconds from their pursuer's confusion and the chance to gain distance or hide.

Hooper's bracelet screamed with a high-pitched whistle as they reached the alley.

"Fuck!" He smacked furiously at his wrist as if it would silence it. He even tried to cover it, but it failed to silence the whistle.

Colton looked up and down the street as the bracelet screeched even louder. It was bright blue, pulsing with beats of crimson and glowing in time with the screams.

All at once they heard a chorus of undead. It sounded as if the zombies were approaching from every direction, just out of sight.

"Come on!" Colton turned to Hooper. "It's not gonna stop. We have to run."

Hooper nodded, and for the first time Adam thought the giant looked downright terrified. They ran down one short alley, then turned down a longer one as the armed players and zombies gave chase behind them.

The long alley ended, branching right and left.

They stopped behind a van with no wheels at the alley's end, not knowing which way to go. It was as if the Outback had suddenly become a maze. The groans of zombies echoed from seemingly every direction, along with the whooping of players eager to kill them.

He hoped death would be quick and not too painful. He thought back to his flight in the building before meeting Hooper and Colton and wished for a window.

"It's okay," Colton lied.

"*Go*. Take the kid and leave. I'll run that way." Hooper nodded toward the right.

There was a holler from behind, then the van windows exploded above them, followed by a hail of bullets. Colton pushed Adam lower to the ground before he popped back up, along with Hooper, trading gunshots with their attackers as zombies flooded the streets.

Even if they managed to kill the half dozen players — it wouldn't be easy, the group had found cover behind a pair of dumpsters — the zombies would surely end them all.

Adam could barely afford to consider himself, but still he thought of Zelle scared and alone on the roof. He wondered how much colder it was that high up, and if she could hear all the gunshots below. He hoped she was okay, even though he knew she wasn't. He wondered if he imagined the connection he felt between them — the sins of the father as Colton had said.

Adam wanted to see what was happening in the alley but felt pressed to the cold ground by the sonic assault. Hooper's bracelet kept screaming, and too many zombies were howling right back. The gunshots were deafening, as Hooper's blaster belched one eruption after another, answered by volleys from across the street and the steady *THWAP! THWAP! THWAP!* of Colton's series of muffled shots.

Adam tried to stand, but a bullet pierced the van's metal to his left and sent him back to the ground, heart in his throat. He felt helpless, like a kid. He ought to help out, but he only had a small blaster pistol, not designed for long shots like both men's weapons.

He had to focus on staying alive, on not letting down his new friends — and Zelle — and on escaping the Outback.

After a few minutes the volleys finally started to fade, then stopped altogether.

"Did you get them?" Adam stood, seeing the bullet holes above, where he would've been shot had he stood to fight. Amazingly, neither man appeared injured.

Colton looked at Adam, nodded, then gestured out into the street without daring to look out. Nothing left of the dumpsters but twisted metal and pluming smoke. What little he could see of the bodies on the ground would be lunch for wandering zombies. There were at least two dozen fallen undead scattered through the avenue, turning most of the white snow dark.

And Hooper's bracelet continued to scream.

Colton looked at him. "Let's go."

Hooper shook his head. "You guys go. You're dead if I'm with you."

There were no players or zombies to keep Colton from argument, but he dropped the argument and reached out to shake his friend's hand anyway.

Hooper looked down at his wrist as if in resentment, then pulled Colton into an embrace. "Take care, and don't worry about me. We both knew what we were getting into. And if I can keep my fat ass from being someone's dinner, I'll find you at the girl's building."

Colton nodded, then led Adam away from Hooper and toward the city's tallest building.

TEN

Anastasia Lovecraft

ANA, Liam, and Katrina were given the use of a double room: four large beds, plus a bathroom — with a working, and surprisingly spacious, tub. They were told to rest before dinner and prepare to take their places as guests of honor.

The last thing in the world Ana felt like was being a "guest of honor." She could hardly tolerate the thought of mingling with strangers while her brother was out in the Games fighting for his life — *if* he were still alive. The longer they stayed in the underground train station, the less hope she had that she'd ever see him again.

But it had been a while since she'd experienced the joy of running water and wasn't about to pass on the opportunity. Ana and Liam bathed first, then Katrina gave them an uncharacteristic wink on her way into the bathroom to take her turn as they lay together, freshly scrubbed atop a bed.

Ana reached up and touched the black leather patch over Liam's left eye. "I'm so sorry."

"I'll be fine. Besides, I always wanted to be an old-time pirate." Liam smiled and laughed.

"You're so amazing." Ana kissed him. "No matter what you're forced to go through, you always find a way to keep from falling apart. You lost your eye, Liam, and you're acting like it's not a big deal."

"So I lost an eye. I've still got you, and look around — we have a warm room, hot water, food, and kind people around us. We're okay, Ana."

"But for how long? We can't stay here. We haven't found Adam."

"I know." Liam ran his hands through Ana's damp hair. "But we'll worry about that later. Right now, we've got … well, right now."

Ana could hardly believe this was the same Liam who routinely lost his temper at microscopic slights. He was hardly a pacifist, but ever since Hydrangea, he had calmed down significantly. Liam was still a tough-as-nails soldier outside in the world, but alone in these quiet moments when they were fortunate enough to find a soft spot to sleep, he was so calm. Almost tender.

"What happened to you, Liam Harrow?" Ana asked playfully.

"What do you mean?" He sat halfway up and leaned on his elbows.

"You used to be so … wild. And now, you're almost, I dunno, domesticated."

"Love does that to a man." He had been sweet in recent months, but he hadn't exactly been declaring his love with poems or bundles of freshly picked daisies. He met her eyes and cleared his throat. "I don't know, Ana. It's hard to live in the moment when you're always worried about what might happen next. That's been my life so far: plotting, planning, trying to stay a step ahead of the enemy.

But after that night when I thought I'd lost you for good, then you woke up cured in the morning … I don't know. Now I just feel like I'm supposed to enjoy whatever moments we have. Life is cruel enough without me dwelling on the horrors that *might* happen. I'll fight when I have to, and," he smiled, "love when I can."

Ana crawled on top of his body and kissed Liam again. She felt him harden against her, but with Katrina in the bathroom behind a paper-thin door, there was barely any privacy, let alone time for a quickie without getting caught. That wasn't unusual. There was rarely time for sex since their flight from Hydrangea, which made these moments being so close, in such an intimate setting, all the more excruciating.

As if on cue, Katrina pulled the drain plug in the bathroom. She'd be coming out soon. Ana closed her eyes and sighed.

"Why do you have to be such a sexy pirate?"

"Sorry, I just can't help my sexiness."

She pictured his smile, then opened her eyes, saw it was real, and kissed him again, allowing her hand to travel down to his pants with caresses.

"Stop it," he whispered.

The bathroom door opened, and Ana pulled herself off of Liam, laughing.

"Sorry," Katrina said, emerging fully dressed in a long-sleeved black shirt over black pants. "Didn't mean to interrupt."

"You didn't interrupt anything." Ana wasn't sure why she felt the need to explain herself. Maybe a part of her felt guilty to have found love with Liam while Katrina had no one.

Not that Katrina ever acted like she wanted a man — or anyone, really. She seemed tough, in need of neither love nor friendship. Ana had tried to get close, but Katrina always kept a distance between them. Her arm's length wasn't exactly cold, but it was undeniable. The warrior clearly enjoyed their company, and she *had* risked her life to spring them from Hydrangea, turning on Sutherland — a maniac unable to handle betrayal — to help two people she'd barely known.

Katrina was a good person but clearly damaged.

Ana had seen proof of that a few months back. One morning she'd woken up early. The three were staying in a cabin they'd been lucky to find and secure well enough for three weeks of safe harbor. Liam was asleep, but Katrina wasn't in the house. Concerned, Ana grabbed a blaster and went outside to look for her. She spotted Katrina bathing in the lake … and noticed her striated chest, vicious with long, intersecting scars. Who could have done this to her?

Ana had wanted to ask Katrina about the scars ever since but couldn't find a way to broach the topic without feeling like she was invading her privacy.

Clearly Katrina was thinking along similar lines. She sat on the bed, opened her backpack, and began sorting her supplies. "I'll see if they'll give me another room tonight. You two deserve some time alone."

"Thank you," Liam said, before Ana could dismiss her.

Ana met his eyes and smiled.

Katrina nodded, then turned to Ana. "So, what do you want to do? Are you going to stay like Egan asked?"

"We're leaving in the morning. I can't stay here while Adam is out there helpless."

Katrina drew a blade from her backpack and strapped its sheath to a spot on her back along her waistline.

"But I don't think Egan will tell us where Adam is if I *don't* stay," Ana finished.

Katrina smiled. "Give me two minutes with him. I'll get him to talk."

"We don't need to hurt anyone," said Liam, sitting up.

"You're no fun." Katrina grinned.

Ana tried to ignore their flirty banter. This was their way, and she had no reason for jealousy. Katrina had never shown the slightest interest in Liam, nor had his eyes been on her. But Ana couldn't (and wouldn't) have blamed him if they were. Katrina was gorgeous, exotic, with more than enough years on Ana to make her much better under the blankets.

"Maybe you *should* stay here," Katrina said with a shrug. "Oswald's here. And we need to find a cure, right? You're too important to keep putting yourself at risk. I bet Egan will let Liam and me go if you agree to stay. We can bring Adam back here and we'll *all* be safe."

"We're a team, the three of us. I can't ask you guys to go save Adam while I hide here. My brother, my responsibility. It's enough that you're helping. I can't ask that you go in my place."

"Katrina has a point. We've no idea what we'll run into. I'd rather you stay here safe too."

"No!" Ana said. "Besides, now you're half blind. You *need* me."

"Even half blind, I'm still a better shot." Liam laughed.

Katrina laughed too, and Ana tried not to glare at her.

"I'm going," Ana said, as a knock at the door cut into their argument.

"Come in," Katrina called out.

Calla opened the door, joined by the older, olive-skinned boy with bright golden eyes: Elijah. He was tall, but didn't look much older than Calla. His belt hung low from his blaster's weight — their contingency plan in case the girl turned.

"Dinner's ready," Calla said.

THE TABLE WAS long and perfectly centered in a room that was even more gorgeous than the one Ana had seen when first introduced to the Station.

Somehow, the old and no-longer-abandoned train depot — with its musty-scented mineshaft corridors, chunks of wall either rotten or missing, and chipped tiles scattered along the wall leading into the common area — still looked more like a home than any Ana had seen since the one she'd grown up in. She still pictured her childhood home each day, often with her mother wearing the old ice-blue apron with the silver script that read *Molly Knows Best.*

The ceiling was ivory and hung low with a coil of colored lights strung from one corner to the other, on both diagonals and crisscrossed through the middle. The walls were yellow, in various shades of gold, daffodil, and canary. The many yellows made Ana think of the fancy fabric stores on the bottom floor of the stores on Park, back in City 6.

Calla sat across from Ana, with Egan by the girl's side. A brown-haired dwarf introduced to her as Father Truth was sitting beside Egan and mumbled only a word or two after she sat, seemingly unable to move his eyes away from any one of the three newcomers. It felt as if he were analyzing them for some reason, and that sent a flutter up her spine.

It didn't help that the rest of the room was pretty empty. There were two dozen chairs, most unoccupied — Egan wanted dinner to be for those closest to him and his special guests, so they could speak freely.

Liam sat to Ana's right, squeezing her hand under the table in support. She loved that he sensed how hard it was for her to sit near a girl she was likely consigning to death by her departure. Oswald sat beside Katrina to Ana's left, and the two of them were chatting about everything that had happened since his flight from Hydrangea. Sutherland had apparently gone into a rage after they left, accusing everyone — including Oswald — of conspiring to help them flee. After the trials he'd hanged the guilty.

"Oh God," Ana said.

"I felt awful but wasn't about to step forward and admit my guilt. I made plans to escape myself instead."

"Thank God." Father Truth raised his wine glass to toast their success.

Ana followed, though she wasn't feeling very celebratory in the least, as did most of the others around the table.

"So, have you made a decision yet, Ana?"

She glared across the table at Egan. How dare he put her on the spot in front of Calla like this? She wondered how much the girl knew. "I already gave you my decision. I have to find my brother."

Egan lifted a hunk of bread to his mouth and took a bite. "I can tell your friends exactly where to find him and can even lend you another body — along with some useful gear, food, water, blades, guns and ammo — if you would like."

Calla punched the table, causing her cup to jump and splash. "Don't force her, Father! If she wants to go, let her. I'll be fine."

Liam squeezed her hand harder.

Egan turned to his daughter. "How do you know what we're talking about?"

"I'm not stupid. I hear things. I know you're trying to

get her to stay so Dr. Oswald can find a cure. But you have to stop trying to force people to do stuff! Haven't you learned anything?"

She rose from the table and started to walk away.

"Calla!" Egan called after her.

She turned back to Ana. "Your brother's in the Outback. That's where the Games are being played." Then she left the room without looking back.

Egan turned to an open-jawed Elijah. He waved his hands, as if to remind the boy of his duty to shadow her. Elijah swallowed and bolted from the table wide-eyed, calling after Calla.

Egan turned to Ana with a sigh, a sour expression wrinkling his face. "I won't lie, I have thought about making you stay. Having my people take the three of you at gunpoint and forcing you to remain here until Calla has been cured. I'm considering it even now."

Ana turned to see Katrina's clenched jaw. Surely she was flinching for her blade. She'd seen Katrina lodge her knife into a bandit's neck from twenty feet away. Egan might have men — and kids — with guns, but Katrina was a force of nature who could probably kill every man, woman, and child in the Station. Then leave without a scratch on her.

"But my daughter would hate me if I stopped you," Egan continued. "And I don't want to do anything to cause more stress. Keeping her spirits up and her life as normal as possible is important to maintaining the serum's effectiveness. I'll give you supplies and even let you take a skidder. You can go in the morning. Just, please, promise you'll return."

"I promise we'll return," Ana replied, blinking back her tears. "Thank you."

Egan grunted and returned to his dinner.

The remainder of the meal unfolded mostly in silence.

Ana could barely eat, though something inside her was surely eating her.

ELEVEN

Sutherland

SUTHERLAND STARED at the throne room trying to decide what was bothering him.

It was spacious, well placed on the tenth level of Hydrangea, and consumed what had once been two dining halls. The walls were red and black, lined with torches and sconces, with several strands of gold garland sprouting up and over the room's many columns. A plush crimson carpet striped the floor leading to the throne. Ornately carved wooden benches lined the walls on either side, where the citizens of Hydrangea could gather for their most important meetings.

The throne, gold and black as well, rested at the top of five long steps, a high perch from where he could survey the room and those who were eying the proverbial, if not literal, crown.

Gallus stood beside him, eager for a reaction. For praise, like a child. Sighing, Sutherland finally turned to his second in command. "I don't know. It seems a bit too ... formal."

The young man's face nearly melted. "But, sir, I

thought you *wanted* formal. I thought you were tired of the informal nature of the dining hall meetings. That is what you said, right?"

"Yes, yes, I know what I *said*, but you were supposed to know what I *meant*."

Gallus looked like he wanted to say something but knew better than to cross Sutherland. Gallus, just nineteen when Sutherland handpicked him as Hydrangea's second — to replace the traitor Katrina — was young, strong, and well respected among the citizens. But he was still a damned child, which made him half idiot, and Sutherland should've known better than to trust a brat still missing the tit with details as important as a throne room.

Sutherland approached the throne and ran his hands along its ornate golden frame and dark-blue cushioned seat and back. "Is this real gold?"

"Of course, sir."

Sutherland traced his fingers along the carved laurels. "It is quite nice."

"Have a seat, sir. I trust that you'll find it to your liking."

Sutherland sat. It *did* feel good. Though not good enough to give Gallus his praise. "Not bad." He looked out around the room, imagining it filled with his citizens learning to respect — and fear — him again.

Yes, they were still the Patriots of the New Revolution, part of a community spread across the Barrens in nine separate camps. But Sutherland was no longer the leader. Not since he'd allowed Katrina to escape with Ana and Liam. In a vote by the Council of Patriots, which he'd once led, Sutherland had been replaced at Sagebrush by that foolish old bastard Jeffries.

But Jeffries wasn't fit to lead a raid, let alone lead the Patriots. He was trapped in the past, and too afraid to lead the Patriots in the bold direction they needed to go if they were to ever live as truly free men and women.

But the council had made its decision, and there was no recourse for Sutherland. Jeffries had the audacity to say, "You're lucky to stay as Hydrangea's leader. Remember that, and get your camp in order."

Ever since Katrina's betrayal, too many people had trafficked in whispers, wondering at Sutherland's effectiveness. They didn't think he heard them, but he hadn't risen to the top without having ears and tentacles everywhere.

When Oswald followed her flight a few months later, the chatter grew louder. Some idiots even considered holding an emergency "election" of all things, to select another leader for the camp. Of course no one was bold enough to approach him and suggest such a thing. They were still fearful of crossing him — *for now.* But Sutherland had to do something before the rabble began to clamor more vocally for his removal.

He had to make a statement. This throne room was a start. It *was* ostentatious, but it wasn't as if Sutherland was a stranger to extravagance. As he sat on his throne, he enjoyed it — and his place above the people even more. In the worlds before the Old Nation, throne rooms were necessary, providing a majestic setting for a ruler to display his power. A king could hold official court and grant audiences to the rabble, award high honors and offices to the worthy.

The throne room proved his station. "This will do quite nicely, Gallus."

"Thank you, sir." Gallus stood as if waiting for additional praise, rather than leaving like Sutherland wanted.

"Yes?" Sutherland said.

"Well, sir, if you're ready, Captain Horrance has news for you."

"Oh?" Sutherland clapped. "Then bring him to me."

Gallus left to fetch Horrance. Moments later, the two men returned to the throne.

Horrance, a large ogre of a man with a smooshed face that would embarrass his mother spoke first. He wasn't nearly as stupid as most people believed — though not a third as smart as Gallus — which was why Sutherland liked having Horrance in charge of his soldiers, the Black Guard.

"Greetings, sir." He bowed his head slightly.

"Yes, Horrance?"

"I saw something in the Barrens, over near Quadrant 11."

A long sigh. "Please, Horrance, can you be more specific, or do you delight in prolonging the agony of each moment I spend in your presence?"

"I saw Katrina and the escapees."

"Ana and the boy?" Sutherland leaned forward in his throne.

"Yes, sir."

"And you didn't attempt to capture them?"

"They were with bandits, sir."

"I should've expected that whore Katrina to scurry back with vermin. And? Do you have a location?"

If Horrance had a tail, Sutherland was sure it would've been wagging. "I do, sir. I followed them to what appears to be an old train station."

"A train station? Are you sure it's not another installation like this? One of the nine camps?" Maybe this idiot was dumb enough not to realize that *their* base was connected to a train station.

"It's not one of ours. And I don't know if it's just an old station or maybe a base, sir."

"How many bandits?"

"I can't say for certain until I can go back. I was on my own and didn't want to risk capture before you had word."

"Good job, Horrance."

Horrance kept smiling, displaying two uneven rows of ruined teeth.

Sutherland tried not to let the man's ugliness sour his appetite for dinner. "Gallus? Please take Horrance to the whores. Let him have his pick — any except for mine."

"Yes, sir," Gallus said.

"Thank you, sir." Horrance's smile grew bigger and uglier.

"You're welcome." Sutherland tried not to imagine the beast on top of any woman, fouling them with what he imagined would be a misshapen cock. "Come back later and we'll plot our next course of action against the traitors."

Gallus escorted him out.

Sutherland sat in his throne room, alone with his excitement. Soon he would capture the traitors. And once he had Ana back in his care, he would hold all the cards and ensure his return to head of the Patriots.

He smiled, deciding to avail himself of his whores.

Anastasia Lovecraft

LIAM AND ANA left Oswald and Katrina behind, heading to their own room while the doctor led Katrina to the one he'd promised before dinner. She would be on the other side of the tunnel, a loud yell away if needed.

Her heart began to beat faster as Liam closed the door behind them. They were finally alone. She wondered if it would be different with him missing his eye, if he would be self-conscious about his wound when he didn't need to be. Liam was fierce and bold, then suddenly shy without warning. A wonderful lover, though she had no one to compare him to.

She looked in the mirror, pinched her cheeks, and again thought of her mother. Ana remembered her prettiest nighties, the ones her mom had said were her father's favorites. She remembered her mother telling her that one day she would have her own favorite nighties, more grown up than the little girl ones in her dresser then, and that her man's favorites would probably be her favorites too. She remembered feeling excited. Now Ana wondered if she'd ever have a favorite nighty or even a shabby dresser to keep it folded inside.

She finished in the bathroom, then emerged in a long white bed shirt as Liam was entering the room. He closed the door and turned to Ana.

"Where'd you go?"

"Katrina came back, right after you went into the bathroom. She wanted to let me know she'd be sleeping with one eye open tonight. She thinks Egan might try pulling a fast one."

"Do you agree?"

Liam shook his head. "I think he was telling the truth. He'll let us go." He sat on the bed beside her, peeling off his shirt. "Are you sure you want to come?"

"What?" Ana didn't want to talk. She wanted his lips on hers, then everywhere else. She wanted no words to interrupt them.

"That little girl could die."

"So could Adam." She traced her fingers along his skin, circling his nipple and then dipping down past his waistline to tease him. "Please, don't make me feel worse than I already do. Can we not talk … now?"

Liam opened his mouth, then swallowed his words like a good boy. "You're right."

As his mouth found Ana's and his hands cupped her breasts, months of tension melted to nothing. He pressed himself against her, lowering her down to the mattress and pulling the blankets over their heads like a tarp.

"I love you, Liam," Ana panted.

He mashed his lips hard against hers, making love to her mouth for a moment with his tongue.

"I love you too," Liam said — a long time later, when they were finally done.

Ana felt herself falling asleep, naked, his warmth against her skin.

This was the way it should be. Forever.

She usually fell asleep slowly, most of the time wondering what the next day would bring. But here in the warmth of the tunnels, lying safe in a bed, breathing long shallow breaths beside Liam, an ounce of worry seemed like a pound too much. Next to Liam, everything seemed more than okay. She had to get Adam, then everything else would settle into place.

Her father had always told her to enjoy the moments they had, because one day they'd be gone, no matter what. Good advice she should finally start taking.

Who knows what tomorrow will bring? We are here now. Together.

Ana fell asleep.

When she woke in the morning, Liam was gone.

THIRTEEN

Adam Lovecraft

"Tell the truth," Adam said. "Do you think we'll make it?"

Colton peeked out the door and into the street. "I don't see any zombies and the building is just a few more blocks ahead."

"You didn't answer the question."

"No." Colton shook his head without meeting his stare. "Probably not. But if we don't try, we don't stand a chance."

Based on what they'd seen earlier and the movement of the zombies, it seemed like the swarms were all headed toward the tallest building. Zelle was at the top. There would be plenty of fighting and pain before they could find her, if they were lucky enough to reach her at all.

Zombies were impossible to cut through once they started moving in a wall, and they'd be several layers deep so close to the building.

"Are you ready?"

"Yes," Adam answered, as if he had a choice, following

Colton out as light flurries of snow began to fall in the darkness.

The empty street allowed Adam to imagine for a moment that they really could make it the rest of the way without running into anything else. Maybe they would find a way to get inside the building. Colton was a great shot. Plus, he was smart. He would think of a way.

Maybe there was power in the building. Or an elevator that went to the top. It didn't make sense that Zelle would have climbed so many stairs by herself. Adam had asked Colton how tall he thought the tallest building was. He'd said he didn't know, so Adam had tried to count. There were maybe forty floors. Unlike most of the other buildings in the city, the tallest one seemed mostly unbroken, with only a few windows missing near the top. Not only was it the tallest, but clearly it was the strongest too.

"I wonder if Hooper made it out alive." Adam didn't believe it, but it seemed like Colton had lost hope for them both. Saying impossible things out loud might make things better.

"Hooper didn't make it. No way. There were too many."

"You never know."

Colton stopped walking. He turned to Adam, pulled a small black square from his pocket, and jammed his thumb on the middle of it. A small blinking circle with the number *51* in it appeared and moved toward two other circles, *17* and *88*. Tiny chirps bleated from the box's small speakers.

"What is that?"

"This is a mini-radar I got in the Opening Rush. It shows you a few blocks' radius around your location. That "51" is the number assigned to Hooper's bracelet in the game. These other two dots are us."

"He's alive!" Adam said, smiling.

"Well, maybe. We don't know if he's infected."

They watched the dot coming closer as the bleats grew louder.

"He's moving pretty straight forward. Zombies don't tend to walk like that, do they?"

Colton nodded. "Maybe the bastard did manage to get away. Let's stay put and wait, though, to be on the safe side."

The bleats grew louder. Colton and Adam looked down as a fourth dot, one without a number, suddenly appeared on the screen behind Hooper.

"What's that?" Adam asked.

"Not good news. Either a zombie or a bandit."

Colton handed the radar to Adam, then knelt, swung his rifle in front of him, lowered his eye to the scope, and scanned the darkness ahead.

"Is it him?"

"Yeah!" Colton exclaimed. "He's running, he's not too far. He'll be here in a minute."

More beeping as several more dots appeared on the screen, all behind Hooper, and none with numbers.

"There's a bunch more dots," Adam said, looking up to see Colton's face, staring wide-eyed and slack-jawed through the scope as he registered what Colton had spied on the radar.

"What?" Adam asked.

"He's got a whole damned horde behind him."

"Doesn't he see them?" Adam looked down at the now dozens of dots on the screen.

"I don't know, but he's going to lead them right to us. *Shit.*"

His body tightened, watching Hooper appear at the

end of the street. He was too far away for Adam to detail his injury, but he wasn't moving like an infected man.

"Guys!" Hooper called out, waving his arms, seemingly oblivious of the threat behind him.

Adam turned to Colton. "Aren't you going to shoot them?"

Colton said nothing, eye to his scope.

Just when Adam thought he would have to ask again, or else suffer death from anticipation, Colton pulled the trigger.

THWAP!

But it wasn't a zombie he shot.

Hooper dropped to the pavement.

Adam stared, barely able to believe his eyes.

"You killed him!" Adam stared straight ahead as the zombies descended on the fresh kill.

He could hear their ravenous grunts as they tore into Hooper's flesh.

Colton turned to Adam, put his hands on both Adam's shoulders, and shook him. "Come on, or we're their next course."

With no time to mourn, they ran.

FOURTEEN

Keller

KELLER OPENED his eyes to a raging headache and an empty bed. He threw the covers from his body, stumbled to his feet, and wandered out into the living room of their spacious City 1 loft, one of the more obvious perks of being the State's Provisional Leader, a title he'd assumed even though Jack Geralt was dead.

The Elders determined that it was better to maintain the illusion that Geralt was still alive rather than to appoint Keller as the State's One True Leader. And, as Keller's understanding of the power structure's *true* inner workings expanded — a few Elders secretly pulled strings behind the scenes — the decision made sense.

It also left the taste for government sour on his tongue.

Keller had never thought it would be possible to mourn his old life as City 6 chief, a position he'd done everything possible to get promoted from. But mourn it he did, every damned day as he woke to City 1's glistening paradise, and then through the evening, into the black of night when the burn of scotch helped him to sleep.

Jacqueline was happy enough, with her new friends and shopping trips. She was living in luxury's lap and couldn't understand why Keller's mood had been so consistently negative, especially considering he had always promised this very move would be the one thing that might heal what was broken.

Things had been different between them since Joshua's death. And though she'd never said it, Keller knew a part of her blamed him. Whether the blame was for not spotting the bomb or the Underground scum who planted it — or for the State's policies which the Underground opposed — she'd not looked at him the same since losing their son.

So he buried himself in work while she filled the void in ways he didn't want to think about.

"Promotion means a new life, Jacqueline," Keller had said aplenty. "We'll have different things to see and different things to do. Everything will be better."

But nothing was better. Even though Jacqueline seemed happy when keeping herself busy with friends and shopping, he could tell in their moments alone that things still weren't right, and now likely couldn't be.

Just admit it: you're thinking about Adam.

Despite just having gotten up, Keller poured himself a drink — a small one now, more later — to silence the inner voice that wanted to dwell on betrayal and scold him for allowing the kid to get close, letting him occupy a spot in his heart opened by Joshua's death.

Adam will never be half the man my son would've been.

But it wasn't just Adam's betrayal that kept him low. There was something else — something he couldn't quite put his finger on. He didn't think it was the politics of City 1 leadership, at least not exactly. Keller had kissed ass long enough to understand the game. It wasn't the new stresses of having to deal with the privileged City 1 citizens and their many demands. He often wished he could take a few of them into an alley and set them straight. But his hands were tied: everyone in City 1 knew someone who knew an Elder.

Sometimes Keller wished Jonah had taken out more than forty percent of the place. Really, what would have been the harm to the State if he'd taken out the whole damned city and left them to start over?

The law was solid, practical, necessary. It kept people safe. But it was poison to know the truth about the people behind it. These esteemed Elders he had only seen once or twice a year prior to coming here, and now suffered on a daily basis. He never saw their pettiness and damage before, now those qualities shimmered.

Rules weren't just made to maintain power. They were also used to punish personal enemies, usually for the most trivial of things. These were rich, powerful men who were not used to refusal. Keller had yet to question his oath to the State, but he did question those in seats of power, and wondered if improvements were possible.

He dared not say it publicly, but Keller was looking for a chance to bring new blood into the Elders Council, to find at least one other who truly believed in properly running the State.

Keller entered the kitchen and saw a note on the cupboard's digital face. "Gone out with Evia. Be back for dinner."

Good. Now he could get nice and drunk.

Keller left the kitchen and went into his office. He sat at his desk and pulled the half-empty bottle of scotch from its home behind the bottom drawer, along with the tumbler he'd been using for days, pretending that Jacqueline didn't count or notice it missing. He filled the glass and wondered *why* Jonah had unleashed the virus.

It had never made a lick of sense, and even with a full tumbler of the State's best scotch it wasn't any better. No part of Keller believed the official story — that Jonah had decided to topple City 1 on his own to hit the State where it counted. Keller could easily see some of the more radical leaders of the Underground pulling such a cowardly move, but never from Jonah.

He was a good man, despite his radical leanings. No matter how angry Jonah was over his wife's murder, his framing for the crime, or even Ana's fate, Keller couldn't imagine what would drive an honest man to murder so many innocents. Assuming the Underground *had* planned the attack — and Keller had no reason to suspect anyone else — he couldn't think of a way they could ever have managed to drag Jonah into the scheme.

Yet somehow they had, and now nearly half of the State's crown jewel was a memory.

Keller had studied the footage from Jonah's attack over and over for hours at a time. The State wasn't lying about the skeleton of facts: Jonah had definitely *done* the deed. He was the one on the train unleashing the virus. The guilty horror was clear on his face.

But Keller also thought that Jonah seemed uncertain, and he didn't think it was the Underground that had given him the helpful shove. But someone had helped Jonah get into City 1 and orchestrated the attack. Someone inside City 1. Someone trusted by the State?

Keller assumed that the Elders had wanted him to solve the crime, in addition to taking over as the Provisional Leader. But as he poked around, asking questions, his investigation was stonewalled by the Elders, who didn't want a word whispered about any alternate possibilities.

Go about your lives, ladies and gentlemen. Nothing to fear here in City 1.

But Keller was too smart to believe the lies he was forced to tell.

He took another swallow and wondered yet again who his true enemy was, and when they might strike again.

FIFTEEN

Adam Lovecraft

EARLY MORNING LIGHT pounded on Adam's eyelids, almost forcing them open as he slowly woke to the sound of movement. He managed to keep them closed. Something might be wrong, and if it was, then feigned sleep beat opening his eyes to danger.

He kept his eyes closed, barely moving his fingers, hand slowly inching toward his blaster. Hand around the butt, Adam finally dared to open his eyes. He was ready to shoot … but didn't need to. The "danger" was only Colton, who knelt a few feet across from him, stuffing his pack with supplies that probably weren't worth the weight on his back.

The old store where they'd been staying had been picked dry, who-knew-how-many times across who-knew-how-many years. Packing his bag with scraps made Colton seem as desperate as Adam knew he probably was.

With a guilty flush, Adam remembered that he had fallen asleep on the job. After Colton declared that they needed to rest before attempting to reach Zelle, Adam was supposed to take — and stay awake through — the final shift.

At first, Adam had only pretended to sleep. After arguing with Colton over the necessity of shooting Hooper — which Colton insisted he had to do to save both of their lives — Adam wanted time to think.

And think he did, over both Colton's seemingly heartless action, and whether or not Adam would do the same thing if put in that position. Wondering was the last thing he remembered before nodding off and sleeping through the night despite the sporadic gunshots, screams, and rolling groans that seemed an ever-present soundtrack in the Outback.

"Why didn't you wake me?"

Colton turned to Adam. "I wasn't tired."

"Really?"

"That so hard to believe? You may be young, kid, but I'm in the prime of my life. There's an old saying: 'you're only as old as you feel.' Well, I feel fantastic, son. Top o' my game." Colton stood with loudly creaking knees.

"Yeah," Adam said with a grin. "Might wanna grease those rusty gears."

After so long without laughing, the two of them doing it together was like sun melting snow. He had suffered isolation too long.

"What's the plan once we find Zelle? How will we convince her to trust us and escape the Outback without us all getting killed?"

"One step at a time," Colton said. "First we need to reach her."

"But you do have a plan, right? You're not just making this up as we go."

"Trust me."

"My dad said to never trust a man who says 'Trust me.'"

"Your father was a smart man. If only he had taken his own advice. In the end, it comes to trusting the *right* people, those who prove themselves, which I've done quite nicely by saving you. Your father trusted Liam Harrow blindly, and that got him into trouble. Liam ratted him out, and that led to Keller ordering your dad to kill your mom."

"What do you mean?"

"Keller had a chip put in your dad. It's in all Watchers. They activated your dad's and forced him to kill your mother."

Plenty of Colton's words sounded — and *felt* — wrong, but the cloth was too large, and Adam didn't know where to start cutting. "W-w-why would Keller do that?"

"Because your father was part of the Underground and a threat to the status quo. And you know what they say about the status quo?"

"What?"

"That men at the top will sell their souls, kill their brothers, and destroy nations, so long as they maintain their power."

The sound of clopping hooves came in from the street.

"Shit," Adam said jumping up and heading to the window.

Colton was there a beat before him. They stared through the glass as Adam's heart gathered speed. A black and red stagecoach pulled by four armored horses was on the street below. A man in a black hat and matching trench coat clutched reins like a cowboy from the Old Nation flix atop the stagecoach.

It was hard to see inside the carriage, through the thick, drawn curtains and grime-coated windows. But Adam was most horrified by what he saw behind it — two women in blue Darwin Games jumpsuits being dragged by chains. One of the women was older and had dirty, matted blonde hair, but the other was young, with long dark hair. She reminded him of Ana.

The women wore large metal collars — evil black bands circling their necks and attached to thick black chains that looked to be around seventy feet long. Both looked exhausted, eager to die.

Adam had seen some horrible things happen in the Games. Of course, there was murder — the Darwins were "Kill or Be Killed," after all — but there were also the rapes, which Adam hadn't really understood when he was little, but as he got older, he saw how they presented a new level of barbarism as mass entertainment. With the Games being held in the lawless Outback, crawling with depraved bandits and worse, the Darwins were throwing meat to the wolves.

Adam wondered if the women were sex slaves or if they were being dragged behind the stagecoach as zombie bait. His father had always said that no matter what, you had to do what was right, even if it was hard. *Especially* when it was hard. Adam had never stopped believing that, even when he couldn't believe in anything else.

He turned to Colton and looked up into his darkening eyes. "We have to do something."

"No, we don't. We sit tight until they pass."

"But those women look like slaves! We can't just watch from the window."

"There could be as many as four in the carriage, and old Big Hat on top. I don't like the looks of this — at all. We need to hit the building where Zelle is this morning and can't afford to take unnecessary chances."

"I saw your shooting. You could take two or three of

those bandits out before they knew where the shots were coming from."

Colton looked down again, as if assessing their odds, then met Adam's eyes. "Do you see the guy driving the coach? You know what that is there beside him?"

Adam peered over the sill again and saw a long thick black rifle, like nothing he'd seen at the Academy. "What is it?"

"It's called a Hellweaver. It fires ammo in bursts over a target, and those bullets explode above you. It's like raining fire. One shot up here, we're done for."

"Then you hit him first," Adam said as if raining fire meant nothing.

"And what if they have more Hellweavers inside? What if the coach is bulletproof? We're not doing anything, kid. Getting into a gunfight with them isn't just stupid, it's suicide. We're too close to everything right now. The building's just up ahead. We need to reach it. Dealing with the swarm of zombies at the bottom will be bad enough, the last thing we want to do is invite other players, bandits, or zombies to give us attention. I'm not trying to be cold, but there's too much at stake. We can't afford to let anything stop us from finding the girl."

Adam couldn't believe his indifference. "But if we do nothing, those women will die."

"We were all dead the minute we got here." Colton turned from Adam, looking down, then out the window. "You can't save everyone."

"Maybe not." Adam stood. "But I can save *them*."

He grabbed his blaster and turned toward the stairwell, making it one step before Colton grabbed him hard by the arm, dug his fingers into his flesh, and yanked him back toward the window. His face twisted into a scowl. "You're putting both our lives at risk."

"Let me go!" Adam shouted, loud enough to attract the bandits below.

Colton let go of his arm, eyes wide. "Think about what you're doing, boy."

"I know what I'm *not* doing: sitting up here like a scared old man." Adam turned and ran down the stairs two at a time until he reached the street below. He heard Colton bounding after him, but he was too fast, and by the time he hit the door, Colton had already realized the folly of chasing him into the street.

SIXTEEN

Anastasia Lovecraft

ANA STORMED into Egan's office.

"Where are Liam and Katrina?"

Egan sat at his desk, hands folded as if awaiting her arrival. One of his youngest soldiers stood behind him, a skinny kid with thick glasses, hand resting on a shock stick hung loosely at his belt. Ana glared, as if daring him to raise it, and made him find something on the floor to stare at.

Egan spoke softly, "Please, Ana, sit."

She didn't want to sit, damn it. "Where are Liam and Katrina?"

"They went to the Outback. To look for your brother, of course. Before you woke."

"I was supposed to go with them! You said we could take a skidder and you wouldn't stop us."

"Yes, I know what I said. But after speaking with Katrina last night, and then Liam ... they were both concerned for your safety. *They* asked if I would give them one of my men if they left you here."

"Damn it!" Ana said, kicking Egan's desk. She couldn't believe Katrina had tricked her like that. And that Liam had gone along with it.

Katrina's move was an unflinching betrayal; Liam's a knife in her back.

"I'm not staying here when my brother's out there."

"You won't be going anywhere."

"Are you going to stop me?" Ana glared at the skinny kid, wishing he'd give her an excuse to grab his shock stick and use it on him, then maybe on Egan. Or there was always her blaster.

Egan remained infuriatingly calm. Like he was dealing with a child. "You'll never reach the Outback if you leave on foot. And you're certainly not taking one of our vehicles. Clark, Katrina, and Liam have already gone with one of our two skidders."

"Who the hell is Clark?"

"A citizen kind enough to volunteer himself to go in your stead."

"I didn't ask for any volunteers! I don't need anyone to *go in my stead. I* should be there. Adam is *my* brother. *My* responsibility."

"I appreciate the sentiment, Ana. Your father would be proud." Egan gave her a smile that she wanted to carve from his face with a knife. "But sometimes the right thing to do is the hardest to choose. For you that means staying put even though you don't want to, so we can develop a cure for the virus. *That* is what's best for us all."

She felt a sense of déjà vu, hearing her father: *sometimes the right thing to do is the hardest.*

Ana wanted to keep raging, but Egan was basically right. Maybe not about her duty — her brother would always come first — but about her options. She had no idea how to find the Outback on her own, how far from the Station it was, or how long it would take her to reach it even under the best of circumstances.

She could escape the Station, but where to then? Where would she be safest? Besides: if Liam and Katrina managed to find Adam, they'd immediately return to the Station.

Ana couldn't risk not seeing her brother again. It was bad enough that she'd lost her parents. Adam was all she had left, other than Liam. Of course Egan was calm, knowing he had her.

She spent several seconds glaring into his smile, then left his office without another word.

ANA WAS SITTING on her bed, back to the wall and mind full of darkening thoughts, when there was a quiet, barely audible knock on her door.

"Yes?"

The door opened and Calla timidly stepped into her room. The girl's constant companion loomed behind her, like a Grim Reaper in waiting.

"She's welcome to come in, but you are not."

"Excuse me?" he asked.

"She can come in my room, but you may not."

"I'm supposed to watch her. I can't just—"

"You can wait outside. It's not like she can go anywhere from here." She gave the kid her coldest stare.

The boy looked nervously back and forth.

"It's okay, Elijah. I feel good."

He swallowed, "I don't know if I should—"

"It's okay," Calla repeated, reaching up and touching his hand sweetly, like a little sister.

"Okay. I'll be right outside the door."

"Thank you," Calla said.

He sheepishly left and Ana felt her morning's first victory, minor as it was.

She looked at the girl expectantly. Calla smiled, stepped the rest of the way into Ana's room, peeked her head out into the hallway and said something to her shadow that Ana couldn't hear, then slipped back inside, quietly closed the door, and walked over to the bed.

Calla sat on the end, looking little like she had when they met. Before, she was hard as a box of nails and dirty as a bandit. Thick clothes were her shield from the world. Now, sitting slouched and freshly scrubbed, wearing a long blue dress with a single yellow flower on her chest, she looked like the frail little child she was.

"He means well."

"He means to kill you if you turn," Ana said.

"I know, and he's right. He *should* kill me before I hurt someone."

Ana swallowed a lump as she considered the girl's bravery.

Calla pulled up her dress sleeve and showed Ana a bandage: white gauze wrapped around her left bicep. Eyes haunted, she said, "They say you're the only one who has ever survived infection and fully recovered. That true?"

Ana cringed at the bandage, remembering Duncan as he ripped into her flesh.

"Yes. Oswald was infected, too, but he chopped limbs off, so he doesn't consider himself to truly have fought off the virus."

"What happened?"

Ana didn't know what to say and wished she could say nothing. She felt oddly shy and uncomfortably ashamed. Though she hated talking about such an ugly reality with a child, she felt compelled to give Calla the truth.

"I was bitten. It was bad right away, then quickly got worse. I was weak and every bone felt hollowed out and stuffed with pain. Most of the time it felt like my body was on fire. I begged Liam to kill me, but he wouldn't. Without mercy, I spent every second hoping for death, angry that I couldn't find it. Then, one morning, right after it was at its worst, I felt suddenly better. I still don't know why."

"Dr. Oswald says it's something in your blood. That your blood reacted to the virus by fighting it, and that maybe he can get mine to do the same."

"That would be nice."

Calla stared into Ana's eyes for an uncomfortably long moment. Ana felt like the girl was trying to read her thoughts.

"You don't think I'll live, do you?"

Ana swallowed, regretting the lies even as they left her lips. "I think you'll be fine."

"Please, miss. Don't lie to me. Everyone walks around the Station saying I'll be fine, but I can see in their eyes that they're lying. No one believes it, except maybe Percy the cook. He still won't let me have sweets. If he thought I was gonna die he wouldn't care about my teeth. But everyone else acts like I'm already dead. Even my father, sometimes. Please — tell me the truth: *Do you think I'll be cured?*"

Ana thought back to her lowest point, begging Liam to leave her. She'd tried to run, but he'd kept believing in her, no matter what. She never could have survived without his faith in her, she would have slouched in a corner and waited to die.

Ana stared into the girl's eyes and saw a bright fire that belied Calla's scrawny frame. The child had to believe, and — more importantly — needed someone to truly believe *in* her, without candy or lip service.

"Yes, I think you'll live."

Calla leaped across the space between them and threw her arms around Ana, tears streaming down her face.

Ana allowed herself to cry and hoped she wasn't wrong.

SEVENTEEN

Liam Harrow

As they navigated the alleyway, Liam stayed behind Katrina and the man Egan had lent them. His name was Clark, skinny and pale like a half-dipped candle. Pale except for the fact that every inch of his body was painted with tattoos. Before they'd left, Liam saw that the man's chest, arms, and back wore a blanket of color. Then he donned a thick black jacket like the one they gave Liam and covered all but his head.

On the skidder, and in the two hours since leaving it behind and sneaking in through the only part of the Outback's vast drainage network that wasn't patrolled by orbs, Liam found himself pondering the mystery of Clark's ink.

The tattoos were colorful geometrics, threaded by intricately drawn black vines. Letters bled through the shapes, though Liam couldn't find meaning and didn't feel like asking — or trusting — a man who had barely breathed a word since joining their expedition.

Regardless, Clark was said to be the Station's best shot after Egan and more than made up for Ana's absence in that regard. Liam couldn't stop thinking about her anyway. She would be furious at him for lying and leaving her behind. But Katrina had pulled Liam aside while Ana was in the bathroom and convinced him that there wasn't much of a choice. She was certain that Egan would never really allow Ana to leave. It was best to go with Egan's blessing and give Oswald time to find a cure. So as Liam and Ana made love, Katrina went to Egan and said they'd go, on the condition that they were given another warrior to help keep them alive.

The mission seemed simple enough last night: find Adam and bring him back. But as they crept from the sewers and navigated the crumbling city's crooked corridors, Liam couldn't help but remember nearly losing Ana in the Outback a year before. They would certainly have died on that rooftop if not for Belan's orb.

But there would be no orb to watch their backs this time. If anything, Belan — who was at Paradise, one of Hydrangea's sister camps — might be more inclined to help Sutherland hunt Liam down.

Odds were against them: they faced bandits, players, and a city thick with undead, plus whatever orbs the State had sent to monitor the Games. The State couldn't afford to have Liam, of all people, pop up in the middle of their precious Games, so he would be exterminated on sight.

He hoped that his hair — much longer than it had been a year before — along with his scruffy beard and the eye patch would disguise him enough. Thinking of his eye made it itch even more. He pressed the leather patch hard against the socket, to kill the itching with a shot of excruciating pain.

Katrina held out a hand to halt them.

Liam's gaze tracked her finger, aimed at a bank of windows overlooking the street. So far they'd been walking along a windowless row of decaying buildings. They would be exposed unless they moved through the building beside them, which held dangers of its own.

Then she pointed toward a door dangling by one hinge from a wet and rotting frame. Clark nodded as he opened the door one-handed while aiming his blaster inside.

Clark slid into the building's darkness, then emerged a moment later and said, "Clear."

Katrina followed, with Liam taking the rear.

The only thing he hated worse than navigating the Outback's roads was crawling through the city's dark interiors, which were teeming with the wrong types of life — rats, bandits, zombies, and even the occasional wolf.

They crept along the building's bottom floor, stepping over debris and slowly making their way through the littered space, ducking in and out of shadows, quiet like scurrying mice.

Liam's heart was pounding like a warning in echo. From somewhere ahead — the floor above, behind a wall, in the next room, he couldn't be sure — he heard the rumble of zombies, the murmur of the undead who no longer spoke and could only croak their haunting cry of death that had yet to claim them.

He looked over to Katrina, then to Clark. Both nodded. They heard it too. Katrina didn't bother with the hybrid rifle or the blaster at her hip. She clicked both her wrist blades to life like six razor-sharp claws eager to shred.

Liam wished like hell that he had something cooler than his crappy blaster.

As they passed through two more rooms, the moaning grew louder. Katrina stopped at a door, shook her head, and twirled her finger through the air, motioning for them to turn back around.

Liam was now in front, leading them back toward the

door. Too late they realized the moaning was rolling in from every direction.

A zombie crashed through the doorway, rabid and frantic on its way to fresh meat. It gnashed and clawed toward Liam, the closest living human. He made the mistake of looking to Katrina for direction, hoping she'd give him some miracle clue.

She shot him a sharp look: *pay attention, eye in front!*

More zombies spilled in as the leader — an ancient-looking man wearing crusted jeans and nothing else — launched himself at Liam.

They landed hard on the splintered wooden floor, zombie on top. Liam's gun also lay too far away as its jaws opened and closed, desperate for flesh.

For the attack's first few seconds he held out his thick jacketed arms, keeping the zombie away from his skin. They'd each wrapped several layers of cardboard and cloth around their forearms and wrists before leaving Hydrangea, both to protect from bites and to give them something to push the zombies away with.

With all of his strength, he pulled his arms back, then shoved forward. It wasn't much: he still felt off balance with only one eye, and the zombie had most of the leverage, but Liam was able to tip him backward enough to use his momentum and shove the zombie from his body.

Liam scrambled to his feet and stomped hard on the zombie's head, once, twice, three times — then four and five — harder and harder until the zombie's face looked like mashed pumpkin.

He might have kept at it if he hadn't heard another three zombies approaching. Liam leapt back toward his gun, grabbed it off the ground, and turned to shoot. The closest zombie — a tall woman in pigtails, who looked like she might have been a kindly mom some once-upon-a-never-again — would have killed him for sure, but she flew by Liam on her way to something behind him. He managed to pop a shot between the second zombie's eyes, disintegrating its face and sending the undead body twitching to the floor. The third zombie was on him and ready to bite.

Liam, caught by surprise, yelled out as if his scream could somehow scare the zombie away.

It opened its mouth, putrid rot falling forth as Liam struggled to guard his face. It was inches away when a blade split through the front of the zombie's jaw, nearly slicing Liam's cheek, and then the corpse was yanked away from him.

Clark turned on the zombie he'd just killed and swung his machete, grunting with every hack, cutting into the creature's head, chest, and arms until he leaned over in exhaustion, hands to knees.

Katrina stood behind him, slinging blood from her wrist blades onto the wall before sheathing them.

Liam stared at the litter of corpses — a wet, messy circle around them, seven full bodies and a couple in parts — dispatched mostly by Katrina and Clark.

"Are you okay?" Katrina's voice was kind behind Liam.

He looked over his still-shaking body, trying to catch his breath. "Yeah, I think so. Thanks."

Seeing he was fine, she lost her softness. "Well, be more fucking careful next time. You'll get us killed."

"What did I do?" Liam had done his best, followed her lead, turned when he was supposed to, handled the attack to the best of his ability. The problem was *her bad idea*.

Katrina said nothing. She had been cold ever since the three of them had left the drainage tunnels. She'd always been a mystery, and he didn't have time now to read between her many lines. He figured that probably more than anything, Katrina was more scared than she wanted — or was willing — to admit.

Liam didn't want to think there was anything more, that maybe she harbored resentment towards him, or perhaps regretted going on this mission. He hated politics and niceties in the best of times and certainly didn't care to navigate them now.

They walked back toward the exit in silence, prepared to go back into the snow, pausing at the door to stare out at a world that had grown louder around them, filled with gunshots, screams, and perhaps the most chilling of all sounds, man's laughter as he committed atrocities against others. Danger was too close to risk being out in the open.

"We can't go out there," Katrina said, confirming his thoughts.

"Then where?" Liam asked.

She nodded across the room. A door, open. Beyond it, stairs. "Up."

Liam didn't argue. Instead, he fell into a soft gait behind Katrina and Clark, shoving the stir in his gut as low as he could, shaking his head from the memories of climbing to a roof where he and Ana were nearly killed a year ago.

EIGHTEEN

Sutherland

SUTHERLAND WOKE to the sensation of being shaken.

His head pounded from a gallon too much of last night's hooch. That and whoring.

"Sir, sir!" Gallus sounded urgent.

Last thing Sutherland needed was to hear his braying into the morning.

"What is it?" He sat up and pulled the red silk sheets up to cover his cold, naked body, then looked over to where Nat's curly, dark hair concealed her face beside him. "Well?"

Gallus stood by his bed like an idiot. "The throne room, sir. Someone's … well, I think you should just come see."

Sutherland sighed and looked over at his whore, then slid on his clothes from the night before — black dress pants and a burgundy shirt — and pulled his long red hair into a ponytail. He tied it back with a thin strip of leather and fastened his belt with the blaster. He considered grabbing his sheathed sword but thought better of it. He still had to bathe and didn't feel like fussing with more than he needed to.

Sutherland felt suddenly hungry. Though damn near empty, he ignored the growl on his way to whatever faux emergency Gallus was whining about.

As his number two led him through the crowded hallways, too many eyes were like spiders on his body. Hydrangea's air stank of something Sutherland didn't like. He was about to ask Gallus if he could report what he'd seen, without the mystery and ballyhoo, but he couldn't stop and demand to know in front of the others.

So he kept his eyes on the idiot and kept marching behind him until they reached the throne room's double doors where two of his men stood guard.

They met his eyes as he entered, then quickly looked down.

He was about to demand their reason for not holding his gaze, but swallowed the words when he saw for himself: someone had smeared two words on his new throne with feces.

King Shit

Sutherland stared, feeling his face redden, skin on fire. He inhaled as slowly as he exhaled, swallowing the lump of betrayal, then turned to Gallus. "Who did this?"

"I ... um ... don't know, sir."

"Don't know?" Sutherland snarled as if he couldn't believe that Gallus had the nerve to admit something so stupid.

"No, sir. We're looking into it."

"When did this happen?"

"We don't know, Sir. Therault and Harris came down here this morning to let in the builders so they could finish the design. The doors were open when we got here."

"Where's Connor?"

"Who?"

"Connor Vinson, the sneaky rat bastard who tried to rally support for an election earlier this year. Find him. Now. Bring him to me. Five minutes."

Gallus left and Sutherland stared at the shit. His blood rolled to a boil.

From behind, just outside the room, he heard suppressed laughter from one of the two men at the door. He spun, drawn to the men's laughter like a falcon to a fat and filthy rat.

Sutherland stood in front of the men, knowing neither of their names. One was thin and in his thirties with dark circles under his eyes that made him look like the sobbing whore his mother most certainly was. The other was fat, his extra pounds weighing him down with expendable sloth. He looked twenty or so. Both men looked frightened as Sutherland paced before them, his arms crossed.

"Is something funny?"

"No, sir," said the whore's son, his dark-rimmed eyes staring at an imaginary puddle of his own reeking piss.

"How about you, Piggy?" Sutherland turned to the fat one. "Something funny?"

"No, sir," said the sloth, growing more expendable by the second, still staring at the floor and his own imaginary puddle of ammonia-scented fear.

"Well *someone* was laughing." Sutherland scrunched his face. "Unless I'm hearing things." He paused, leaned toward them. "I'm not hearing things, am I?"

"We weren't laughing," said the pig.

Whore's son kept his eyes to the floor.

"So are you calling me a liar?" Sutherland was an inch from Piggy's face.

"No, sir."

"But *someone* was laughing. And you two are the only

ones standing here, right?" He feigned surprise. "Did I miss a gaggle of school children skipping by laughing on their way into the City? Is that it? Did I miss the frolicking wee ones?" He shook his head and clucked his tongue. "Such a shame to have missed them. There's always much to learn from an innocent's whimsy."

Sutherland stared into Piggy's beady eyes. "Did you make me miss an innocent's whimsy, or are you a lying pig who said something behind my back?"

The man's jowls shook as he shivered. "I don't know … sir."

"You don't know if there were frolicking children, or you don't know if you said something yellow when you thought I couldn't hear."

"I don't know, sir," Piggy repeated, one heave from tears.

Sutherland smacked the pig across the face and watched him tremble, too terrified to reach for his gun.

"I'm going to ask you both once more. Who was laughing?"

The two men traded glances. The bastard slowly raised his finger to Piggy. "He was, sir."

"I was laughing at a joke, sir!"

"A joke?" Sutherland said with an exaggerated smile. "Well, why the hell didn't you tell me? I love jokes. Go ahead. Tell me the joke."

Piggy shook his head and pointed at the skinny man. "Jim told it to me, sir."

Sutherland spun to Jim's face and stopped just inches from it. "Make me laugh, Slim Jim!"

He bristled and shuddered, hemmed and hawed, then said nothing worth a damn. Finally, his eyes lit as if he'd conjured the perfect joke to cover the fib from his hog of a friend.

"How can you spot a zombie whore?" He paused a beat, then finished. "Because she's the one moaning."

"What? Well, that's not a very funny joke, Jim. Which means that you, Piggy, have a horrible sense of humor!" He jabbed his finger into Porky's chest. "Now, please tell me the truth before I make you uncomfortable with something sharp. Was that *really* what you were laughing at?"

Piggy said nothing.

Sutherland turned to Jim. "Ten seconds: I want the truth or you'll both lick shit from my throne before I cut you."

"No, sir," Jim finally said. "He wasn't laughing at a joke. He was laughing at the throne."

"So you just lied to me, Slim? Why'd you go and make up a joke to cover for your fat friend?"

"I … um, don't know, sir."

"At least you could've had the decency to think up a good one. Not that god-awful zombie whore joke. Tell you what, Slim. I've a guaranteed chuckle you're both sure to love!"

Piggy and Slim Jim both visibly swallowed.

Sutherland whipped out his blaster and fired it into the whoreson's stupid face. His head puffed in a sick splash of blood and ash as the pig screamed like he was stuck.

Piggy finally reached for his blaster.

"No, no, no," Sutherland said sweetly, shoving his own in the man's face. "Now, tell me who in the hell did this."

"I don't know, s-sir," Piggy said as his friend's headless body spilled to the floor, finally pissing himself.

Sutherland sighed as he shoved the blaster so hard past Piggy's trembling lips he broke a tooth on the way into his mouth. "Once more … *who did this?*"

Piggy mumbled something.

Sutherland pulled the gun from his mouth.

"C-C-Connor Vinson!" Piggy spit.

"Who else?"

"I don't k-know. Connor asked us to borrow the keys last night. Said he had a surprise for you; a gift."

"Are you really that fucking stupid?"

Piggy said nothing and proved it.

Sutherland asked again and Piggy nodded.

Sutherland shook his head in disgust, sighed, then reached for the man's blaster. Piggy's fingers tightened on the gun, then Sutherland met his eyes and the grip relaxed as Piggy closed his eyes in surrender.

"I'm going to give you a chance to redeem yourself. Would you like that?"

"Yes, sir."

"I want you to dispose of Slim's body, then return when you're done. Got it?"

"Yes, sir."

Sutherland held up a finger. "No, that's yes, King Shit."

Piggy looked at Sutherland wide-eyed, like he wasn't sure if he should be prepared to die, or laugh. He did neither, frozen and mumbling. Sutherland loved it. He laughed and smacked Piggy's back. "Now, that's funny!"

Gallus came walking up with Connor Vinson.

Connor's eyes were dead.

"Hello, traitor." Sutherland smiled.

NINETEEN

Adam Lovecraft

Adam crept along the wide city street, running hunched from one hiding spot to another, trailing the coach as close as he dared. Hiding behind one of the many hunks of stripped cars shoved to the side of the street, while trying not to tremble from the wind as much as from his fear, he was surprised that the noises of clopping hooves, turning coach wheels, and metal chains scraping on the ground weren't attracting any nearby zombies.

Maybe whatever was keeping the swarm gathered at the base of the building ahead was responsible. The closer he inched to the carriage, the more certain he grew that the women were being used as zombie bait of some kind, even if they weren't yet doing their job.

He wondered what the bandits did once the women were attacked. Was the purpose to keep the riders safe through the assault — give the zombies easy prey to distract them — or something darker?

Did the bandits sit and watch? Or place bets? What happened next? How would they deal with the horde?

Maybe that's when they'd pour from the coach and start hacking the undead.

Adam realized with an uncomfortably large lump in his throat (suddenly missing Colton more than he cared to admit) that this looked like something bandits designed for sport.

Alone in a cell for more than a long half year, it was finally easy for Adam to figure out how much of his Watcher training was mere propaganda. Still, as Michael had said before his murder, there was truth inside every lie, otherwise they were hard to believe. Adam had learned plenty about the packs of bandits that lived as subhuman savages, haunting the Barrens with murderous intent, so this sort of thing shouldn't have been a surprise.

Crouched behind a wall of warped metal and ancient tires — now just rims in the snow — Adam found it easy to accept the City Watch rules about bandits:

Never trust a bandit.

Shoot first. Ask questions later.

Never sympathize with one of their women or children, lest you be tricked and stabbed in the back by one of their men.

At the time of Adam's training, he had secretly wondered if perhaps the anti-bandit stuff was just a warped City Watch perception. He had never been outside the Walls but figured that the people in the Barrens couldn't be all that different from citizens living inside the Cities: people were people, after all. Anyone who spent their life on the lookout for zombies while scavenging for limited resources in a dead land could be turned into a savage. Still Adam had always figured there was something human left in them. But not any longer.

No one who chained women and dragged them through the streets deserved an ounce of sympathy. They deserved to die in the worst way imaginable — shot but not killed, left to be dined on by zombies.

He darted from behind his metal rampart to a slab of rubber and concrete that reminded him of the partitions that kept City 6 stuffed behind Walls. He made it to within twenty feet of the chained women, when he realized that his idea — using the blaster to separate the chains — might not work. Blasters fired energy strong enough to disintegrate men, but he'd never used one to shoot at inorganic matter. If he were wrong, and the chain didn't break, he'd be forced to take out the bandits — as many as five — entirely on his own.

And if any one of them got a shot off with a Hellweaver, Adam would be a dead man.

He peeked around the partition's sheared-off edge, making sure the bandit riding atop the stagecoach wasn't looking back, then launched himself forward to close the distance between himself and the women.

His heart slammed against his ribcage as he drew nearer, sucking in icy breaths that stung his lungs. He wondered how long he'd been chasing the coach, and more importantly, how much distance he'd put between himself and Colton.

He looked back, but the rotten buildings all looked similar, with one crumbling facade mirroring the next. Seeing everything lined in a row, he couldn't remember — or determine — which building had held them for the night.

Adam cursed his impulsive stupidity. He had managed to piss off the one guy in the Games who not only didn't see him as an enemy but who was also his path to possible freedom *if* they could find Zelle and make it to the Gardens, which might or might not exist.

Adam rechecked if the coast was clear, then darted to

the left, crossing the street for a better look at the windows on the right, trying his best to see Colton.

Nothing seemed familiar. They'd barely glanced at the exterior as they ducked inside the night before, happy to find a place away from the screaming, a few alleys up and away from where Hooper had been made into a feast after Colton put him down.

Even if everything looked different when cast under the bright morning light reflecting up from the snow, Adam didn't think his memory was sharp enough to draw their particular hovel from the line.

The coach pulled farther ahead. Adam sprinted again and this time kept running until he pulled up even with the girls, some seventy feet behind the coach.

They looked at him, startled. The older woman cried out.

Adam put a hand to her mouth and shook his head.

"I'm here to save you," he whispered, just above the icy wind, hoping like hell no one in front had been able to hear him.

The younger woman, the one who looked even more like Ana up close, seemed relieved. "Please, help us," she whispered, looking ahead at the stagecoach.

He showed his blaster to the women. "I'm going to try and shoot your chains off. Once I do, run into one of the buildings and just keep running. Can you do that?"

The older woman shook her head violently before she finally managed, "They'll k-kill us."

"I won't let that happen." Adam was surprised by his own boldness and the unreasonable belief that he might be able to handle the bandits.

"Do it," said the younger woman.

He aimed at the long thick chain linking body to collar, then angled down to the road, and back up to an iron rung at the stagecoach's rear. He had to aim low, or risk killing the women if the disintegration spread in either direction.

He fired and missed. *Shit.*

Adam didn't bother looking ahead to see if the driver had heard the blast, though it was hard to believe that he hadn't, even if the horses weren't spooked. He fired again and a section of chain burned bright blue before it faded, leaving a heap of smoldering ash as the connection broke.

The girl's eyes widened, relieved as she pulled up the remaining feet of chain still connected to her collar and raced toward the open door on the building to their left.

A yell came from up front. The clomping stopped and the stagecoach lurched to a standstill. Adam looked up front and saw the man in the black hat turn back toward him.

"Hey!" he screamed, then aimed a gun — a blaster instead of his Hellweaver — at Adam.

The second woman, still chained, cried out, "I didn't do anything!"

Adam fired at the driver. He missed, then dove to the ground, expecting the bandit's shot to tear through his body.

But Top Hat missed.

Adam had popped up, ready to fire another shot, when the carriage doors burst open and another three bandits poured out, all aiming their weapons at him.

The chained woman screamed, though Adam didn't know if she was yelling for him to save her or because she was sure the bandits wanted her dead.

He scrambled toward the same open door where the younger woman had fled. Dirt kicked up at his feet, chips of concrete sprayed his body as chunks of wall burst to dust around him.

He kept running, then dove through the open door and slid hard into a wall.

Pain splintered his head as he struggled to stand.

Then hands were on him, pulling him up from behind.

"Well, well, well, looks like we've got another member to the party," said the man in the black hat before punching Adam in the nose.

Unbearable pain — like everything was breaking all at once — tugged at his consciousness. He considered the horror of what would happen to his body if his mind couldn't fight.

It wasn't enough.

Adam fell and knew he would die.

TWENTY

Liam Harrow

LIAM WATCHED as Katrina's light bobbed along the stairwell walls. Without a light of his own, he was forced to keep close to her and Clark or risk getting left behind in a tangle of shadows, maybe missing a step. There was nothing he hated more than the idea of climbing stairs in the dark, one-eyed no less, with danger in wait both above and below.

They'd climbed three flights so far but had yet to run into more zombies. As they continued upward, Liam's chest kept constricting. He hoped Katrina would choose the next floor to leave the stairs, yet she kept climbing and climbing.

"How high do we need to go?" he finally asked.

She turned, aimed her light at Liam, blinding his eye. "What do you mean?"

He raised a hand, and she lowered the light toward his chest. "Why are we climbing?"

"Because." She spun the light from Liam, shined it up the stairs and kept walking.

"Thanks," Liam grumbled, falling in step behind Clark.

The stairwell stank of death. They climbed another three floors, hearing scratching from the hallways past the stairwells, before they reached a quiet floor. Katrina insisted they climb another two floors to the tenth. Clark agreed — although he gave no indication why — giving Liam little choice but to follow and nod.

On the tenth floor she opened the door and held it open for Liam and Clark. The room was oddly empty. Most rooms Liam had seen in the Outback were littered with Old Nation debris amid the few remaining relics of desperate survival. This room was barren except for dust like a carpet on the floor. The room was relatively bright, lit by a long row of oversized windows displaying the city's horrors below.

They went to the windows and looked out into the wasteland. Liam wondered if his face looked as hopeless as Katrina's and Clark's. He saw zombies, players, and orbs. No hope. From ten floors up, in an office building that had managed to stay reasonably tall while so many of its siblings had crumbled to nothing, they could see much of the chaos.

An orb flew by the window, one floor below, then burst into a smoky plume lit by azure sparks. The broken machine swirled through the air on its descent to a few feet above the ground, where it was chased by a huddle of bandits.

Liam turned from the window to see that Katrina was gone. "Where did she go?"

Clark shrugged, still staring out the window. Liam stared with him, until a few moments later when Katrina returned.

"Floor's clear," she said. "There's some stuff in the

other rooms. I suggest we check it all out, see if there's anything we can use. This area's too neat. My guess is someone lives here. It's worth checking out. Agreed?"

Katrina said it like a question, but Liam knew it wasn't. Clark probably knew too. Both men nodded without a word.

They split up and, as expected, Liam found nothing. He did think Katrina was probably wrong — the area *had* been someone's home but had long ago been abandoned. He found a room lined with shelves and neat rings in the dust. Outlines were faint but Liam was sure they had once harbored cans. One shelf read Water. He swallowed to kill his sudden thirst.

"Find anything?"

Startled, Liam looked behind him. Katrina was standing in the threshold, arms crossed, gaze and posture as sharp as her tone.

"What in the hell is your problem?" Liam finally asked.

"I don't have a problem." She crossed her arms tighter, and her scowl seemed to deepen. Everything about her said the opposite of her words.

"Yes, you do. And if we're all working together, it would be great to know what's crawled up your ass."

"Nothing's *crawled up my ass*, Liam. I just want to get this over and done with."

"Over and done with? You knew what we were going to do. You *wanted* to go find Adam. So why did you volunteer if you were afraid?"

"Who said anything about afraid? Besides, it's not like I had much of a choice. What was my option, to let you go alone? Or go with Ana? You'd both be dead, and we still wouldn't have him."

Liam wanted to lash out, angry that she doubted him so much. Who was to say that he couldn't have found

Adam on his own or with Ana's help? He didn't know much about a past Katrina wasn't willing to share, but much of her life was spent surviving the elements, predators, and zombies, while he'd grown up relatively safe behind City 6 walls.

He was ready to change the subject, but a deafening gunshot tore through the morning and took his chance, followed by another immediate two.

"Clark?" Liam said, knowing it wasn't.

"No." She shook her head, arms now uncrossed and reaching for her weapon. "He has a blaster, not a lead shooter."

As if to answer Katrina and the gunfire, a blaster echoed the shots before a tiny voice cried, "Sorry, I thought you were a zombie!"

It sounded like a little girl from far off. But up close, Liam saw he was wrong.

She was much taller than he pictured from her voice. He could only see her from the back as he and Katrina approached, but her voice was smaller than her size. She was at least a teenager, if not an adult, and wore the blue that Egan had told them all the players were wearing.

"Put the gun down or I'll shoot you," Katrina said.

The girl held her gun on Clark, who looked as confused as Liam did. She half-turned from the tattooed man to the newcomers, saw that they were both armed, and that Clark still had his blaster aimed at her. She aimed the gun to the floor, extended her arm, slowly squatted, and rested her gun on the floor.

"Please don't kill me."

"Get her gun," Katrina instructed Liam.

He went over, keeping his own blaster trained on the girl, and bent to grab her old revolver. Then he stood, his heart nearly skipping a beat as he met her eyes and saw the girl's face for the first time. "Chelsea?"

"You know her?" Clark said.

"She's from City 6. We grew up together. She was a friend of Ana's a long time ago."

Something crawled onto Katrina's face and died. Her eyes darkened and her mouth curled down at the corners. Her soured silence gave Liam a thirst to slap her. He turned to Chelsea.

She peered at Liam, studying his face. He wondered if she knew who he was, then figured his voice hadn't changed. She struggled for words and stuttered, "Liam? I thought you were dead!"

"That's what the State wanted you to think. How did you end up in the Games?"

Her face relaxed, ever so slightly. "Do you remember Alfonso Frailey?"

Liam thought, then shook his head.

"He's your age. We'd been going out for a while, turned out his dad was in the Underground. Alfonso wasn't, me neither. I didn't even know his dad was until all of us were arrested — his mom and little sister too. I haven't seen anyone but Alfonso since we were brought in."

"They took you in? Just like that?"

Chelsea nodded. "The new chief, Ives, he's been going crazy since Keller left. Alfonso thinks it's because he has something to prove. We weren't doing anything wrong when City Watch came, just looking at old flix. They stormed in and dragged us off. I can still hear Samantha screaming."

Liam ignored Katrina's growing impatience. "Have you seen Adam yet or anyone else from the City?"

"No. I spent last week alone in a cell, then was driven

here in a van with six others, two more girls and three guys. But I didn't know any of them. Only person I recognized at the Opening Rush was Alfonso, but he was all the way on the farthest side of the line and didn't see me. At least, I don't think he did."

It looked like Chelsea was trying not to cry. She swallowed, then seemed to catch herself. "What about you guys? Are you in the Games?"

Liam's back was still to Katrina, but he could feel her stare and imagined her tapping her foot. "No, and neither of my friends are. They're helping me."

"Helping you with what?" The question left in a whisper, harsh, as if afraid of his answer. "And what about Ana? Is she alive too?"

"She's safe." He nodded toward Clark. "They're helping me find Adam. We have to—"

"That's enough," Katrina cut him off. "We've wasted too much time here already."

Liam smiled at Chelsea, awkward and apologetic, then said, "I'll be right back," and walked to Katrina. Clark held his blaster on the girl as Liam pulled Katrina to the side and whispered. "We need to bring her along."

"Absolutely not."

"You can't be this cold," he argued. "If we don't help her, she's dead."

"You don't know that, Liam. She could be fine. Plenty of people survive. We're on a mission. Last thing we need is to be looking after some kid."

"She's not a kid, Katrina. She's the same age as Ana and me."

"And you've survived fine."

"Barely, with a lot of help, and now a missing eye. She's not a fighter — we're consigning her to death if we don't help her."

"Exactly. She's not a fighter. She'll slow us down at best. Or worse, consign *us* to death."

"How can you be so selfish?"

"I'm not the one who's being selfish, Liam. You're putting your need for warm fuzzies above the practical truth: your little friend could slow us down or get us killed. You left Ana so you could bring her brother back. How do you think she'll feel when you bring *that* back instead?"

Katrina nodded at Chelsea, as though she were a bag of garbage waiting for the dump. Again he wanted to hit her. "I'm not just leaving her to die. If I can help someone, I will. What harm could one more person be? Another set of eyes and ears, more senses to help us stay alive."

"Another mouth to feed or scream too loud."

"I'm giving her my gun. It's the right thing to do. If you're so concerned about our odds of survival, know that your choices are making them worse."

"This is your choice, Liam. And a stupid one. Why give up *your* weapon, just to prove a point?"

Liam turned from Katrina and walked over to Chelsea, drawing his weapon on the way. He made his eyes as kind as he could. She opened her hand as if by instinct and Liam set the gun on her palm. She wrapped her fingers around it.

"I'm sorry, but you can't come with us. We have to find Adam and can't afford to take anyone. We've been out here for a while, and know what to expect. Your coming with us is too big a risk.

"But I can't be alone." Her voice cracked as she tried not to cry. "Please, you can't leave me. You can't go. You can't do that to me."

He squeezed her fingers tighter around the gun. "This will help you." Then, knowing exactly what he was doing, Liam added, "Do you know how to use it?"

She shook her head and burst into tears. "No!"

Liam wouldn't turn to see but felt reasonably sure that her vulnerable wail, trying hard to stay strong, had to have *some* effect on Katrina. Plus, no way he would use that peashooter Chelsea was carrying. He looked at Clark and saw the man's resolve to side with Katrina slipping.

"I'm sorry," Liam said sadly, setting a hand on Chelsea's shoulder. "We have to bring Adam home and make sure he's safe. We have to go."

She tried harder to choke back her tears, but lost them anyway. "What do you mean *home*? Where are you living? *Please*, you can't do this. Please take me with you. I'll shoot whoever I have to, I'll do whatever I can to help. Just please don't leave me!"

Liam looked back at Katrina but didn't give her a chance to recant before turning back to Chelsea. "Sorry, we just can't. We have to go."

Liam patted her on the shoulder, then turned toward the exit. Chelsea burst into fresh tears behind him, then audibly choked them back, forcing herself into steady breath, seemingly unwilling to lose any more pride than she already had.

"You can come with us." Katrina dipped down, grabbed the girl's gun, and snatched Liam's blaster back. She threw it to him and turned to the girl. "Stay in the middle and keep your eyes out for everything. Got it?"

"Got it." Chelsea vigorously nodded.

Katrina nodded at Clark, then the door, gesturing for him to go first. He stepped through the doorway, then Chelsea behind him. Katrina pulled Liam back before he could follow and whispered, "If she slows us down even a little, I'll put my sword right through her."

Liam stepped through the doorway and muttered under his breath, "I don't doubt that at all."

TWENTY-ONE

Sutherland

SUTHERLAND MADE a wide smile that Connor couldn't see and stepped from the room's only light, out of the shadows and into the dull flicker coming from behind the traitor.

Fingers woven in front of him, he made a long and loping orbit around the room, circling Connor's lonely chair in the middle, hoping to drive the traitor's temperature higher with every lingering pass.

Once finished, the throne room would be Sutherland's favorite room in Hydrangea. For now, this confession room was the one he thought of most. It was special, because only here did people always find their god ... before telling him truths they'd barely dared to whisper before.

All men were willing to sing the gospel once they had someone to show them the song.

Connor Vinson remained impressively frozen in his seat. Sutherland knew the man wanted to struggle or squirm, yank his restraints, and pull away from the chair. But he wouldn't give his captors the courtesy of a cracked exterior. It would be admirable if it weren't so explicitly stupid.

Connor was cuffed, hands behind his back, metal bracelets digging hard into his flesh. Gallus stood by the door, on the other side of a thin tangle of shadows, as required by the Patriots Constitution: a dog sitting by its master's feet wagging its tail, while the master did as he pleased to the stray bitch trying to usurp his land.

"I won't give you more than one chance. This is it, Vinson. Spend it as you wish. *I'm innocent, I didn't do anything, I don't know anything,* or even *I'm sorry*: none of these are acceptable. I want a full confession. And if your confession meets my satisfaction, I might leave you alive, though probably not. I'll spare you from the zombies, and that's something, right?"

"I didn't do anything, and I don't know a thing." Connor's lips cracked into a thin smile.

Connor and his stupid, stupid balls. Sutherland would have to slice them from his scrotum, then make the traitor eat them with jam. He chuckled at the thought, still grinning into the man's treasonous glare. "You didn't dare to say you weren't sorry."

It dangled in the air like a question. In the room's near silence, Gallus swallowed. Sutherland looked thoughtful. He brought his fingers to his chin and started to stroke it. "Wasn't it you, Connor Vinson — *traitor extraordinaire* — who tried to drum up support to get the good people here to rise up and vote me out?"

Connor looked at Sutherland like a petulant child.

"Do we still have that ear kit?" Sutherland asked. He turned to Gallus. "The one we used on Sallinger last September?"

Gallus nodded like a good little number two.

"Never mind, it doesn't matter." Sutherland returned his eyes to the traitor. "Hearing problems have a way of working themselves out in here." He cleared his throat and repeated, "Weren't you the one rousing the rabble to vote me out of Hydrangea last year?"

"I don't have to talk." Connor looked like he wanted to spit.

"Oh, but *you do.*"

"I demand to see my representative, as afforded by law, and stated by Article 19 of the Patriot's Constitution."

Sutherland barked laughter. "Article 19! How did you know that one was my favorite?" As his laughter settled, he added, "Of course I could never forget Article 19. Gallus is your representative, *as afforded by law, and stated by Article 19 of the Patriot's Constitution.*"

Sutherland nodded to the man in the shadows.

Connor was brazen and stupid enough to laugh. "Gallus isn't my representative or anyone's. He's your little bitch and nothing more."

Sutherland gasped and slapped his hand over his mouth as if suppressing laughter. "Oh, my." He looked over at Gallus. "You're not going to let him get away with that, are you?"

For the first time, Sutherland was happy to see terror crack through the traitor's veneer. "You may think he's nothing but a bitch, and I suppose you'd be right, but only if you compared Gallus to me. Compared to you, he's nothing of the sort. Gallus would never wait until a man's back was turned to scrawl profanity in feces on his favorite chair, nor would he commit acts of betrayal that are likely to get him killed. Gallus is more of a man than you'll ever be, traitor, because he has enough balls to face his enemies. Are we enemies, Vinson?"

Sutherland leaned toward the traitor. Connor said nothing to him, though, just turned to Gallus and hissed, "You're his little bitch, you know that, don't you?"

Sutherland barked more laughter. "You're not going to

take that, are you, Gallus? Go ahead and hit him — he's practically begging you."

Gallus looked uncertain.

"You can't intimidate me," Connor said. "I know my rights."

"Show the man his rights." Sutherland laughed. "Go on, Gallus. Hit him as hard as you can across his stupid traitor's face. Then maybe we can start talking."

The traitor stayed frozen as Gallus marched over, probably still stupidly certain this was an act. He barely reacted, until Sutherland's number two's fists were bashing his face on both sides.

"You have no rights!" Sutherland roared. "You are in this room until I'm finished with you. And you *will* confess. All traitors eventually do."

"This is bullshit," Connor said, his jaw already swelling and probably throbbing. "I can't just disappear. People will look for me. They'll know where I went. You can't get away with this. You're not even the leader." Then as if it just occurred to him: "I demand to speak with Jeffries."

"Oh, my," Sutherland said, as if worried. "You mean you didn't hear?"

Connor's bottom lip twitched.

"He hasn't heard." Sutherland turned to Gallus and spoke in a hush. "Do you think we should tell him?" Then he turned back to Connor and smiled. "Jeffries has been replaced by King Shit."

Sutherland was pleased to finally see the traitor struggle in his restraints, making a valiant yet impossible effort to leap from his chair.

"You won't get away with this! My people will never allow it."

"*Your people*?" Sutherland repeated. "May I ask *what people* you might be referring to? Last I heard you had no one. Your wife was too stupid to keep near the borders, and your daughter, well, it's unfortunate that she was eaten so early, before the age of seven — so many of life's best parts she never experienced. But I suppose that's a father's just desserts for not being careful. So, traitor, we've established that there's no one to mourn you. Tell me, who are *your people?*"

"You can't see it," Connor said, looking like he could murder Sutherland with his eyes, "but there's a revolution in Hydrangea happening under your nose. People don't respect you. They want things back like they used to be — you're just too drunk and buried in whores to notice."

Sutherland knelt in front of Connor, daring the man to butt his head or try and bite his face. Instead, the traitor did nothing, waiting for Sutherland's next move.

"Do you really believe you can take me out? I assure you, better men have tried."

"You're a fool and a dictator, abusing your power. This isn't how it's supposed to be. The Patriots stand for freedom and for living a true life outside the Cities. But you're as bad as the State, forcing outliers to surrender earnings, bleeding them dry for nothing in return."

"You must be joking." Sutherland stood, genuinely affronted. "*Nothing in return?* The Barrens are badlands, offering little chance for survival. This is Hydrangea, the best of all the camps. We live in a state-of-the-art facility, outside the Cities, where people are safe, unless they do something stupid, as your family is prone to do. Before me, this place was no different from the others. Now it's the safest place outside the Cities — and free. That makes it better than anywhere in the world. Do you really think I don't deserve respect for that?"

Spittle flew from his lips onto the traitor's unblinking

face. "Fine! I'd like to see how well you rats can scurry without me." Sutherland turned to Gallus. "Leave us."

The traitor's face drained quickly of color. Sutherland could see its pallor even in the dim room. "No. Don't go. You can't leave me with him. You *know* what he'll do. This isn't the work of a Patriot!"

Gallus was already on his way to the door. And still the traitor pled.

"You can get me representation, Gallus. You don't have to do this. You're better than that!"

The door closed behind Gallus, sealing them inside.

"You shouldn't have called him a bitch." Sutherland winked. "He's quite the delicate flower."

He turned from the traitor and walked to the room's only piece of furniture other than the chair — a small end table bolted to the corner floor with a small metal box resting on top.

Sutherland lifted it, holding his eyes on Connor. "Would you like to know what's in here?"

He waited several seconds for the traitor to speak, then shrugged. "This box has seventeen ways for me to get you talking. I'm certain at least one will work."

Sutherland brought the box over to Vinson and showed the traitor his many species of pliers and knives.

TWENTY-TWO

Adam Lovecraft

ADAM FELL HARD to the ground, hands flying to his nose, screaming as he tried to stop blood gushing between his splayed fingers.

"Come on!" One of the men grabbed him roughly by the back of his jumpsuit, dragged him from the building, then dropped Adam to the icy ground where he landed a devastating kick to the young man's soft middle.

Adam scrambled for his blaster, but he couldn't see where it had fallen with all the red blurring his eyes.

"Should we look for the one that escaped?"

Adam blinked toward the gravelly voice as he tried to recover. It belonged to a pug of a man, waving a long blade.

"No," said Black Hat. "We don't need 'er. We've got a replacement."

"What?" Adam gasped before taking a second kick to the ribs.

"You heard him." Pug yanked Adam up to his unsteady feet before throwing him back to the ground just behind the horses. Pug leaned in and pressed his gun barrel into Adam's temple.

"Careful," a gray-bearded man said to Pug. "He looks like a wily one — might want to watch your hands."

Gray Beard nodded toward Pug's full mitts, one holding the sword, and the other freshly outfitted with a blaster.

Pug said, "He'll be no trouble. If he is, I'll cut him to pieces."

Gray Beard grunted, then went to the coach, grabbed another chained collar, attached one end to the back of the carriage, and approached Adam.

Adam screamed, hoping to capture Colton's attention — assuming his companion was still back in the building where Adam had left him before running off like a fool.

Pug put his blaster to Adam's skull, holding him down as the other man opened the collar and lowered it onto his neck, laughing as he clamped it shut.

"Let me go!"

"Shut up," Black Hat snarled, his whisper harsh. "You'll attract the zombies!"

As if on cue, a wave of moaning rolled in from behind them. Adam turned and saw six zombies shuffling one by one from the building back close to where he'd left Colton. To his minor relief, they were the slow-moving sort, but they were still close enough that they could easily catch the group if the carriage didn't get rolling.

"Looks like the show's gonna start early." Black Hat ran back to the coach and climbed to his spot up top as the other men followed, all diving inside.

The woman Adam hadn't set free wailed as the zombies approached, still twenty feet off but closing in quickly. He scanned the snow, searching for something — anything — he might use as a weapon. But he saw only puddles and some debris awkwardly piled against the side of the building (which was impossible to reach anyway). He'd have to fight the undead bare-handed.

The woman, still screaming, backed away from the approaching zombies. Adam balled his fists, heart racing, bracing body and mind for certain attack.

He thought through his training at City Watch, which involved precious little close-quarters combat and virtually no unarmed fighting. But Adam had spent the past half dozen months in solitary confinement going over and over moves on his cell's cold concrete floor, until ducks and parries were automatic reflexes. Whether or not those moves would be effective …

The three zombies in front flailed with outstretched arms and tromped through the dirty snow toward the woman. Adam readied himself to kick at the closest monster's knees. He'd deaden the undead's legs, then kick its skull into mush once it fell.

But just as the first zombie was about to make its move, it fell back, covering its ears as if in excruciating pain, shrieking an unholy cry like an animal trapped.

The zombies just behind and beside it did the same thing. The swarm receded like a wave from the shore, all six zombies backing away from the still-screaming woman.

What the hell?

Adam turned and saw Black Hat half-grinning, holding a small red cylinder high in the air. Whatever it was seemed to be emitting some sort of frequency — or *something* — that only the zombies could hear.

Black Hat reached into his coat, retrieved his blaster, and hit three zombies in three shots, their rapidly disintegrating husks dropping to the ground. The second row of zombies were still backing up, shrieks growing louder as Black Hat fired another trio of shots. The undead fell into bloody chunks, plumes of steam rising from the snow.

Adam was impressed — and horrified — by the man's accuracy. He turned back to look up at the stagecoach. Black Hat returned the blaster to his coat and looked down at Adam.

"Don't thank me just yet, kid."

If he was going to die, Adam was determined to be brave on his way. He straightened his shoulders. "What do you mean by that?"

Black Hat chuckled, then turned, sat on the wooden bench and snapped the reins to set the horses in motion.

Adam screamed from behind the stagecoach. "What do you want with us?"

He ignored him as the horses moved, the chain pulling taut and jerking Adam forward.

After the stagecoach had passed two empty alleyways and was slowly approaching a dangerous-looking third filled with tons of hiding places in the form of broken trucks and cars along with open doorways into dozens of buildings likely filled with zombies, the woman turned to Adam. Her eyes red and wet, she asked, "Why didn't you free me first?"

Without any idea what to say, Adam told her the truth. "Because the other girl looked like my sister. I'm sorry," he forced himself to hold her gaze, instead of looking down at the ground, "I thought I'd have more time."

She scowled. "You done pissed them off."

"Who are they?"

"I don't know. They came up on us and killed the man we were teamed with, then they put us in chains and forced us to follow."

"How long have you been chained up?"

"An hour before you came."

"And you have no idea what they're planning?"

"Whatever it is, it ain't good."

Adam stared at the back of Black Hat's head while thinking about all the stories he'd heard at City Watch about bandit slavers in the Barrens. He'd figured it was a myth, since the ones who told the stories had never seen it with their own eyes. Now, here in the Outback, being dragged behind a black-hatted devil, Adam wondered if death might be better than the godforsaken hell these men might be taking them to.

He imagined the pug bastard trying to have his way with the woman … or with him. He looked like the type to rape slaves … and maybe eat them once finished.

He looked back again, hoping that Colton had forgiven his reckless decision.

But Adam saw no sign, and after another minute of walking, decided: *death beat slavery.*

TWENTY-THREE

Sutherland

SUTHERLAND RETURNED the knives and pliers to their box, one by one — partly because he preferred that his favorite tools always stay neat, and partly because he enjoyed the ritual of show, making each movement matter as the traitor stared captive from his chair.

Sutherland wondered how well Connor could see him, with blood filling both of his eyes and all that flesh around them so crimson and bloated. He snapped the lid shut, thinking of Oswald. The doctor had never had a stomach for torture, either as participant or observer. Leadership wasn't for the weak. Men in charge had to be capable of doing what others would or could not, including the extraction of the information required for survival.

He walked to the door without any parting words to the traitor, wondering if Connor had really surrendered all there was. Perhaps he would return later, to see if an evening alone with his pain might make the man even more talkative.

Sutherland stepped out of the chamber and fell immediately back against the door, startled. He straightened his shoulders as the four men approached, feeling suddenly stupid for not having his sword. Something Gallus would do: an idiot's move. Now that very idiot was marching down the corridor with three men walking as guard. His gait, and the way he was looking directly at Sutherland like a child looking to unseat his older brother, gave him away. Gone was his subservience. Gallus was about to betray the one man who could keep Hydrangea safe.

Sutherland squinted, trying to get a better look at the three men walking a slight step behind Gallus. No use — he couldn't remember their names, no matter how hard he tried to dig back in his memory. Their hands brushed against their sidearms, almost caressing them as they walked. The three men drew, barrels leveled at Sutherland as he stepped toward them, then stopped a few feet shy. Only Gallus held no weapon, and yet his betrayal was loudest of all.

"What's going on here?" Sutherland demanded.

Gallus was only a kid and wore his gumption like another man's hat. The harder Sutherland glared, the more difficult it would be for the turncoat to hold his composure. He would snap the man like a twig, then throw him into the fire to burn. Once down, the other three would crumble like loosely packed dirt.

But Gallus' voice didn't crack. Almost booming he said, "You have violated Article 19 of the Patriot's Constitution and are hereby under arrest."

Sutherland laughed, trying not to bristle. "Don't be ridiculous." He waved his hand at the three men and their silly guns. "And please, put those away. This place reeks of danger. Traitors are growing like weeds." He narrowed his eyes and peered at each man in turn, before settling on Gallus. "We must cease the mutiny *before* it occurs. Right now there's still time for everyone to make the *right* decision. The one that will keep you and your families safe."

"Under the law, I am acting leader until such time that a free election is held."

It was one thing to be stupid, another to suffer such delusions of grandeur. If Sutherland didn't feel the moment's true danger, he might almost feel sorry for Gallus and his potentially fatal mistake. If the man backed down this instant, Sutherland *might* spare his life.

"Enough of this!" He thrust out his arm, planning to grab a weapon from the closest soldier — *what was his name?* — but the guard flinched back and fixed his aim harder on Sutherland.

Sutherland looked at Gallus. "Don't do this." He kept his voice bold and did not show any sign of weakness, let alone beg. "You're making the worst mistake of your life. You know who I am, and you know what I'm capable of." Sutherland lowered his voice to a low murmur, almost a growl. "You know what I'll do, to you and everyone else involved in this coup."

Gallus turned to his left. The name *Benson* leapt into Sutherland's head.

"Don't you *dare*," Sutherland snarled, taking a step back and hating everyone in the hall — himself most of all — for forcing his retreat.

Sutherland opened his mouth to give Gallus one final warning, a chance to cease his stupidity and perhaps save his pitifully insignificant life. But before he could form words, two of the three guards circled behind him while the third — and surliest-looking of the three — raised his weapon to Sutherland's forehead, silently daring him to move.

All four were fools to believe they could usurp him.

"You are a traitor, and you know what happens to traitors at Hydrangea." Sutherland held his even tone, eyes still drilling into Gallus. "You will pay for this, boy."

Gallus looked past Sutherland, toward the two guards behind him. "Take him into custody and free Connor Vinson," he said, without the slightest quiver.

Sutherland allowed his hands to be shackled behind his back — no need to tussle with no chance of winning. Let Gallus have his little victory. He'd be less prepared when Sutherland sprang into action.

Softly, almost sweetly, he purred, "I am going to slowly peel the skin from your body, everywhere but your face. That I'll save for last. Oh, the fun I will have."

Gallus turned his back on Sutherland. "Our options are clear, gentlemen. If he violates any of our laws *as we see them*, pull the trigger and shoot him dead."

TWENTY-FOUR

Anastasia Lovecraft

ANA SAT on Oswald's examination table. His office was in a
secure section of the Station, several tunnels down from
the living quarters. She looked around, surprised at how
much the room resembled a City 6 doctor's office, clean
and sterile. She wondered if Egan had been able to
smuggle medical equipment from one of the Cities or if
the old train station had been built with a doctor's office
inside it.

So far, Oswald's office — and the long hallway leading
to it — was all she'd seen of this sector, which was sealed
off by a barricade and a pair of guards who had apparently forgotten how to smile. The hall sprawled for some
distance leading into darkened corridors where Oswald
said he'd conducted experiments on infected subjects found
in the Barrens. Ana felt a slithering chill at the thought of
being so close to infected subjects — and perhaps to
already-turned zombies.

Somewhere deep inside, likely in cells forever altered by
the virus, Ana could still feel when the undead were near.
Like now, an anxious patter of her heart that swore some-

thing wasn't right. The hammering thud tightened her chest and made her feel like she was sweating more than her clammy brow suggested.

She wasn't sure if her reaction was to Oswald, who himself had partly turned zombie before arresting his transformation with the robotic enhancements, her brain messing with her because the doctor had informed her of the infected down the hall, or if she truly felt them nearby.

Oswald went to the adjoining room to check on something, leaving Ana to nurse her rising anxiety. She closed her eyes and tried to think only calming thoughts. But closing her eyes brought visions of zombies: chomping through the guards at the checkpoint, then snarling on their way toward the living quarters, feasting on the men, women, and children who lived here until there was no one left.

Perhaps even worse than the thought of zombies rampaging through the tunnels would be for the virus itself to spread through the population like the filthy disease that it was. One that had wiped out most of humanity so long ago, and still seemed eager to finish the job.

For all the Station's precautions, Egan was still undermining his people's safety by not quarantining Calla in the secure area with the rest of the infected. If the girl turned before someone noticed, she could make the Station a memory.

Oswald entered the room and looked at her oddly. "Are you okay?"

"I just feel really nervous. My heart won't stop racing." Ana paused, swallowed, then went ahead and asked what she didn't want to. "Are there zombies nearby?"

Oswald looked at her, something playing at the corner of his mouth, a decayed eyebrow slightly raised. "You can sense them?"

"Yes." Ana nodded, now meeting his eyes. "Ever since I was bitten. I can feel them when they're close."

"There are zombies topside, roaming the Barrens. I feel them all the time. But at the moment, we've only one subject, infected but not yet turned."

"How close are you to finding a cure? Be honest. I want to know how long Egan plans to keep me prisoner here."

She knew the word *prisoner* sounded ugly, but Ana said it anyway. The doctor sighed, not correcting her. "I can't say for certain. We're taking it day by day, but without more human subjects, it's difficult. No one is more motivated than Egan to find a cure. It's his daughter's life on the line."

"I know," Ana said, conflicted. "How *is* Calla doing? How long do you think she has?"

"I can't say."

Ana looked at Oswald's robotic hand and half-metal face, suddenly getting an idea. "If she does get worse, can't you replace her limbs with bionic parts, like you did with yourself?"

"I didn't operate on myself. I had others, trained surgeons, to help me. We don't have the staff here, let alone access to the required parts or equipment. Besides, in most cases, the virus infects the brain early on, which would render any attempts to salvage limbs pointless. While much of my body had atrophied, the infection hadn't yet affected my brain. The odds of that being the case with anyone else, especially Calla, are statistically impossible. I can probably keep the virus at bay a while longer. Maybe as long as six months or with luck even a year. But I hope your blood will be the key to a cure before that."

Ana hoped that was the case: she didn't think she could

stay in the Station another year — not without her brother and Liam, or something to make the tunnels feel like her home.

"I need you to roll up your sleeve," he said.

She turned away as he moved the needle closer to her arm. Ana had never been particularly afraid of needles but couldn't stand to watch them puncture her skin. She waited patiently as he filled four vials and placed a small bandage on her arm. Then he thanked her and carried his tray of vials through a large sliding metal door, beyond which she saw a room full of coolers.

She sat in silence, wondering how Liam was doing. Wondering if he'd found Adam. Earlier, Egan had offered her access to a monitor — one of the screens he didn't allow the Station's residents to watch for fear of exposing them to State propaganda. He told Ana that she could watch the Games to see how her brother was faring. She'd thanked him, but had said *no*, unable to bear the thought of seeing Adam while she was helpless to save him. Instead she asked that he report anything of note; he knew what she meant.

No one had heard news on the mission yet — not surprising since Egan had said that communications in or around the Outback would be simple for the State to pick up, so the rescue team would be observing radio silence until after leaving the ancient city.

She heard clanging above as the heating system kicked on and warm air poured through the vents. Ana looked around the lab, reconsidering her earlier stance of wanting to leave when Liam returned. The Station was filled with safety, electricity, running water, food, and company — all luxuries in the Barrens, particularly in winter. Then again, she couldn't see herself settling in another underground community led by one man who decided all. Even if things seemed fine now, how long before they ran afoul of Egan? What would stop him from becoming another Sutherland?

Oswald returned and thanked her again for giving blood.

"How is Egan to live with?" Ana asked.

"What do you mean?"

"After what happened with Sutherland, I'm leery of moving into another underground installation run by one man. What is he like?"

"He's as fair a man as I've ever worked with."

Ana laughed. "That sounds … diplomatic. What is he *really* like?"

"He has a few issues." Oswald shrugged. "But who doesn't?"

"What kind of issues?"

Oswald pursed his lips. "I'm not comfortable discussing this, Ana."

She leaned forward. "What do you mean? Should I be worried?"

"No," Oswald said. "Trust me. If anyone's safe here, it's you."

"But?" Ana waited for the doctor to color his silence.

The door opened behind her. She turned to see Calla, surprisingly alone.

"Where's Elijah?" Oswald asked.

"I ditched him," Calla said, smiling mischievously. "I wanted to see Ana."

"What did I tell you about ditching Elijah?" Oswald pointed a metal finger at her. "Your father will be ticked."

"I'm a girl. I need privacy. Girl time. Ana understands, right, Ana?"

Ana smiled. "Boys can be totally annoying."

"Thank you!" Calla nearly squealed. "Just the other

day I was trying to read, and he kept talking to me, like *nonstop*. He wouldn't shut up."

"Maybe he likes you," Ana said playfully.

"Gross!"

"Okay, ladies, I think this is my cue to leave you two alone. Let me call your father and tell him where you are before he—"

A siren stopped his thought.

His eyes went wide as a red light over the door started to spin, casting the room in a strobing red hue.

Ana tensed, looking around. "What's happening?"

Oswald scrambled back into the office where he'd taken her vials, then returned moments later with a pair of blasters. He handed one of them to Ana. "Can you use this?"

"Of course."

"Good, get in there." He pointed to the adjoining office. "And wait."

Oswald shoved her and Calla toward the room with the vials, then answered once they were safely on the other side of the sliding metal door.

"A zombie has infiltrated the Station. You protect Calla, understand?"

The door slid shut and locked her in before Ana could answer.

TWENTY-FIVE

Sutherland

Sutherland stared at his cell door, seething.

He was surprised to see that Gallus had grown a pair. How, he had no idea. His *brussels sprouts* had barely been *peas* while serving as Sutherland's second.

How *dare* they take him into custody and lock him away; how *dare* they think they could do this to him; how *dare* they so arrogantly think he was powerless to stop them?

What made Sutherland angriest was the time it must have taken to plan the insurgence. It seemed as though it had come from nowhere. Gallus had apparently left the chamber so that Sutherland could take care of business. It was impossible to believe that his betrayal had been born in that moment. Gallus had to have been nursing thoughts of treason before then. Maybe he was the one who had allowed that "King Shit" crap to happen.

Sutherland was plenty familiar with betrayal. The weak and petty hid like snakes in the grass, waiting to sink inferior fangs into superior strength, but in all his years and with all he'd given to Hydrangea, Sutherland had never been stabbed in the back by his inner council. He'd been blind to trust someone so young. In retrospect, he should've seen the man's sycophantic behavior as a raw thirst for power. Such thirst could never be sated by serving one man, no matter how noble the cause.

As the hours ticked on, Sutherland's hunger began to swell. He was starting to feel lightheaded. He hadn't been in this cell all that long, but he also hadn't eaten since an early dinner the evening before. A night with plenty of brew and his favorite whore had emptied him out. Morning had gone from the shit with his throne right into the traitor's interrogation.

He stared down at his bed and the toilet, the dimly lit cell's only two pieces of furniture, wanting to kill someone. Many people. All deserving.

Soon, I will have my chance.

He kept repeating that to himself, because to think anything else would allow the doubt inside. A mortal foe when stuck in a cell. He needed strength and resolve. The longer he sat, the more Sutherland was able to piece together the conspiracy's puzzle.

The shit-covered throne was a catalyst designed to move him into action, get him to "break the law" so they could wag their crooked fingers between him and the ink marring the Patriot's Constitution, a document they clearly did not understand. His opposition knew he would do what had to be done to keep Hydrangea safe. What cowards — to stage their coup while he was busy with the job they were all too yellow to do.

Sutherland hated that he'd been so blind, trusting when he shouldn't have. He wondered how long they would make him wait to stand trial. Would they seek to hang him or merely send him out into the Barrens to fend for himself? They might think the latter a harsher punishment, but it would be their undoing. Sutherland could survive the winter, return in the spring, and burn Hydrangea to nothing.

The thought of Gallus and the other traitors sitting in his new throne room, commanding his officers, gorging their fat faces on his delicate food, sleeping in his chambers, screwing his whores — was a blade in his gut, and every hour twisted it deeper.

These people weren't leaders. They were usurpers, taking advantage of a situation, of Sutherland's leniency following Ana, Liam, and Katrina's escape. And, of course, Oswald after that. He should have come down harder, perhaps sealed the base like a drum. He was weak for not going further, and that weakness had landed him in this cell while another ass sat on his throne.

He should have held *everyone* responsible for helping the traitors flee … and stuck a handful of heads on pikes in the dining hall to keep the rest from their whispers. Instead he was forced to sit in this cell like a rat in a hole, waiting for his chance to run.

But his first and second round of interrogations after Oswald fled had produced nothing, so he had quit searching, assuming the rot had stopped with the zombie doctor. Clearly, it hadn't. Clearly he had failed to eliminate every cancerous cell.

They would never get away with this. He wondered if that old fool Jeffries knew about the coup, and had somehow orchestrated it from Sagebrush. Whatever the case, neither he, or Gallus, or anyone else appointed could hope to run Hydrangea or keep it from devolving into chaos. Nor would they know what to do with the potential zombie solution Oswald had been working on. Sutherland wasn't a praying man, but he hoped they wouldn't discover the canisters of weaponized zombie virus before he could reclaim his position as leader. If knowledge of the canisters got back to Gallus or Jeffries, things could get ugly. The Council of Patriots would never approve of his plans to attack the remaining Cities.

Following the deaths in City 1, the other leaders had lost their backbones, second-guessing themselves and believing that maybe they'd made a mistake. They had ordered Sutherland to surrender his remaining canisters, which he did without argument.

But Sutherland hadn't earned his position by listening to others. Little did they know he had planned ahead and squirreled away enough to end every City three times over. It was maybe four hours — though it could've been twice that — before the door finally opened and Horrance the ogre shuffled in with a plate.

"Horrance!" Sutherland said, happy to see him, assuming Horrance wasn't also a traitor.

"Hello, sir. I have your dinner."

Sutherland noticed a second guard standing by behind Horrance, palm to the butt of his rifle. Of course the bastards wouldn't trust Horrance alone.

Sutherland took the tray and looked down to see two slices of bread, a piece of overcooked meat, half an ear of old-looking corn, and a tin cup of water. He licked his lips, imagining the metallic taste as the sight of food stirred his appetite hard enough to raise an audible growl. He hated himself for being so weak but felt grateful it was only Horrance.

"Thank you." Sutherland stared past the giant to glare at the other guard as he took the tray from Horrance's massive paws. "You need two guards to keep me in line now, is that it?"

Sutherland pictured himself slicing the silent guard's throat. If they'd given him utensils, he might have tried.

They left without a word. Sutherland thought to call after Horrance, *You've betrayed me too*, but the giant might still be on his side.

He lifted the meat for a bite and saw a piece of brown paper folded beneath it. He dropped his meat to the plate, grabbed and unfolded the paper, then read the message: *Tonight we will right the wrong.*

Sutherland stared at the awkward scrawl, unsure if it was a threat from his captors or a sign from his supporters that help was on its way.

He wolfed down his food, trying not to worry that he could be chewing through his final meal. All he needed was a little help, a small nudge, and he could easily tend to the rest. Surely there would be people out there who knew which side was right, men — or women — willing to stand up for what was true in this world.

It was impossible to believe that traitors had infiltrated every level of his council, or that every guard was a turncoat. Perhaps Horrance was gathering troops all along. He laughed at the notion that when things went bad, the most loyal man in the camp might be Horrance the Slow.

At least he had been smart enough to keep the canisters from everyone else. Staring at the empty plate, Sutherland realized that not only had Horrance brought him a meal and a message, he'd also hand-delivered a weapon.

He picked up the plate, then let it shatter on the floor. He looked down, found the sharpest, longest piece, grabbed it with a smile, and shoved his new shiv under a pillow just as his cell door opened.

Piggy, the guard he'd dressed down outside the throne room, peered inside.

"Sorry," Sutherland said, "slippery fingers."

Piggy looked him up and down, then called for another guard. A second man appeared in the doorway, tall with a monobrow and iron jaw. Sutherland wondered if his old guards had been replaced, and if so, how they had failed to get rid of Horrance?

Maybe because Horrance had betrayed him too.

"You'll pay for that." Piggy scowled and yanked the shock stick from his holster. He aimed at Sutherland, then fired a blast before Hydrangea's true leader could move to defend himself.

He fell back into bed, pain chewing through his cells, unable to move save for his twitching.

Piggy came toward him, smiling like he'd just found a table full of fat. "Oh, yeah, I thought of a funny joke, King Shit. You're gonna love this one. What happens when a fool underestimates the people whose protection he relies on?"

He shoved the shock stick into Sutherland's chest and delivered another arc of pure electricity.

Sutherland tried to fight it and stay conscious, but he couldn't do either.

TWENTY-SIX

Adam Lovecraft

THEY'D WALKED for about an hour when Adam noticed the shrinking buildings on either side of the long road, three and four stories tall now rather than ten and fifteen. Doors and windows on the nearest buildings were boarded shut — the first time he'd seen anything like that since fleeing the arena and entering the old, broken city at a sprint.

He wondered if the structures were now hovels, homes to bandits, maybe even homes to the devils driving the coach that dragged him behind it. Adam tried to spy movement in the dark spaces nested in the sliced recesses between planks, but he saw nothing: no blinking residents or sympathetic souls to take mercy on and help them, not even another prisoner like himself, staring out from his own boarded cell while waiting to die.

Adam heard one of the horses whinny, then the one beside it did the same. The carriage came to a stop. His heart beat hard against his chest as he looked ahead and saw the road blocked by a large cargo truck, its rust peeking out from the blanket of snow. Its bulk swallowed much of the alley, leaving barely enough room to squeeze by on foot.

Adam looked closer, noticing that the debris wasn't just the normal garbage they'd seen strewn through the city. The taste of copper coated his tongue as his eyes tried to make sense of what they didn't want to see — hundreds of bones and mounds of bloodstained clothes poking through the snow.

Black Hat stood atop the carriage and surveyed the road like a baron. Appearing satisfied, he grunted, then reached down and picked up a pair of lead pipes each about two feet long. Then he turned to Adam and the woman. "End of the line, folks."

He loudly clanged the pipes, one against the other. The sound echoed, then bounced off the alley walls and rolled with the wind for who knew how many miles.

Black Hat began to mimic Kirk Kirkman's familiar voice: "Hear ye, hear ye, residents of the Outback! It's time for another edition of the Outback Games! Let's see if these lazy City folk — who look down their noses at us — can last one round in a *genuine* game of skill!"

Black Hat threw the pipes to the snow and got louder. "If you can fend off the zombies for five minutes, I'll sound the disruptor and send them off. Let you go on your merry ways."

Adam scanned the windows and doors, still seeing no one. He wondered if there was in fact an audience beyond Black Hat and his unmerry bandits.

Subtle movement farther down the alley, coming out of the doors and windows that hadn't been boarded. At first a few crept out, then dozens. The bandits must have boarded the closest buildings to keep players from escaping, assuming they could somehow break their chains. It probably also allowed them to funnel all the zombies toward the other end of the alley, making escape that way impossible as well. The only way out was to fight and kill them all.

Dozens of undead groaned in a chorus as they ambled out into the freezing wind and toward their waiting dinner.

Adam grabbed the nearest pipe and watched as the woman shakily grabbed hers.

But instead of preparing for the zombies, she did something stupid, begging for mercy from men who clearly had none. "Please, you don't have to do this. I'm a mother!"

The man's smile was blacker than his hat. "Nothing personal, lady. But just so ya know, I didn't care too much for my mama." He thought about it for a minute. "Maybe it *is* a bit personal."

Black Hat crossed his arms and watched, smiling at what was unfolding below like a man surveying a row of arcade stalls.

Men were peering through the dirty curtained windows of the upper stories. Even with their faces shrouded, Adam could imagine their smiles, grinning from front row balcony seats, waiting for the show.

He stared back at the horde — then down at his measly pipe. There was no way to bash them all before one managed to rip into his flesh. He could only hope that they attacked the woman first, so he could maybe pick them off one at a time before they turned on him.

A wicked, merciless thought crossed his mind: *If I hit the woman and knock the pipe from her hand, the zombies will focus on her first.*

He stared at her as she stupidly screamed, "Go away!" and swung her pipe at the first of the undead, as if they would listen or she might be able to reach them from thirty feet away. The woman paid him no mind. He could easily do it. Knock her out and buy himself some time.

He hated himself for losing his mercy. He'd risked his

life to save the girl who reminded him so much of Ana. And now, maybe an hour later, he was willing to kill the mother.

A gunshot thundered off the walls.

Adam half-expected to look down to see a gaping wound in his chest and his blood adding more dark red to the bright white snow. Instead, he heard Black Hat tumbling from the carriage top and falling to the ground between the horses as they whinnied and bucked in their harnesses.

"Get the Hellweaver!" a voice shouted from the rooftop.

Colton! Adam turned and ran toward the carriage.

The left side door swung open and Pug came out, sword in hand. He looked around for Black Hat, saw Adam racing toward him, screamed, and swung his weapon.

Adam stumbled, lost his footing on the slippery ground, and fell hard onto his back.

Pug rushed him, sword raised, hate gleaming in his ugly brown eyes as spittle flew from his mouth.

Another gunshot, this time taking out the back of Pug's skull. He fell to the ground.

Adam scrambled to his feet, slipping, sliding, before finally finding purchase on the asphalt, cracked and covered with snow.

Noisy chaos erupted behind him: Colton firing shots, zombies moaning, and the sound of metal *thwacking* into rotting flesh. He wanted to look back and see if zombies were about to fall onto him. He wanted to look into the carriage as he passed the open door to see if the other two bandits were taking aim from inside, if they'd come out to try and stop him, or — if they were smart — if they'd run like hell.

But Adam saw only the fallen twisted body of Black Hat getting trampled by the horses as they struggled for freedom. He *also* saw the Hellweaver beside Black Hat in the snow but couldn't see the red disruptor required to drive the zombies away.

His momentum died as he moved toward the horses. He looked back to see Pug's corpse, heavy on top of the chain that bound Adam to the carriage. A zombie was tearing into the dead man's face, and there was no way he could pull them both off and get slack in his chain. He struggled to pull, just to gain a few more feet.

The collar bit deep into his neck as he stretched the chain, tight as it could go. He reached out, still three feet shy, as the horses cried louder, more frantic, shaking and bucking, stomping Black Hat's flesh into pulp.

Suddenly, arms fell onto Adam's shoulders, a growl hot on his neck.

He spun, pipe tight in his fist, driving the metal into the zombie's skull and shoving it to the ground. From the corner of his eyes, Adam saw the woman go down in a pile, zombies atop her as death cries mingled with the sound of her choking on her own blood.

Horse cries found a new pitch behind him. Adam spun to see a pack of zombies circling to the other side of the carriage, several already tearing into equine flesh.

One of the two remaining bandits shoved the zombie feasting on Pug and fired his blaster into its body. The zombie fell, and the bandit looked down to see that Pug was past saving.

He looked up at Adam and raised his blaster to fire.

This is it. The thought tore through his mind as he stared into death. The bandit fired …

And missed.

Or, as Adam realized a moment later, he'd been firing

at a zombie approaching Adam from behind. He hit his target and sent the creature to the ground. Adam had no time to wonder why the bandit had chosen to save him, or if maybe he had in fact missed Adam and accidentally shot the zombie instead, because the man was suddenly buried beneath the weight of another three zombies.

Fate smiled and sent the bandit's blaster flying from his hand to just inches from Adam's feet.

He fell to the ground, grabbed the blaster, and checked his perimeter. He saw a zombie approaching on his left and fired, tearing a wide hole in its chest and sending the rest of its body on a short trip to the ground.

Adam grabbed the chain in his left hand, yanked tight, then fired three inches below his grip. He missed the first time, sending chunks of melted asphalt flying from the ground.

He heard undead shrieks behind him, closing in. Footsteps inches away. He ignored the sound of imminent death, focused on the shaking length of chain in his hands.

Focus.

He fired again.

Adam fell back as the chain split, ripped, and set him free … tumbling into a pack of undead.

He fell straight through them to the ground and somehow managed to hold onto his gun. As the three monsters turned to catch the prey that had slipped through their rotting fingers, he fired three blasts, taking them all down.

His heart pounding, he leapt up, wondering where Colton was, but with no time to look.

Bodies littered the ground around him, moving, groaning, reaching, clawing, biting.

He raced toward the horses, all kicking and chomping their teeth in battle with raging zombies. He could scarcely make out anything among the heaving masses of moving flesh and blood but noticed that the horses had managed to yank the stagecoach forward about ten feet, enough to leave Black Hat's trampled corpse unmolested, face down under the carriage.

Adam raced forward, slid to the ground, and grabbed the Hellweaver.

He could feel its awesome power in his hand. But the weapon might not be enough. He had to get the disruptor. Adam set his blaster aside and reached into the bloody, wet clothes, desperately searching the man's pockets, fingers closing around plenty of stuff, but none of it feeling right.

He heard footsteps behind him — more zombies. But he couldn't turn before finding the disruptor. His fingers seized an object that felt right in size and he started to pull.

Black Hat's head turned and his eyes popped open.

For a moment, Adam thought the man was still alive, but his groan said otherwise.

Zombie Black Hat lunged his head forward, gnashing at Adam.

He raised his feet and kicked Black Hat in the chest, propelling himself away and out from under the carriage. The Hellweaver tight in one hand, disruptor in the other, Adam looked up in time to see no less than twenty zombies surrounding him, all rushing forward.

He felt a button on the disruptor's slick, bloody surface and pressed it, raising it high as Black Hat had done. The zombies stopped in their tracks, all slapping rotten hands on their ears as they shrank back, shrieking.

Adam held the device in front of him, stepping forward to carve a path through the mass of rotting monsters.

He slowly marched forward, careful not to slip on the ice, feeling his pulse pounding in his neck. The undead's shrieking grew louder as he neared. The crowd parted for

Adam, clearing a path through an alley full of even more of the creatures as he prayed that the device didn't have some sort of time limit, or worse, that the zombies would too quickly become immune to whatever held them at bay.

Eyes darting between zombies, he scanned the alleyway, windows where more bandits might be lying in wait to attack, and rooftops searching for Colton. He saw the man nowhere.

Adam felt a sickening certainty that his father's old friend was dead, shot by the bandits or killed by the zombies, leaving Adam to fend for himself.

"Colton!"

The only response was an uncaring wind blowing through a dull gray sky.

He pushed the zombies farther back as he marched toward where they had come from, hoping Colton was waiting. He turned, checking behind to make sure that no undead were sneaking up on him. He saw the creatures backing away from the disruptor, content to feast on horses instead.

One of the wooden boards to Adam's right pushed open.

He turned, aiming the Hellweaver, even though he had yet to check the ammo or fire it once and could only hope it worked the same as any other gun.

Adam didn't bother to fight his smile as he realized it didn't matter. He wouldn't have to fire.

Colton stepped out of the building, shaking his head. "I hate to say I told you so."

Adam wanted to break down and cry hard, wanted to hug him and thank him for saving his life, wanted to confess that he was so very, very sorry.

But Adam only nodded, hanging his head low as he followed Colton into the building's dark shadows.

TWENTY-SEVEN

Sutherland

SUTHERLAND OPENED his eyes as someone lightly slapped his face. Several thoughts erupted at once, then suddenly he remembered the worst — what had happened, where he was, and the sour truth that he was waiting for mercy or death at the hands of another.

Sutherland told himself that the shard under his pillow would be enough. He needed only patience and the right opportunity. But someone had cuffed his hands and legs to the iron bedposts.

He tried not to panic. As soon as he opened his eyes all the way, he saw it was Connor Vinson slapping him — the man who Sutherland had been torturing not too many hours before.

He thought again of the shiv and saw himself running it first along Connor's throat, then doing the same thing to Gallus. He would go slower with the second, taking his time to let the man bleed out, just as the traitor had taken his own sweet time while crafting betrayal.

Connor leaned down and smiled. "Well, hello there. Glad to see you're awake."

Sutherland cleared his throat and spit, catching the traitor's puffy red eye. He'd earlier pulled the lid back far enough to make Connor scream like a baby in a boiling bath.

Connor calmly wiped his eye and leaned forward, practically daring Sutherland to try it again. He held his saliva, licking his lips while picturing tearing into the bastard's throat with his teeth, then feasting on his face like a ravenous zombie.

"I knew this moment was coming," Connor whispered. "Anticipation was enough to pass the minutes, knowing that the next time we were alone in a room, things would be so much worse." He opened the door. "For you, of course."

He entered Sutherland's cell and quietly closed the door behind him looking almost … sad.

Gallus walked straight to Connor, set his hand on the puffy-eyed traitor's arm, and leaned toward his ear. Connor nodded as he whispered, then stepped back to the door as Gallus took Connor's place beside Sutherland's bed.

Gallus looked down at Sutherland's restraints, then up into his eyes. "Can you talk?"

"Of course I can talk," Sutherland snarled back. "Do you think I'm an idiot?"

"I mean can you be reasonable? Are you able to have a conversation?"

Sutherland wanted to yell and scream, to ask Gallus how he dared to be so bold and stupid. But his hands were restrained and both Gallus and Connor were armed. He'd have to be patient.

"I'm always reasonable."

Gallus continued to prove his new brazen nature as he sat at the edge of Sutherland's bed. His voice was calm and collected, thick with authority in a way that Sutherland had not heard before.

"This is all rather unfortunate." Gallus took a moment to breathe before continuing. Sutherland had time to wonder if he was supposed to agree. "Things didn't have to be this way."

"What way?" Sutherland barely held his spit. "You were supposed to be my second in command. Yet you *deceived* me. How else was this supposed to go?"

Voice still cool, Gallus said, "You had to be deceived, sir. This is all your fault and a long time coming. It's your fault for being so selfish. It's your fault for the throne room. It's your fault because you've displayed reprehensible leadership when all of us needed you most."

"You *still* need me. Everyone knows it. This place will fall to either zombies or bandits without me."

"No, we don't need you," Gallus said, as Connor nodded behind him. "The only one who thinks you're an effective leader is you. It wasn't hard to turn your most trusted people against you."

"You're lying. I *will* be missed. I've been gone since last night. If I'm not seen at dinner and am still missing tomorrow, people will ask. Word will get out. The people, *my people*, will demand my release."

Gallus laughed, sad more than mocking. "Do you really believe that? Do you really believe the people still love you? Can you really not see that they think you're a joke?"

The words cut him like the shiv under his pillow, but he wasn't defeated yet. "Weak minds are easily twisted. It is clear to see what has happened. Fortunately, there are always those who can see the danger we're facing and are sure to see how grossly you have misjudged this situation. I demand to speak with Jeffries."

Connor laughed from behind Gallus, clearly louder than Gallus liked, judging by his face. "Oh, now it's *you* making legal demands. That's rich."

Sutherland again pictured his shiv and imagined somehow breaking free, sweeping it from beneath the pillow before launching from the bed to slice the traitor's throat.

Even restrained, he refused to stay quiet. "You think you're better than me? You think that somehow your injustices shine with a brighter light than mine? You preach from up high, yet you're no different, denying what's rightfully mine, legally and otherwise. Clearly we're more alike than you think."

"We're nothing alike," Connor said.

Sutherland laughed.

Gallus raised his hands to Sutherland, an awkward plea for peace.

"And you're an idiot who has dug his own grave and fashioned his coffin."

"Say what you will, Sutherland. It changes nothing." Gallus shook his head, still looking sad.

"I knew you were stupid but had no idea that your reason had decayed enough to put you on the wrong side. History will prove me right. You'll beg me not to kill you. But I won't listen. When I'm freed, you will all hang like the cowards you are."

Gallus sighed, stood, then turned away from Sutherland. He went to the door where Connor was standing. Connor opened the door and held it for Gallus. Then Sutherland's former second stepped through.

Conner turned to Sutherland and whispered, "Good luck making it to trial."

The door closed and Sutherland made a vow: *Connor would either be the first, or last, to die.*

TWENTY-EIGHT

Anastasia Lovecraft

Ana paced, fuming as she stared at the locked lab door — pissed that Oswald had told her a zombie was on the loose, then stuffed her away like some sort of precious child instead of letting her fight like she'd done since her ejection from City 6. Ana was probably as good, if not better with a gun than most of the Station's residents. She could be out there, contributing, doing *something*. Not babysitting Calla.

The room was twenty feet long by ten feet wide with giant metal refrigerated coolers on either side. The lab also had a desk and a chair where Calla had sat for the ten minutes since being shoved into the chamber.

"Don't worry, we're going to be okay," Calla finally said.

Ana stopped pacing, not wanting to make the little girl any more nervous or frightened than she might already be. If Calla could somehow stay calm, then she had to try and do the same.

"You're right. I just don't like being stuck in here."

Calla looked up. "I understand you not wanting to be stuck in here with me, when I could … you know."

Ana shook her head. "I didn't mean that at all. I want to be out there, *helping*. I don't like being told to sit out while others are fighting, like I'm a …" She stopped, wanting to say *helpless child*, but here in the Station children were anything but.

"Father has been doing the same thing with me ever since I got bitten. He almost never lets me go on hunts or anything. Not anymore. I had to fight hard to rescue you when we did."

"He's just trying to protect you. Liam's like that. Same for my father. Maybe it's a man thing. Or maybe it's just how you are with the ones that you love and want to protect."

"Your father was very nice."

For a long moment, it seemed like Calla was going to say something more, as if she had a specific story to tell. Instead, she looked down at the floor. "I like your tunic."

"Thanks. Rosemary gave it to me."

"She's nice. She's been kind of like a mom. She's not with Father or anything, but she's always been there for me."

"What happened to your mom?"

"She died a long time ago, back in City 6." Calla shook her head. "But I don't want to talk about that."

Ana looked down. "Sorry."

"It's okay," Calla said, still staring at the floor.

An internal gnawing insisted that a zombie was near. She'd felt the sensation earlier but had lost it once locked in the room with Calla. Here it was again.

She looked down at the blaster, made sure it was charged, then eyed the door as if expecting it to slide open at any second. She could hear nothing on the other side, only the whir of warm air pressing through the vents, blending with a steady hum from the wall's bank of refrigerated units. Her heartbeat sped up as she resumed her pacing.

"What's wrong?" Calla asked.

Something's coming. Can you feel it? She didn't want to frighten the girl, especially if there was no way a zombie could enter their room. "Nothing."

She heard a loud popping and looked up to see the metal air duct vent fifteen feet above her swing open. Seconds later, a man dropped down from above.

Ana screamed, barely managing to dodge out of his way as he fell. She tripped, landed hard beside him. The blaster slipped from her hand and skidded across the floor.

She reached out to grab it but was too slow.

The man yanked it from the floor, turned it on Ana, and barked, "Get over there!"

He was wearing nothing but a thin white shirt and only slightly thicker white cotton pants. He looked maybe thirty, thin, gaunt even, with medium-dark, curly brown hair and a short beard. His eyes were brown, but the whites were red, like his swollen lids.

He aimed the blaster between them, moving it ever so slightly side-to-side, ushering Ana next to Calla. She stood slowly, putting herself between the girl and the gunman. "It's okay. We're not going to do anything."

The man looked back at the door and pressed the green button on the wall beside it.

"Why won't it open?" he shouted, turning back to them, gun shaking.

"We're locked in," Ana said, "to protect us from the zombie."

The man laughed, wildly shaking his head. He seemed crazed, as if on drugs. On TV, she'd seen people in the

Dark Quarter acting weird like this guy. They'd been described as extremely dangerous and to be avoided at all costs. *Vermin, just as likely to slit your throat as rape you. Beware and report.*

"Is there a way out of here?" he asked.

"Not that I know of. Like I said, we're locked in."

"Not this room," he hissed, glaring at her. "Of this *place*. Wherever the hell we are."

"You're not from here?"

"NO!" That bitter laugh again. "They brought me here!"

"What are you talking about, mister?" Calla asked.

Ana looked back at her: *Do not attract attention to yourself. Let me deal with this.*

"They fucking kidnapped me. They've been doing experiments or something."

Her heart pounded faster as she realized that the man must be the infected subject that Oswald said they found in the Barrens — the zombie she'd sensed nearby, the one that had made the siren scream.

Only he didn't seem to know he was infected. Looking closer at the man, she tried to determine how close he was to turning. His red eyes reminded her of Duncan's. He was shaking and sweating, but she couldn't tell if he was about to turn now, with her and Calla in a locked room, or if he was merely frightened.

She had to calm him before his frazzled nerves caused him to change — or shoot them.

"I can help you get out of here," Ana said.

"How?" asked the man.

"If you go back up into the air vent, you can crawl another twenty feet or so that way, and drop down into the room next to this one. Open the door and I can sneak you out of here."

The man looked at Ana as if considering her offer, but then he shook his head. "No. The girl goes up. She can unlock the door from the other side."

Ana was about to argue, but why? His idea got Calla out of the room, away from danger.

"Can you go up there, crawl into the next room, and open the door?" Ana asked her.

"Yes," Calla almost whispered, her chin trembling, clearly terrified.

"I'm going to move the desk under the air duct, then climb up with Calla and lift her to the vent, okay?"

"Yeah, yeah," he said, irritated, running a hand through his sweaty hair and squeezing it tight.

Ana pushed the desk over, climbed up, then waited for Calla to scramble up onto the desk, sweating and shaking.

"It's going to be okay," Ana reassured her before turning back to the man. "She goes free once we're out of here. I'll take you to the exit. No one gets hurt."

The man chewed his lip, hand still shaking, and tugged at his hair in thought.

"All right?" Ana repeated forcefully.

"Yeah!"

Ana lifted Calla and whispered, "Don't open the door. Go get help."

The girl nodded as Ana lifted her up. She watched as Calla crawled into the duct, listening as the sound of banging metal faded away from their room and then stopped entirely.

Calla had probably dropped into the other room on her way to find help. Ana had to stall and keep the guy from figuring out what they were up to.

"So, what do you mean they took you and experimented on you? What happened?"

"Don't act like you don't know."

"I'm not from here. I only arrived a couple of days ago. They took me in after I got sick. They helped me get better. Are you sick, too?"

"I wasn't!" He glared at Ana as if she'd been the one to take him. "They grabbed me in the middle of the night, stole me and another two from our camp. We didn't do anything to deserve this."

"Two others?"

"I was with Johan and Filner, two longtime mates. We have, or had, a camp near Yath River. Not a big place, but we managed. They came in the middle of the night and grabbed us all. I'm the only one left."

"What happened to the others?"

"They turned 'em into zombies, then killed 'em."

"They're trying to help. Are you sure you weren't infected before?"

"Hell no." The man moved closer, spittle flying from his mouth through his anguished, angry cry. "They injected us with something! They turned my friends into monsters!"

Ana stared at his gun, now only aimed in her general direction. If she could inch closer, she might be able to snag the weapon from him.

But then the door suddenly opened and Calla stood there, alone.

Ana stared in disbelief. Why hadn't she run off and gotten someone?

Ana was shocked enough that she missed her chance to disarm the man. He aimed the gun at her again. "Okay, girl, now you get me out of here."

He waved his blaster, instructing Ana to move ahead.

She did, feeling him behind her, looking down at Calla leaning against the exam table, holding her stomach.

"I don't feel good. I'm so cold."

The color had left her face. She was sweating, her body shivering uncontrollably.

"What's wrong?" Ana reached out to touch her. Calla was burning up, despite her claim.

"I don't know …" Calla swallowed and looked up at Ana in terror. The infected man, through either proximity or inoculation of fear, might have caused Calla to change. "I think it's happening."

TWENTY-NINE

Sutherland

SUTHERLAND STARED at the door for hours, waiting for someone to come and free or kill him.

He drifted in and out of sleep, unsure of how much time had passed.

He couldn't be caught off guard. He had to stay …

At some point, he must've fallen asleep again because the door burst open and movement came in a blur. He tensed as his eyes adjusted, revealing the men in the room: Horrance and two others, Finch and Wormwood. Good men, if they hadn't been turned by the cancer in their ranks. They were both older men and had fought bravely in the Battle of '32. He wanted to believe that older meant wiser and that the pair of battle-tested soldiers, along with the giant, could easily see Gallus's folly.

"My men," Sutherland greeted them, hoping that they were, in fact, still that.

"Sutherland," Horrance said with a nod and understanding eyes. The other men looked at him the same way, giving him hope that they were indeed on his side.

"Have you come to free me?" After a too-long pause,

he added, "We can go arrest the traitors. Everything will be back to normal by morning."

Finch stepped forward. "We can't. It'll never work."

"Why not?" *Cowards!*

"Because," Wormwood said. "There aren't enough supporters left."

"Impossible!"

Horrance sighed as he freed Sutherland from his bindings. "Gallus has turned nearly everyone."

"How could he turn *everyone*? Surely these people remember who stood by their side! Who has helped them survive, nay, thrive, when the rest of the world is still shit!"

"If you go out there, they'll kill you." Finch nodded toward the closed cell door. "These people think *you're* the problem. And they think that Jeffries is the only one who can help."

Sutherland could hardly speak. The weight of their words was too much. How could all of his people turn on him like that? He swallowed as he stood, then found Horrance's eyes. "Is it true, Horrance? Is Gallus right? Have I lost touch with my people? Am I wrong?"

"No," Wormwood, the strongest and smartest among them said as he stepped forward. "Gallus is wrong. You're the only one with the balls to do what must be done. You're the one with the courage. These others are ungrateful parasites that take and take, but never give when it's their time to pitch in."

Sutherland held back tears of joy as the men all nodded in agreement. "Well then, gentleman, what are we to do?"

Wormwood spoke. "We can help you escape. We have another five men who also believe in you, in the cause."

"Then what? Where shall I go? Where shall we go?"

Horrance replied. "The train station. Where Ana is."

Sutherland brightened. "You think we can take it?"

"Easiest thing in the world," said Finch. "We can do what we done to City 1. Can you get your hands on more of the zombie gas?"

"Can you get me to the lab?"

Horrance nodded. "Yes, sir."

"Then let's go fix this clusterfuck."

Moments later, Horrance was accompanying Sutherland to the lab. He stayed cuffed to keep up appearances, but they were loose and would come off if he needed them to. He'd shoved the shiv into his pocket, and couldn't wait to use it on the first traitor to stand in his way.

They descended two floors and turned several corners down, and approached the lab where two guards stood in front of the door.

The first guard stepped forward and held out a hand. "What is *he* doing here?"

"Gallus asked me to bring him to the lab for a test."

"Test? I didn't hear anything about a test." The guard looked them up and down. "What sorta test? It's the middle of the night."

The guard turned to his partner. "Hey, you hear anything about a—"

Sutherland thrust the shiv into the man's throat.

Then Horrance fired his blaster, dropping the second guard before he could signal for help.

Sutherland knelt down to watch the life drain out of the first guard's eyes, then yanked the blade from his throat, stood, and turned to Horrance as he waved the big man through the door to the science lab. "After you, sir."

～

SUTHERLAND AND HORRANCE hefted the four black bags onto the service elevator where Finch was waiting.

"Good lord," said Finch. "I thought you might've held back some, but not *this much*."

"Just because the other camps stopped fighting doesn't mean the war is over. There are still six cities standing last I looked. The wheels of power barely skipped a beat. It's time to take them down once and for all."

Finch smiled. He'd lost his brother and sister in a State raid when they were escaping City 3. He knew exactly what they were fighting for. He, unlike the others, had not forgotten. "And what about the antidote? Do you have enough?"

"Enough to spare the deserving. Enough to start things over and do them right this time."

"Good," Finch said.

They stepped into the elevator. Wormwood was about to press the button marked GARAGE when Sutherland told him to wait. "Are our loyal people out?"

"Yes," Finch said. "They've taken out the guards in the garage and are ready to take us out of here."

"Good. Go to Level 7."

Wormwood's brow furrowed in confusion even as he pressed the button for LEVEL 7. "Civilian living quarters? Why?"

"Hydrangea is now as complicit as the State. I made the mistake of being lenient once, ignoring the very cancer as it spread beneath my roof. I cannot allow that to continue."

"What are you gonna do?" Wormwood asked.

Sutherland reached into a bag and grabbed gas masks for each of them. "I suggest you put these on."

Horrance paused. "Are you sure about this? Aren't there kids and stuff?"

Sutherland's voice deepened as he stared into Horrance's eyes. "Are we not at war, gentlemen? Because I've never known a child that didn't grow up to become a man or woman. If we don't wipe them out now, they'll keep coming, forever hunting us like animals. You are all heroes, but they'll see you as villains, as traitors. They will not stop until they murder each and every one of us. Do you understand?"

Horrance looked at his feet. "But … they're kids, sir."

Sutherland grabbed Horrance by the collar and pulled him just inches from his face. "Do you really think these people are worth saving? You've heard the names they call you, haven't you? Even these *innocent* kids. Freak. Brute. Mutant. You really want to spare their cruel lives?"

"No, sir." Horrance finally shrugged.

"Good." The elevator doors dinged open. "We finish this, then the train station is ours."

THIRTY

Liam Harrow

THE SUN LEFT and took forty degrees with it. A chill shot through Liam. He wondered if they could build a fire in their building without drawing the eyes of zombies, bandits, or other players.

From their spot on the fifth floor of an apartment in surprisingly stable condition, they had an excellent view of a main avenue. According to Egan's roughly drawn map, the five-mile stretch of six lanes zigzagged north and south, staying just straight enough to split the Outback's heart roughly in half. The meandering road was littered with ancient transports and starving zombies, making it impossible to pass without a vehicle to cover distances quickly and provide immediate cover.

"We should leave the buildings if it snows. The streets should be less crowded. Probably safer." Liam turned from the window to Chelsea. "How's your ankle?"

She stood from her chair, wincing. "Still hurts, but I can keep up."

Liam didn't bother looking at Katrina, sitting on the floor in the corner beside Clark at the window. But he could feel her stare. Chelsea twisted her ankle while the four of them ran from zombies a few hours ago and was thus responsible for slowing them down. It wasn't Liam's first choice, but his only other option was to leave the poor girl to die. Yet, without any idea where Adam was, resting didn't really change things.

"I'm sorry," Chelsea said to Katrina. "I don't want to slow you all from finding Adam."

Katrina ignored Chelsea as she continued to rotate the dial on the box screen provided by Egan, searching through the twenty or so network feeds from orbs flying through the city. They'd stopped every half hour or so to cycle through channels, but had yet to find any sign of Adam.

Liam tried not to become discouraged, telling himself that didn't mean he was dead. The Outback had plenty of places to hide, no shortage of hovels where a resourceful guy like Adam could bury himself, then wait for the others to eliminate one another before reaching the Mesa, wherever that was.

"Thanks, Liam," Chelsea said, filling the silence left by Katrina. "I know we lost touch over the years, and weren't really all that close before. This is really kind of you. All of you." She breathed through a beat, then repeated her gratitude. "Thanks."

Liam could practically feel Katrina rolling her eyes.

"No problem," muttered Clark.

"I was rooting for you and Ana in the Games. It broke my heart when they showed you both dying. I was so glad to see you today, and realize it was a lie."

Liam nodded, not knowing what to say, uncomfortable with her fawning. She'd been lathering him with compliments ever since he'd managed to convince Katrina to bring Chelsea along. Liam wasn't sure if she was truly that grateful, or afraid that he'd realize what a liability he'd invited into the group.

Chelsea had tried to appear tough when they found her, but clearly wasn't cut from Ana's fabric. She had a clerical job in City 6, useless in training for the Games.

"I found him," Katrina said, holding up the box screen so Liam could see. "There."

Liam walked over and looked down where she pointed. Adam, creeping through an alley alongside another player, trying to pass a horde of zombies swarming the front of a tall building with large letters carved into its stone face: *Apex National Bank.*

Katrina cranked the volume to see if Kirk Kirkman had anything to say. He didn't. Liam figured they were likely watching one of the many feeds the State kept from the audience, meant for monitoring players internally. Adam's feed would probably go to broadcast the moment he and his companion crashed into trouble.

"Look for an Apex National Bank," Katrina said to Clark as he scanned the skyline with infrared binoculars.

Liam turned to a trembling Chelsea. "You okay?"

"Just cold," she said through chattering teeth.

Katrina, Clark, and Liam were prepared for the freeze, all covered in thick black coats. Chelsea had only the Darwin coveralls, thin as they were.

Liam shook the coat from his shoulders and slipped it around the girl.

"You sure?"

"Yeah, I'm good." He returned to his spot beside Katrina.

She looked up at Liam, not so subtly shaking her head. He focused on the screen as Adam and his companion took cover behind a small wall to survey the zombies.

From the camera's angle, it seemed like they could have easily sneaked past them by turning down another alley.

"They could have kept going," Katrina said, confirming his suspicions. "They must be trying to get into the bank."

"Yeah. But why?" Liam asked.

"Maybe one of 'ems cold." Katrina looked up at Chelsea and then back at Liam before her eyes returned to the screen. He continued to bite his tongue, avoiding a scene.

Clark said, "I found the bank. It's gonna be a trek."

Katrina turned off the box, slid it into her backpack, and stood. She pointed at Liam. "You, come here."

Liam followed her from the room, down the hall, and into a bedroom where she clicked on her flashlight.

"Your girlfriend stays." Then she barreled on before he could argue. "She can't keep up. We've got a line on Adam, and need to reach him before he's gone or dead."

"She said her ankle's fine."

"Do you even hear yourself? Where the hell is the Liam I met last year?"

"She's not some stranger, Katrina. She's a friend."

"That girl doesn't give a fuck about you. She's saying whatever will stroke your ego, and keep me from kicking her out of the club."

"Maybe you shouldn't be so eager to leave her behind."

Katrina burned her gaze into his. "She's a liability, Liam. Tell me she's not." He couldn't lie, and she seized on his silence. "You want to tell her or should I?"

"Why don't we tell her to stay put and we'll come back for her?"

"We're not coming back for her, Liam. We're going to get Adam and then go to the Station, so you and Ana can settle down, start a fucking family, or whatever it is you soft people do after you wave your white flag."

"What's really bothering you?"

She shook her head and looked away.

Liam grabbed her by the arm.

She twisted from his grip, and turned her fiery gaze back on him. "I heard you and Ana talking when you thought I was asleep, about how you can't wait to stop fighting and finally settle down somewhere *safe*."

"And there's something wrong with that?"

"I risked everything to break you both out of Hydrangea. And I did it because I thought the two of you could help hurt the State, maybe even cure the zombie virus and bring down the Walls."

"You helped us because you wanted to get away from Sutherland, too. Because you knew Ana was in danger, *same as you were*."

"No." She shook her head, arms crossed. "I wasn't in danger *until* I helped you."

"Do you wish that you hadn't? Are you saying that you weren't happy to get away from that crazy fuck?" He stared at Katrina in disbelief. "The guy wiped out a city! Men, women, children. You're okay with that?"

"I don't approve of his methods, no, but he's the only real chance the Patriots have of making genuine change. He's the first person to come along who isn't just spouting off at the mouth. There's plenty to say about Sutherland, but he's never been afraid to put words to his thought and action to both."

Liam couldn't believe his ears. All this time that he and Ana had traveled with Katrina, he had never suspected that she regretted her decision. He couldn't believe she would condone what Sutherland's insanity had done to the innocents living inside City 1.

"He wiped out a city!" Liam repeated.

"I'm not arguing with you, Liam. What's done is done, no matter what *I* think. Right now we're going to go out there into the other room, and one of us is going to tell your friend goodbye. So, who's it going to be?"

A loud beeping echoed from the other room.

Katrina and Liam raced back to see Chelsea shoving the screaming bracelet on her right wrist deep into Liam's jacket in a futile attempt to muffle the racket.

But the bracelet was too loud, inviting zombies, bandits and other players to end them. Network orbs would surround their bodies to broadcast their imminent death in moments.

"Get out of here!" Katrina screamed, raising her gun at the girl. "Go!"

"No! Please. It'll stop soon. *Please.*"

Chelsea's second *please* sounded so desperate, it tugged at something deep inside Liam. It had no such effect on Katrina.

"GO!" she screamed louder.

Liam thrust himself between the women, hoping Katrina wouldn't shoot him in the back. "Let me see it!" He yanked off the jacket to get a better look at the screeching bracelet.

Chelsea's arm shook as she cried, "Stop it, please, stop the beeping."

He ran his fingers along the seam. "What is this?"

"They put 'em on all of us. It's got an alarm that pops off at random."

"Oh, great! Get her out of here!"

"No!" Liam yelled at Katrina. "I can get it off."

Clark rushed over, and for a moment, Liam thought he would shoot her. Instead, he looked at the bracelet, inspecting the metal with Liam as the beeping continued to scream in their ears.

"Hold on," Liam said, "I'm going to get my knife from your jacket."

Chelsea nodded, eyes wide, tears painting her face as the death sentence kept screeching its promise. He found the blade in his pants pocket as she slipped from his hands.

Katrina yanked the girl from his grip, spun her around, and raced her toward the window.

Liam screamed, "Don't!"

But Katrina held her momentum and shoved Chelsea through the glass.

Liam cried out as she disappeared over the ledge, plummeting five flights down to the snowy street below. His gun was aimed at Katrina before he knew what he was doing. "What the fuck!"

Clark drew his gun precisely at no one. He stood roughly between them, his weapon hovering somewhere in the middle, clearly nervous.

Katrina looked the opposite of sorry. She glared at Liam, eyes daring his challenge. She wasn't even reaching for her gun. "You weren't going to do it. Would you rather we all ended up dead?"

He had to swallow his desire to pull the trigger and deal with the consequences later. He couldn't remember ever feeling so suddenly shocked, or mercilessly affronted. He wanted to kill her, not just for what she had done to Chelsea, but for how she had so instantly smothered his trust.

But the weight of Katrina's stare pressed down on his arm. He didn't stand a chance. A wrong move, and Clark would have to shoot him dead.

She dared to laugh. "What are you going to do, Liam — shoot me? *Really?* You couldn't eliminate an obvious threat, yet you expect me to believe that you'd kill me in cold blood. Sure you *want* to, but you won't. *You can't.* And that's exactly the problem."

Her eyes flitted to the window. "Look outside, Liam, and what do you think you'll see? Zombies dining on your girlfriend's guts. Those same zombies would be eating us right now if I didn't stop it from happening. Tell me I'm wrong."

Liam felt his finger twitching against the trigger, still desperately wanting to pull it. Clark lowered his gun and walked over to Liam. "Put the gun down, man. She's right. And we all know you're not gonna shoot her."

They *were* right: there was no way he would kill Katrina in cold blood. He wasn't a murderer like her. But it felt good to hold it in her face, to aim at someone who made excuses for monsters and could kill the innocent without flinching.

Clark holstered his gun, then slowly set his hand on top of Liam's weapon and gingerly lowered the barrel.

Chelsea's bracelet finally stopped screaming outside.

With another angry glare at Katrina, he shouldered by her on his way to the window. Just as she had predicted, Liam saw a small horde of zombies painting their faces with Chelsea's blood. He could imagine the racket of their feasting.

"It stopped. We could have made it out alive. All we had to do was wait."

"It stopped because she's dead. Quit being a fool. Your mercy will get us all killed. Are you on this mission or do you want to run back and tell Ana you gave up?"

Liam looked from Katrina to Clark, then back, wishing he was still holding his gun.

"After you." He nodded toward the door.

Katrina looked like she was biting her smirk.

Clark looked relieved as he took the lead and left the room with Katrina behind him.

Liam took one final look out the window, feeling heavy and at least partially responsible for the girl's untimely death. He shook his head and fell into a grim march at the rear, hoping that they found Adam soon so he could kill Katrina and get back to Ana.

"Think about it all you want, cowboy. We both know you don't have the guts."

THIRTY-ONE

Anastasia Lovecraft

CALLA FELL TO THE FLOOR, doubled over in pain, trembling as the siren screamed.

"Come on!" the infected man yelled at Ana, still aiming his gun between her eyes. "You said you'd take me out of here."

"I can't leave her, she's …"

Ana turned to Calla. She remembered her own infection stirring like soup rolling to a boil inside her whenever she and Liam came close to the undead. Even now she could still feel a deep connection to the zombies, a half year after her supposed curing.

What if there was something in her, and Calla, reacting directly to the infected?

"Go," Ana yelled, eager to clear him from the room. "Go straight down this hall and make your second right."

"No." He reached over and yanked Ana roughly by the hair. "*You* take me."

"Okay, okay," she said, allowing him to pull her, holding her hands high in surrender.

As she started to pass him, Calla dropped to the floor

and kicked the man's leg hard, buckling the knee and sending him to the floor in a screaming heap.

Calla leapt on him before he could react. Instead of going for the gun, she chopped at his Adam's apple, causing him to lose his gun as he reached for his neck, gasping for air.

Ana grabbed the blaster, and before second guessing herself, aimed square at his chest and squeezed the trigger. The man's chest caved in and turned his organs to ash.

"Oswald!" she screamed, rushing to Calla.

She fell to the floor beside her, and swiped sweaty hair from the girl's small face, startled to see her eyes rolling into the back of her head. Limbs spasmed and she banged her head against the floor.

Ana slipped her hands beneath Calla's head, cradling it softly to keep her from busting it like a melon. The girl's breathing was fast and shallow, like she might start to hyperventilate at any moment. Ana had to calm her, though how could she soothe the child when she herself wanted to yell at someone — *anyone* — to kill the damned siren?

She petted Calla's hair. "It's okay. He's gone now."

But Ana was terrified about what was happening inside the girl. "Just breathe slow, in and out. Focus on my voice. Nice and slow."

Calla closed her eyes, wincing as she cried out in pain. "It hurts … *so much.*"

"You'll be okay," Ana said, continuing to promise what she couldn't deliver. "Just breathe slowly and don't think about anything you don't have to. Focus on my voice and the things that make you most happy."

Think about the things that make you most happy? She's turning into a fucking zombie! Where the hell is Oswald? COME on!

Ana was desperate to see the doctor, to know he could

hear her and was coming to help, but she didn't dare scream for him again. Calla had finally stopped shaking, now a low, steady shudder, despite the shrill siren still screaming all around them.

"That's it, nice and slow." Ana rocked her. "You're doing so good."

An ugly panic dawned on her: the girl had stopped moving. Her heart froze as she reached for Calla's neck to feel for a pulse.

Nothing. *NO. Don't let her die.*

Ana moved her fingers, hoping she was being stupid and feeling in the wrong spot.

Then it was there, barely a whisper.

She exhaled, nearly collapsing into tears as Calla's bright blue eyes blinked opened and looked up at her. The whites were ringed in an angry red. She looked confused, but mostly aware.

"You're going to be okay." Ana was desperate to believe the words through her smile.

"I'm tired," Calla barely managed.

Ana wasn't sure what she could say. Everything was stupid in her head. Should she let the girl sleep, or force her to stay awake? She had been at her lowest point before losing herself to a sleep so deep that Liam was sure she was dead.

Maybe if she let Calla sleep, the girl would wake up cured, same as she had.

Or never wake up again.

"Calla!" Oswald yelled from the doorway.

He glanced at the fallen body, then dropped to his knees beside Calla as Father Truth appeared in the threshold behind him.

"What happened?" Father Truth asked.

Ana told them everything she could about Calla, while

leaving out everything the infected man had said — that was for later.

Father Truth grabbed a com from his coat pocket, made a call, then told whoever was on the other end that the situation was under control and that the subject was dead.

Moments later, the alarm finally stopped screaming. Oswald picked up Calla and laid her flat on an exam table. He asked, *Where are you? What's your name? How do you feel?* and a dozen other questions, which Calla groggily, but accurately, answered. He never stopped checking her vitals or scribbling notes on a clipboard beside the bed.

"I wasn't sure if I should let her sleep," Ana said. "I was afraid she might not wake up. Or wake up as a zombie."

"It's okay." Father Truth reached into his long coat and withdrew a small brown pouch. He unfastened a leather string, opened the pouch, and poured two tiny white pills into his palm.

"Give her these," he said to Oswald.

Oswald grabbed a bottle of water from his desktop, then helped Calla take the pills and drink the water.

"What did you give her?" Ana asked.

"Something to help her sleep," said Father Truth. "You were right in trying to calm her. From what we've seen, the infected can trigger a rapid escalation in another's virus. As can stress. Together the two are a lethal recipe."

"Could she still change now, or when she wakes up?"

"We can't be certain if she was actually changing, though it would seem from your description that she may have been," Oswald said. "As to whether she still might, we can't say. But I don't think so. She'll fall asleep in a few minutes, then I'll re-inject her with the serum. I should have something ready using your white blood cells by tomorrow, a variation of our Hydrangea experiments."

"Is it whatever you were using on this man?" Ana asked. "Because I'm not sure it was working."

Oswald avoided her eyes, keeping his gaze on Calla instead.

"No, we were giving him an older version of the serum," Father Truth answered. "We have another subject responding quite positively to the new variation."

He seemed kind as he met her upset eyes. His voice was warm enough to make Ana loathe her next question. But she couldn't ignore the accusation, or stuff it inside her.

"The man said that you all infected him. Is it true?"

Father Truth rubbed his hand through his hair, pushing it back as he seemed to deliberate the proper response. Then he finally motioned for Ana to follow him out of the room and into the hallway.

"Yes, it's true," he admitted.

Ana could only stare. Until she found words, even uglier out loud than they were in her head. "You guys are kidnapping and infecting people?"

Father Truth held her eyes. "I'm not proud of it, Ana. But sometimes advances in science require sacrifice."

"Like me?"

He couldn't meet her eyes.

She swallowed her desire to yell. "I want to see Egan."

"Certainly." Father nodded. "I'll take you immediately."

THIRTY-TWO

Keller

KELLER SAT ALONE in the master viewing room, staring at the two dozen screens which peeked onto streets and into resident homes inside City 1, returning to the search he'd all but surrendered four months ago.

There were cameras in every television, on every street corner, and in every public place in the City. They recorded everything, yet somehow, none had managed to show Keller who helped Jonah Lovecraft unleash the zombie virus on City 1.

There was a woman who'd met with him, but she disappeared after the attack, and no one seemed to know her real name.

He stared at the screens, flipping through the day's footage, growing increasingly annoyed with the red squares covering nearly half the screens at any one cycle.

Red squares were a designation from the Elders that the person in that home was not to be spied upon. An electronic block which prevented televisions from viewing or recording anything. Since the most powerful people resided in City 1, they were granted privileges that others were not.

Keller asked the Elders if there were some way to unblock the squares. They said no, the blocks were legitimate and there was nothing that he, or they, could do. They all had blocks themselves, so he doubted their explanations were necessarily on the level.

Regardless, it meant that if whoever helped plan the attack was among the City's Elders or community leaders, Keller was shit out of luck.

After staring at the screens for so long, they all became a blur. He could've stayed home with nothing done. And there, he could drink.

After a few more wasted hours, his com rang — Jacquelyn asking if he'd be home for dinner.

"Yeah, Jackie. I'm heading out now."

He grabbed his jacket and headed for the elevators. Of course his phone rang as the doors closed. Elderman Hesh, one of the six at the pyramid's top. They ran the Elder's Council — the only people above Keller, unless you counted the deceased Jack Geralt, whom the State still pretended was alive.

"Yes, Elderman Hesh?"

"Mr. Keller," Hesh said with his insincere joviality, "how are you this afternoon?"

Keller hated how the council all referred to him — in person — as Mr. Keller rather than by his title, Provisional Leader. It was as if they wanted to remind him at all times that he served at their leisure.

State citizens thought Keller ran the show, as Geralt had before him. But these old men called the shots, disguising their influence with a "One True Leader" so no one would hold them accountable. Nor would the populace know that the council acted in their own interests, maintaining power, wealth, and influence, while doing the same for their friends.

Even Keller had no idea how crooked the system was until he was named Provisional Leader. It was a different view behind the curtain (the curtain behind the curtain). Corruption or no, he had a job to do, and asses to kiss. Better this crooked system than the Underground's unbridled anarchy.

"I'm quite fine."

"I understand that you've been accessing data from the City 1 attack."

"Well, yes." Keller wondered how the hell the man had known that.

"May I ask why?"

"Certainly. I'm following up on a lead."

Keller wished he hadn't said lead. A lead would mean divulging a source he didn't have. And it wasn't like he could make up something which would hold water if the council were to try and verify. This wasn't like City 6 where Keller knew everyone, and City Watch had each other's backs. People in City 1 were interested in themselves — especially since the attack.

While few beyond Keller and the council knew that Geralt was dead, the people could sense empty rungs in the political ladder, and many were angling to climb. It wasn't enough that three of the council had died during the attack, which meant three new appointed Elders. Several State departments were also affected with new faces heading key positions. So many new faces and changes, no one felt safe in their jobs. Everyone was looking to secure their spot — which meant infighting and backstabbing.

The attack was a strike at the State's seat of power, but it hadn't disrupted the flow so much as rerouted the current.

Keller felt like he was onto something, perhaps connecting a few more dots from the attack to someone inside the City. And if his sniffing had drawn attention, he must be closer than he thought.

"What kind of lead, Mr. Keller?"

"Not a lead, so much as a hunch."

"What kind of hunch?"

"I don't know, sir. I was thinking maybe I missed something, so I figured I'd go through the day's footage again."

"And *did you* find anything?"

"No, sir."

"I thought the council had made it clear that you were to end your investigation."

"Yes, sir."

"And yet, here you are? Is there nothing better to do with your time?"

"No sir, I mean, yes, I have better things. I just hate thinking that our enemies are alive to strike again."

"We have our enemy, Mr. Keller. The Underground, led by Jonah Lovecraft. Those were your findings, correct?"

Yes, that's what *the council* decided that Keller had found after reviewing his investigation.

"Yes, sir."

"So, the case is closed, then?"

"Yes, sir."

"Great!" Hesh said. "Glad to hear it."

Keller again wondered how the hell Hesh knew he'd been investigating the attack. He let him stew in the silence. This interrogation technique worked on ninety percent of criminals, maybe it would work on an old man with too much power.

"Some people would like this put to bed, so we can get to the business of moving on," Hesh finally said.

Keller played dumb. "I'm sorry, I didn't realize I was offending any Elders."

"Not *me*."

So it is someone else asking you to make this call? Keller stayed quiet, knowing a name was forthcoming. Hesh *wanted* to tell Keller this — people in the know always wanted to prove their insider status.

"Elderman Sinclair was worried that maybe some of our people would see that you're still investigating this when the case was closed, and perhaps send the wrong message about our priorities — or your fitness for leadership."

Elderman Denton Sinclair was one of the council who came into power following the attacks. For the third time, Keller wondered how the hell Sinclair, Hesh, or anyone else knew that Keller was viewing the feeds.

It had to be someone on the inside, someone angling for his job, feeding information to the council in attempt to undermine him, or prevent him from finding the truth.

He would have to find that someone and take care of them. For now, though, politics. "Should I speak to Elderman Sinclair?"

"No, of course not. That isn't necessary. He just asked me to take care of it because you and I have known each other so long. He figured you might take it better from me."

"Of course," Keller said. "I understand. Please tell Elderman Sinclair that I'm finished. As far as I'm concerned, Jonah was the Underground's head. We've cut that off nicely, and are now inches from total eradication."

Hesh thanked him and hung up.

Keller stared at the comm, then pressed a button on the wall. The doors parted and he entered the garage, wanting to know why Denton Sinclair was so interested in his investigation.

THIRTY-THREE

Sutherland

With their truck parked a safe distance away, Sutherland had been scouting the area surrounding where they believed the Station to be.

He was with the giant oaf — and now his savior — Horrance, as well as the two stooges Wormwood and Finch, and another handful of idiots.

Half of Sutherland was grateful for the lot of them. They had risked plenty to save him, and had trusted him enough to follow his plans to turn on their own people and unleash the virus in Hydrangea. The rest of him saw them for the idiots they were. That half-wanted to strangle them as they clomped carelessly through the woods like they were on a merry jaunt.

"Want us to go find something to eat?"

Wormwood had been asking Sutherland the same goddamned question for the last few hours, ever since they reached the Station's perimeter and turned food into something they'd have to think about later.

"No," Sutherland said, barely holding his pleasant facade. "We'll eat *after* we find the base where Ana Lovecraft is hiding. Now please ..." He tried not to hiss as he forced his lips into the same tired sentences. "Try and keep your voice down. We want to *see before we're seen.* Got it?"

"What?" Wormwood asked loudly.

A sudden rustling in the woods ahead caught their collective attention. Horrance turned to Sutherland, quietly begging for direction.

Sutherland ducked low in the brush along the tree line and ordered his men to do the same with a gesture. They crouched, Sutherland watching and hoping his men wouldn't screw up.

A few of the men looked like they wanted to say something, and point out the obvious, but Sutherland put his finger to his lips and wagged his head. He nodded toward the rustling, growing louder until a pair of people entered the clearing.

Sutherland could feel the smile as it lit his lips. They had to be from the base. They looked healthy, their equipment and clothing were too nice to be scavengers or bandits. One was a young teenage boy, maybe fifteen or sixteen, hard to tell with him bundled so tight. His companion, a girl, a few years older than him. He bobbed behind her like a lovesick pup.

They would be easy enough to question and kill. Each carried a light-looking backpack. Sutherland assumed they were mostly empty, there to transport whatever they killed as dinner for the base. In addition to their matching packs, the pair carried identical weapons — short bows, full quivers, and each had a mini-blaster at their side. The girl wore hers high on the right, the boy had his low on the left.

Sutherland nodded a gesture at Horrance, hoping the oaf wasn't too stupid to get his meaning. The ogre got it, whispered something to Finch, then followed the leader alone, as the rest of the men stayed back behind the trees.

After he and Horrance trailed the scouts for a while, Sutherland felt his smile start to widen, remembering his own days staying alive by killing game. This wasn't all that different, though the prey now came with half as many legs. He continued to follow his quarry.

In winter, even skilled hunters went hungry. The best way to fight starvation — a strategy the couple in front were clearly familiar with — was to hunt among the bedding areas, where deer went to rest. The pair Sutherland followed was hunting smart, and careful.

The hunters spotted a buck, right where the pine trees started to thicken. Sutherland motioned for Horrance to stay back, then kept going alone, knowing the oaf would make too much noise and scare the deer, along with the hunters trailing it.

As he continued to follow, Sutherland couldn't help but be impressed with the hunters. Young as they were, they were patient, not rushing the kill, waiting until they had their shots lined up. With the wind picking up, and a snowstorm brewing, they knew that they might not get another chance if they missed.

Deeper in the woods, with Sutherland's men still far behind them, the hunters turned so quiet they were nearly invisible. The girl drew an arrow from her quiver, notched it in her bow, and aimed.

Too bad she'll never fire.

Sutherland stepped up behind her, no longer worried about stealth. His boot heel snapped a branch, and sent the deer darting into the woods. The girl's arrow sailed toward the deer, too high, and thunked into a tree as the deer vanished into the trees.

The guy never stood a chance. By the time he realized what was happening, Horrance had him by the hair, blade to his throat.

"You can say something. No need to be quiet. Dinner's gone. Dessert, well, that's another matter." Sutherland smiled at the hunters, thinking it funny that they were now prey, then focused on the girl. "If you don't tell us exactly what we need to know, I'll let my boys have all they can eat."

He leaned forward and winked. "But I'll be the one to slice your pretty little throat when they're through."

THIRTY-FOUR

Adam Lovecraft

DARKNESS CLOAKED them as they crept from one set of shadows to the next, sticking close to the walls, ready for anything.

But as night came, and with it fresh snow, life had left the streets — save for the undead variety of roughly two dozen zombies standing between them and the bank, milling around in the lot in front of the entrance of Apex National Bank, the building where they'd tracked Zelle to.

"Why are they just standing there?" Adam whispered to Colton as they hid behind a wall of broken vehicles, rusting across the street.

"Hell if I know," Colton said. "Maybe they were bankers and they just can't stand the thought of leaving their money behind."

Adam ignored the joke and looked at the box screen. "I still don't see Zelle." The girl, who had been on the rooftop until about an hour ago, seemed to be gone. Adam couldn't help but think she'd been found and either killed by another player, or eaten.

"Relax, kid. I'm sure she just went downstairs to get out of the elements when the temperature dropped."

Adam stared at the bank. The building climbed forty stories, with a pointed spire at the top. Most of the building's glass windows were still in place, dark and impossible to see through. The place could be empty, or packed forty floors high with zombies. The closer they got to Zelle, the more he felt an impending doom closing in around them.

"What happens if she left without us?"

"No way she got out of the Outback alone. I'm the only one who knows where the right tunnels are."

"Well, what if she's dead? What then?"

"Then we leave. But we're not doing that until we find out. You're not getting cold feet, are you, Adam? I mean, you almost got us both killed trying to rescue those two strangers, and now you're going to let a few zombies stand between you and saving a girl from your City, *a girl you know?*"

"I'm not getting cold feet," Adam said, indignant. "I just don't want to get our hopes up that she's still alive."

"Don't be morbid, kid. Let's find her."

Colton led the way, Hellweaver aimed at the zombies as they approached. He fired overhead. The shrapnel spun in place momentarily before exploding into a screaming flash of white.

Adam turned from the blinding light, ears buzzing, then turned back, blaster in hand, trying to see if there was something still standing. Before his eyes had adjusted from the flash, something dark began to lumber toward him.

Adam raised the blaster and fired.

After he got his shot off, something hit him from behind. Adam spun, firing blindly at the shape behind him, hoping it wasn't Colton.

His eyes adjusted, and he saw the shredded remains of several zombies on the ground.

But beyond the ashes, Adam was alone.

He turned around, his heart racing.

Colton?

He looked back at the ground, thinking for certain he'd accidentally shot Colton.

Shit! Shit! Shit!

He screamed Colton's name into the biting wind.

"Stop yelling," Colton called from the bank's front doors.

Adam breathed a relieved sigh, then followed.

Colton led the way — aiming his rifle with the mounted flashlight instead of the Hellweaver now strapped to his back — as they entered the lobby.

Even in the dark, the bank seemed larger inside. Colton's light revealed crumbling tiles dangling from the ceiling and half-destroyed walls that turned the lobby into a debris-strewn pit. Adam tried to cover the areas where Colton wasn't focused, staring into the darkness as if he could will his eyes to see more than shadows in the dark.

They inched across the lobby, exposed. Something could be right next to him.

Between the pressing darkness and the sounds of creaking metal, the building felt like a sleeping giant, poised to wake and collapse at the slightest provocation.

Colton paused, his gear's metal clinking to a stop as he whispered to Adam. "Keep your finger on the guard, not on the trigger. We don't want to kill the poor girl."

"Copy," Adam said, sliding his finger from the trigger. He was a good shot, but not great. If zombies came at them in the darkness he might not get a bead on them fast enough to bring them down. But Colton was right. Adam was just as likely to shoot the girl.

Colton swept his light across the lobby and called out, "Zelle. We're here to help you."

Colton led them to the stairs.

Adam wasn't about to gripe aloud about thirty-nine more floors. Colton had come back to save him. He'd spend the next two days searching the bank if that's what it took to find Zelle.

Four more floors of nothing, and what felt like two days before they spotted movement at the end of a long hallway.

"Did you see that?" Colton asked.

"What was it?" Adam had seen *something*.

"Zelle?" Colton called, trying to keep his voice from going beyond their hall.

"What if it's a zombie?" Adam asked, wanting Colton to quiet down.

"Zombies don't run away."

"What if it's a bandit?"

"Could well be, that's why we're careful."

The hallway was in a T formation with the stairway at the bottom of the T — unless there was a broken floor or ceiling, there was no way the person could get away without passing (or killing) them.

"Remember, finger on the guard. Wait for my signal, or fire, to take any shots."

"Got it." Adam still couldn't shake the feeling that they were walking into a trap.

"Zelle!" Colton called out. "We're here to help."

"Go away!" a young girl shouted back, trying to sound tough. "Or my Daddy will kill you."

"Daddy?" Adam whispered to Colton. "I thought you said she was alone."

Colton shrugged. "Call out to her. Tell her your name. Maybe she remembers you."

"Zelle! It's me, Adam Lovecraft! We used to live in the same building. Me and my friend are here to help you get out."

Silence.

Then the girl stepped out into the hallway, a light aimed at them.

"Adam?" she asked, voice still tough. "Come closer so I can see you."

He stepped past Colton even as the man grabbed at him. A blast of energy blew toward his body, barely missing him as Colton yanked him back, eating a chunk of plaster just inches away.

Adam fell to the floor, heart in his throat.

Colton looked down at him, shaking his head.

"Put your gun down!" Zelle screamed, with a shaking light in her hand, fixed to her pistol. She was scared and had probably fired on accident.

Adam looked back to see Colton aiming his rifle at Zelle.

"Don't shoot!" He stood, slowly, hands in the air, gun still on the floor. "Sorry!"

He stepped forward, hoping that she recognized him and wasn't trying to disarm him simply to make killing him easier.

"Adam!" Then she ran over and hugged him like a long-lost brother, instead of the kid who used to occasionally babysit. She pulled back and met his eyes, crying.

"You've got to help my Dad. He's hurt bad."

THIRTY-FIVE

Keller

Keller sat on the chair and stared at the sleeping man, watching, summoning the courage to do what had to be done.

He reached out with a gloved hand, clicked on the overhead lamp, then smacked Elderman Denton Sinclair across the face.

He woke with a yelp. Keller dropped a glove onto his mouth, then a blaster at the man's head. Sinclair looked up, his eyes adjusting to the horror reflected in Keller's helmet.

"Rise and shine, Elderman," Keller said through his helmet's speakers, knowing his voice would come out amplified and distorted.

Sinclair wouldn't know who was in his house. Keller had disabled the helmet's always-on connected features. And there was no way for anyone at City Watch to see where the suit had been. And since Sinclair had blocked the camera feed inside his own house, there was nothing here to record this conversation.

Sinclair regained his composure quickly, or wore a solid

facade at least. Keller almost wanted to give him credit for that.

"What are you doing in here?"

"I've come to talk to you about the attack on City 1."

"Do you mind removing the gun from my head?" Frustration furrowed his brow, and seeped into Sinclair's voice.

Keller sat back in the chair beside the bed, but his gun was still trained on the Elder.

Sinclair started to sit up.

"No," Keller said. "You lay."

Sinclair glared at him. "I hope you see that what you're doing here is treasonous. I'll have your head, *Mister* Keller."

No surprise, Sinclair guessing his identity, but Keller left his helmet on just the same. "You really want to talk treason, old man? I've had a look around your place while you were up here sleeping like the damned."

"What are you talking about?"

Keller reached over to the nightstand where he'd placed a few of the more incriminating papers, picked them up and tossed them at Sinclair. "I've got documents linking you to the attack on City 1, and to a man named Sutherland. I show this to anyone, you'll be in a very special edition of the Games. Unless we can work something out?"

Sinclair paused, eyeing Keller as if he could read expression through reflection. "What do you want, Mr. Keller?"

Keller removed his helmet, and smiled into the man's eyes. "I want what's mine."

"What are you talking about?"

"I want to be named the One True Leader. Not this Provisional shit. I've given my life for this job and yet I'm treated like an errand boy for you people. How am I supposed to command the respect of the other Cities, when you undermine me with this *Provisional* title? Even if people don't know Geralt is dead, they sure as hell know he's not coming back. For all they're concerned, the old man retired."

Sinclair laughed. "Is that all you want?"

"I also want to know why you planned the attack, and who Sutherland is."

Sinclair eyed him up and down. "May I please sit up?"

"Yes," Keller said, watching the old man move into a seated position on the bed. "Now talk."

"First, I need to know something."

"What's that?"

"Have you ever regretted the lives you've taken in the State's name?"

"Not a one," Keller said firmly.

"See, men like you, *like us*, we know the stakes of being too soft. The *why* of the attack is a bit complicated, but the short of it is that I, and some others, disagreed with the council about the State's general direction. It had grown lenient over the last decade. Rebel groups popping up, disgracing and attacking us everywhere. You lost your own son to just such an attack."

Sinclair gave that one a few seconds to sink in.

"That's what happens when you reward aggression as the council has done too often, cutting deals with traitors, and not going full bore to the infestation's root. Before the attack, Elders were considering passing some laws that would have not only ended the Darwin Games, but instituted voting for individual City leaders ... by the populace! We both know that people need a strong council, a strong leader, people like us. Right?"

Keller nodded again. *Exactly — they need* me.

"There are a few of us who still remember the final

days of the Old Nation. A glorious country brought to its knees by weakness, vice, and a cowardice in dealing with the enemy — external and internal. But that all ended with our "great discovery." It was the 1970s, and we'd made a way to slow aging so much it was practically stopped. Overnight we had the technology to live for centuries. Everything changed, but we also found that our blessing was a curse. Death is a key instrument in preventing overpopulation and conserving resources. Nature is balanced. Our playing God threw a wrench in that. Given how society was crumbling already, that government realized that this 'miracle' would only accelerate our extinction. So I, Jack Geralt, and a few others developed a virus to end humanity as we knew it."

Keller's stomach turned as the man nonchalantly discussed killing a species as if discussing the price of tea.

"Anyway, the government created six underground, city-sized bunkers and picked sixty thousand of the best and brightest, people who would contribute rather than leach off of society, and divided these people among the bunkers. Then the government unleashed the virus. Mankind fell, with its most talented thriving underground. We erected cities over these bunkers while those who survived the plague became savages in the Barrens."

"You're saying that you and Geralt unleashed the virus that wiped out humanity?"

"Us and others. Including the City 1 Elders. Within a few generations, we saw the worst of humanity rearing its ugly head among our chosen, and their offspring. Without a guiding hand, humans always devolve into their parasitic nature."

"Yes indeed," Keller said, still trying to process it all. "How was Lovecraft involved?"

"We targeted Jonah early, after discovering his part in

the Underground. We pushed him into a position where he would be sympathetic to 'our cause.' I told him that I 'felt guilty' for what we'd done to humanity. And that I wanted revenge against Geralt and the 'evil State.'"

"And he was okay with this?"

"If only. We programmed him to kill his wife, made him believe that you were responsible, and engineered it so his daughter and son would wind up in the Games, and *still* he didn't hate the State enough to strike back! How weak are the foolish?"

Keller's heart sunk with the realization that he was just a pawn like Jonah. Had his son been part of their plans?

"Were you responsible for Joshua's death?"

"No," Sinclair said with conviction, "that *was* the Underground. A despicable lot with all the wrong reasons and none of the sense God gave monkeys."

"How did you get Jonah to do it?"

"You'll remember Sutherland as Dennis Weaver, a lunatic cult-leader terrorist who wound up living in one of the Barrens' many villages. He's part of some nonsense called the Patriots of the New Revolution. They stand for bringing down the Walls and bringing 'equality' and 'freedom' to all people — like these savages would know what the hell to do with freedom or the responsibilities that come with it. They'd somehow managed to grab hold of the zombie virus, probably left in one of the bunkers. So I decided to pitch myself as an ally, fund them, see if I could use them like the good little tools they are. As to your specific question, Sutherland had Ana, so Jonah had to play ball."

Sinclair smiled with pride. "Getting them to attack City 1 played right into our hands. They thought they'd cripple the government. But I and my companions knew the truth that it would only make us stronger. You must flush the world's detritus and start over every once in a while. It's what we did with the original virus, and what we had Sutherland and Jonah do in City 1. They helped us to eliminate the very people who might have helped them. We made sure that the right citizens wouldn't get infected, and that the appropriate leaders would live to see prominence on the council."

"Genius," Keller said.

"Thank you." Sinclair smiled. "I had wanted to bring you in earlier, but some of the things you've done since your arrival had me worried that we might not be on the same page."

"I'm sympathetic. But I don't appreciate being left in the dark when I can be of use."

"Good," Sinclair said, beaming. "Sometimes, you need a catastrophic event to make people realize what's important — strength, solidarity, and a strong leader. Tell me, Keller, are you ready to be that ruler?"

"I am." He smiled, then turned serious. "I do have one small concern."

"What is that?"

"What's to keep Sutherland from returning? Especially after he realizes — if he's not already — that his complicity only made things worse?"

"Sutherland isn't a threat. So what if he gasses us again? Like I said, the right people won't be infected. We've administered an antidote as part of their routine vaccinations. You've already received it without even knowing." Sinclair chuckled. "Your blood knows more than you!"

"Genius." Keller paused, leaned forward and met Sinclair's pale blue, almost white, eyes. "So, Elderman, do we have a deal?"

"Yes, One True Leader Keller."

THIRTY-SIX

Anastasia Lovecraft

ANA STOOD at the metal rail looking over the surprisingly large underground farm sprawled beneath the large light squares in the ceiling, marveling at what a small group of people had been able to accomplish together. The farm had plenty of potatoes, with carrots, corn, wheat, and several other foods growing in neat rows around the circular room.

"What was this place before?" Ana asked Father Truth, standing beside her as they waited for Egan to meet them.

"It was an unfinished area when the Old Nation fell. We believe that it was going to be a seating area of some sort, but I'm not certain. It took us a while, but we finally managed to get the mix of soil and light just right for each section."

The Station had less than a hundred people, a fraction of Hydrangea's population, but they had managed to form a tight community who truly cared for one another, and create an impressive farm and water filtration system which seemed even better than the one at Sutherland's camp. They left only to hunt, gather supplies by raiding bandits, or wage the occasional campaign to hijack ship-ments from outbound City trucks.

This place *could be* a good home, where she and Liam could make house together, and finally stop worrying about all the tomorrows that might otherwise haunt them.

But she had to be careful. Even the Barrens and all the unknowns outside the Walls were better than settling under another despot. Egan had seemed nice enough, but Ana sensed an edge. He was perfectly kind when sharing a side with him. But it was hard to see him in the same way now that she knew he was ordering the kidnapping of innocents in the name of finding a cure.

She had wanted to believe that Egan was better than Sutherland. But her faith in powerful men was rarely rewarded. He finally arrived and with a few kind words dismissed Father Truth so that he and Ana could be alone.

"Thank you for meeting me," Egan said, as if she hadn't been the one to demand it. He cast his eyes across the underground farm. "I once held your father respon-sible for the death of my wife and son. His superiors had tricked him into doing so, but still he went along."

"What are you talking about?"

Egan finally turned to Ana, eyes wet, as if he might cry, or perhaps already had been. "I hated Jonah Lovecraft so much. It festered for years. I hated him so much that when I found him abandoned and left for dead after 'winning' the Games, I brought him here and … well, let's just say I wasn't very nice."

Ana felt sick to her stomach imagining what *that* meant. The thought that Egan had hurt her father, no matter what he'd done to deserve it, made her want to strike back. But they both knew she wouldn't, not right now.

"Why are you telling me this?"

"Because you deserve to know the truth."

"That my father was bad? That he set you up?"

"No, that he was mortal. That even though he was a good man, when the State required him to do something bad for the greater good, he did what he thought had to be done without question."

"What happened?" Ana asked, only half of her wanting to know.

"I'll spare you the details, girl. Point is, I judged your father, like you're probably judging me. I'm not a fool — I understand that our search for a cure has led to some less-than-noble means."

"Say what you want about my father, but he never kidnapped anyone."

"He may as well have. His actions, and inactions, affected many innocents. Your father *was* responsible for infections. He destroyed families, and caused death. And I'm not even talking about what he did at City 1."

"He was forced to do that by that bastard Sutherland! *That wasn't his fault!* I already told you about that."

"I know, and I don't blame him for it. And while I still *do* blame him for the death of my family, he redeemed himself while here. Your father had a chance to flee. Calla had helped him to escape, actually," he said ruefully. "She liked him a lot. But when she and I were in danger, he came back and saved us."

Ana couldn't help her swelling tears, but stayed strong enough not to wipe them.

"Before Jonah came, there were only six or so of us living here at the Station. Mostly because I was bitter and suspicious of everyone. Your father's departure changed something inside me. For the first time I decided that I would listen to my people, and allow more members into our community. We've grown stronger, and now have everything you see."

Egan turned from Ana to the farm. "Your father reminded me of what it meant to do the right thing, and how I wasn't being a good father to Calla."

"So why are you killing people?" Ana demanded.

"Because sometimes doing the right thing by your family means doing the wrong thing to others. It doesn't mean those things will be easy, or fill you with pride. But sometimes you have to ignore the acid in your gut. Your father understood that more than anyone I've ever met. He would have done the same to save you, and you know it."

Ana shook her head. "He wouldn't have done *this*."

"Then you don't see how deep a father's love runs. Your father *would* have, Ana. I'm certain — the proof is in the graves of City 1. I won't apologize for trying all I can to save Calla. We need uninfected subjects, and I can't ask our own people, not without a riot. So we take from the Barrens. We go after bandits and other bad people who don't even deserve to walk our planet. But I won't lie, sometimes we gather cases that aren't so black and white, like our three most recent captures. I'm not asking for your forgiveness, but I would appreciate your understanding."

"Why is it important if I understand your reasons for killing people?"

Egan met her eyes and tilted his head, as if trying to answer that very question for himself. "Because I hope that Calla will understand, and not see me as a monster."

"She already knows. That man told us everything."

"I suspected as much." Egan's sigh seemed to swell from his depths. "I do hope she forgives me, but I refuse to stop without a cure. I can live without my daughter's forgiveness, just not without my daughter."

Egan looked away, leaning on the rail and staring at nothing, rather than the impressive farm before him, maybe crying. She waited through a long uncomfortable moment before he finally turned back.

"So, now you know the awful truth of what we do here. Will you be leaving?"

"I don't know."

"I respect your decision either way, but will remind you that your presence is good for Calla. Please, consider her in your decision, and try not to let your opinion of me taint your feelings for her."

Ana nodded, and could barely manage to mutter, "Okay."

THIRTY-SEVEN

Liam Harrow

THE SUN WAS DIPPING behind the Outback's desolate horizon as Liam trailed Katrina and Clark with no interest in catching up. They'd been walking for too damned long, and it was all he could do to keep his anger from becoming a scream.

Trudging through the snow along the four-lane highway because they couldn't find a vehicle worth a damn, racing through the city, carefully navigating between cars eternally stalled in their spots, and the ever-present zombies, bandits, and other threats, he felt a deep ache of regret for having left Ana at the Station.

He also felt outnumbered and alone.

Katrina was clearly out for herself. Clark was there to follow Egan's orders, and that meant doing whatever was best for the Station. Which probably meant bringing Liam back alive — that would make Ana happiest, after all, and she was Egan's hope for a cure — but if Liam got in the way, he couldn't count on Clark to have his back.

The terrible truth that he didn't trust Katrina made

their danger more glaring. It sank into his skin like an open wound, her words stinging like alcohol.

Katrina had said that he'd grown soft, that he *couldn't* do what had to be done. She claimed that he wasn't the same man she had met, the man who gave her hope that the State could be damaged, or perhaps even dismantled.

With every step forward he knew she was right.

Liam wondered if he'd felt loyal to Chelsea because she'd been born inside the same Walls. Was it because he knew her before his world had gone to hell? If he hadn't known her, if she'd just been some Darwin Games player they'd stumbled upon, would he have felt so driven to protect her, even considering the inarguable risk?

Either way, Katrina was right: *he* was a liability.

Liam wondered what he would have done if Ana *had* come with them. What if it wasn't just him and Clark, Katrina, and Chelsea? What if Ana had been in the room — would he have been willing to let Chelsea's bracelet scream then?

No matter how many times he asked himself that simple question, Liam's one-word answer was always the same: *NO*. He would have — *of course* — silenced the bracelet immediately. Not with Katrina's stroke of almost gleeful violence, but he wouldn't have hesitated. Ana's life was too important.

He'd been content to pile risk on the three of them, not just with Chelsea's bleating bracelet, but with the girl's sprained ankle that had clearly cast them as easier targets.

He looked up, around, and behind him, then stared at Katrina's back. Clark was walking about five feet ahead of him, and she was another five feet in front of Clark. The part of Liam that knew he was wrong wanted to apologize, but the rest of him felt too pissed to consider it.

He was wrong, but Katrina was wrong, too.

It wasn't just what she had done to Chelsea. Liam could fault her cruelty, but not her decision. Sutherland was different. She *should* hate him. She *shouldn't* regret leaving Hydrangea. That man was a maniac. Totally insane, and solely responsible for Jonah's death. She could argue that he was a good leader, and looking to demolish the State's iron grip on its people, but what good was a leader if he was willing to do things that were equally horrible to the evil he was planning to unseat — or maybe worse (since Liam wasn't sure that the State, awful as they were, would ever willingly poison a city)?

It's not victory when you're swapping one tyrant for another.

He couldn't apologize, because she didn't deserve it. Same for his company. Once they found Adam and brought him to the Station, Liam would be done with Katrina for good. He had to be, if she couldn't see Sutherland for the sociopath he was.

Something bristled his senses and stopped him in his tracks. He may be seething, but his instincts — Chelsea aside — were still there. Katrina and Clark kept walking. Liam looked up and saw movement on a roof ahead.

Shots rang out like cracks in the darkness.

Old-fashioned lead. One, two, three shots plinked into concrete, metal and glass, sending a chunk of something ricocheting into a gash across Liam's cheek.

"Shooter!" Katrina dove behind a snow-covered long car.

Clark had already dodged to the left and ducked into an alley. Liam looked up toward Katrina, then over at Clark, and decided on Door Number Three: a hollowed-out van about ten feet away.

He ran to the van and ducked behind the rear bumper

just as the front windshield of an ancient car exploded across the street.

He peeked around the van and saw Katrina as she peered ahead to locate their shooter. Another bullet tagged the snow on the car's roof, sending her back to a crouch.

Liam reached up and yanked the mirror from the passenger-side door.

Another shot exploded a window that Liam couldn't see. He heard Katrina yell "Fuck" before she returned two blaster shots from her hybrid rifle.

Liam wiped grime from the mirror with his jacket, pressed his back against the tire, then held the mirror up and scanned the street ahead. He saw Clark in the reflection, or at least the man's eyes, barely visible from the side of what Liam believed was a large metal dumpster — hard to tell for sure with it covered in snow.

Liam kept moving the mirror around until he found the shooter — a gun glinting from the rooftop of a modest-sized building a half block or so ahead of them. He turned the mirror, searching for another shooter as two more shots punched holes in the snow beside him.

Liam saw no one, and thanked his lucky stars that their attacker was an awful shot.

He yelled at Katrina, loud enough that Clark could hear from the alley. "Ahead of us, top floor of the building that says *Eats* on the front. Eleven 0'clock."

Katrina gave him a barely perceptible nod, then proved her worth as a warrior. Liam may not have trusted her, or agreed with her allegiance to a madman, but he couldn't question that she was the best fighter he'd ever known.

Another shot from the roof. But unperturbed, Katrina readied her rifle, then rolled out from the cover of the car.

In a single fluid motion she raised the weapon, found

her target — while standing frozen in the snow with a bullseye on her chest — and squeezed the trigger before rolling back behind the car.

The gunner returned a shot into the car's windshield, cracking it and sending snow into the car's interior, missing Katrina by millimeters.

Then, silence.

Katrina peered over the edge and looked through her scope before firing two quick shots.

"Shooter down!" she cried out as she ducked back behind the car. "Anyone else?"

Liam panned the shaky mirror along the roofline where the shooter had been. "Not that I can see!"

"Clark?" she yelled.

No response.

Liam turned toward the alley, looking for Clark, but saw him nowhere. He stood and squinted into the alley, finally spotting a long tattooed arm like a dead snake slithering out from behind a mountain of boxes.

Feeling as though the pile was stacked on his lungs, Liam managed to breathe, "Clark's down."

"Fuck," Katrina said, walking toward Liam.

Another shot thundered in the night, this one a laser blast — bright white light streaking so close that it sent them to the ground.

They rolled behind the van. Depending on the blaster's strength, it could quickly disintegrate their cover.

She risked rising from behind her shield, narrowing one eye into her scope while scanning ahead.

Another blast hit just past them, but Katrina didn't flinch as she found her target, and pulled the trigger. Twice.

"Second shooter down. I think we're clear ... Clark?"

"Clark!" Liam joined Katrina's cry above a growing,

biting wind. He heard a groaning that was either coming from the alley, or his head.

Not quite believing they were clear of danger, but feeling that he had to prove his worth, Liam cried out, "Cover me!" then raced from his relative safe spot behind the van, over to Clark in the alley.

Another blaster shot sizzled through the air as his foot hit the curb.

He ducked into the alley, where Clark had fallen behind the snow-covered dumpster. He was doubled over, clutching his knee where he must have been hit by the first shooter.

"I've got Clark. He's okay — I think he's been hit in the knee, but he's definitely alive." Liam put a hand on his shoulder. "Come on. We're going to be fine."

He turned toward Liam, with bloodshot eyes and a twisted face, growling as he swiped out.

He knocked the gun from Liam's hand and sent him sprawling back to the ground.

With his back in the snow, Liam launched his legs up to batter the monster's chest.

Zombie Clark continued to come at him, gnashing. It fell on top of Liam, pinning his arms as its gnashing teeth came closer.

He wiggled and writhed, trying to push back with his pinned arms, squirming under Zombie Clark's weight, attempting to move a man who was a boulder atop him.

"Help! Clark has turned!" Liam reached up, trying to keep the creature's mouth at a distance. He slipped a hand free, reaching up and shoving his fingers into the zombie's neck, trying to push it back, or rip out its larynx.

Shots traded in the street. Then silence.

Something told Liam that Katrina was dead, and he had only seconds himself. He could practically feel Clark's sharp teeth as he pictured them ripping into his flesh. Death or worse moments away. His cramping arms were made of fire and his heart was a tick from explosion.

Still, silence in the street. Katrina was dead; he was certain. Liam's arms were about to give way and once they did, they'd collapse under Zombie Clark's weight and force.

And then the monster would be at his flesh.

Liam braced himself. He closed his eyes, cocked his head to the side, and accepted the inevitable because he had no other choice ...

Steaming hot blood splashed his face.

He opened his eyes to see Katrina's sword jutting through the side of Zombie Clark's skull. She yanked the blade, pulling the monstrosity off of him and drawing her sword from the thing's head. She wiped the steel against Clark's jacket, cleaning the blood as Liam spit Zombie Clark's blood from his mouth.

On his knees, Liam grabbed a handful of snow, shoved it into his mouth, swished it around and spit, hoping like hell he wasn't infected.

Katrina held out her hand in offering. He gripped it and launched himself from the ground as the sound of too many zombies echoed around them.

"I think I got the last of the shooters. But there's a mess of zombies on their way."

He didn't need any more than that. They took off at a full sprint, running almost blindly through pitch-black alleys, hoping that they were staying relatively on path toward Adam's location, and that they wouldn't run smack into a wall or worse.

His lungs felt near collapse. He could barely keep pace with a racing Katrina, who already seemed like she was going slower than she wanted to.

Relatively safe for the moment, Katrina ducked into a small, one-story mercantile, pulling Liam into the old store behind her.

He tried twice to speak, but she shushed him, staring out into the street as if daring herself to believe in its silence.

Finally, after many minutes she turned from the window and rifled through her pack.

"I'm sorry," Liam said. "For everything. You were right."

She grunted, eyes still in her pack, and handed Liam a bottle of water and ration. She pulled out the box screen and began to stare with a furrowed brow.

"Do you see anything?" Liam asked, knowing she was likely searching for Adam.

"No," she said, her eyes on the screen. "Not yet."

"I'm sorry," Liam repeated.

"It's fine. Now's not the time."

Katrina held her stare to the screen, face creasing deeper.

Liam saw something out the shop's back window.

He gently shook her shoulder, then pointed, drawing Katrina's attention to the spired building across the street with the giant sign: *Apex National Bank.*

"That's it, isn't it?"

She stared, open-mouthed. Like Liam, she hadn't realized how close their flight had taken them to the bank.

In the parking lot, they saw the ashen remains of what they hoped were zombies rather than Adam.

THIRTY-EIGHT

Sutherland

SUTHERLAND CONTINUED to question the scouts.

He'd been going for a while, trying to ignore the grumbling men behind him who seemed more worried about having left the truck unattended and getting a meal than the job at hand. Wormwood still hadn't stopped bitching about his growling stomach.

"I'll ask you again," Sutherland said, refusing to look up from the hunk of branch he'd been peeling to nothing. "I'd like to know everything that you two know about the Station. So far I have Jack Diddly, and if I don't have more than Jack, I'll have to do something to improve my mood. So ... again, tell me everything you know about the Station: how many people are there, what sorts of weapons do you have, what do your supplies look like — both in quality and quantity — and, this one might be most important of all: *where the hell is it?*"

The scouts still refused to speak. Sutherland admired them, though esteem would in no way guarantee their breath. They would answer or die.

He was most impressed with the girl. The boy went out

of his way to show Sutherland that he wasn't afraid, but his mask betrayed his horror. The girl was afraid, but made him work to know it. The boy, because he was a few years her junior, or was born a pussy, telegraphed fear through every blink and nod.

Sutherland was also surprised to find that the two weren't fucking. The way the boy had been trailing the girl like a puppy, Sutherland had assumed that the kid was looking to bury his pecker, but when he suggested that a lack of answers could accelerate the rate at which Sutherland might decide to let his men bury their own, the idiot kid reacted more like a protective brother than a jealous boyfriend. That same melting mask that telegraphed his terror — the twitching eye and quivering voice — told Sutherland that they had the same daddy.

He'd given the kids more than a minute of quiet to think, but neither had lowered their jaw to tell him anything about their hideout, so Sutherland would have to speed things along.

He dropped his peeled stick to the snow, stood with an exaggerated yawn, walked over to the boy, waited for him to finish his flinching, then pulled back and launched a fist hard into the boy's jaw to a chorus of *ooh's* and *aww's* from the idiots behind him.

The kid was a pussy, so of course he started crying. He managed to swallow a yelp, but his eyes went bright red and began to water.

"Still nothing?" Sutherland said, almost kindly.

The boy stayed silent. His sister looked up, eyes colder than the wind.

Sutherland was many things, but a woman beater wasn't one of them. He took no pleasure in striking the inferior sex. He wasn't one of those idiots who believed a man should *never* hit a woman, but he did believe a man should only hit a woman when she truly deserved it.

He looked down kindly into the girl's eyes, smiled a flicker — just long enough to let her believe that all might be swell — then pulled back and launched his fist into her jaw, even harder than he had for her pussy brother.

The girl's eyes were redder and wetter than the boy's, to account for Sutherland's sudden ferocity. Still she said nothing. Her brother behaved exactly as expected.

"Okay! I'll tell you whatever you want!"

Sutherland turned from girl to boy, glad that the encounter was nearing its end. He was cold, and Wormwood wasn't wrong about dinner. He was starting to think that maybe he should have let them fell the deer before accosting them.

He kneeled to the boy as his sister started to scream.

"No, don't say anything, Jaul. Keep it trapped. He'll kill us anyhow."

Sutherland slowly rose from his crouch and turned to the girl, admiring her will as he surveyed and pitied its inevitable departure.

"Do you think that's wise?" His voice was friendly, almost smooth.

She pursed her lips as if about to spit, but said nothing.

"It's okay, you can spit at me if you want to. The world would be better if people followed their instincts more often. You know, those *true* feelings we stuff down inside us because it's easier than staring into their eyes."

He returned to his crouch and brushed a knuckle across her cheek. He leaned in and whispered, "Do you know what sort of things I'm talking about?"

He kissed her before drawing back. Inches away she let go, covering Sutherland in spit, and a rope of saliva ran from one cheek to the other, drizzling his nose in between.

"Don't touch her," yelled the boy, as though the coward could do anything to stop him.

"Oh, you don't have to worry about me," Sutherland soothed. "Not in that way. I'm used to women who know what to do. Your peasant sister is a child, and wouldn't know where to start." He turned to look behind him. "Horrance, would you come here for a moment? And bring your friends."

A moment later Horrance was in front of Sutherland, with the other men standing in a semi-circle behind him.

"When's the last time Little Horrance was wet?"

Horrance, who looked like a dog, actually started to drool. He looked down, as if embarrassed and muttered under his breath. "Just the other day. You gave me one of your … you gave me one of your girls, sir."

"And you?" Sutherland turned to Wormwood and Finch, as if their brains were each so small it took two to make one.

"A month for me," Wormwood said, then as if to prove Sutherland right he spoke for Finch. "And a month for him. It was with Salie, both of us on the same night, same time."

He didn't have to ask the other men. Fear was planted. He twisted his face into an unpleasant grimace and turned back to the girl.

"I've seen all of these men eat and, well, I wouldn't want them anywhere near me if I were you. I can't imagine how ugly the whole thing will get. That's nothing I want to see. Now, you can keep all of this from happening if you're willing to stop being stupid and start telling me the truth. Really, shouldn't we all just get to the inevitable conclusion?"

Again he brushed his knuckle across her cheek. "And

such a pretty girl." He turned to the boy. "You don't really want your sister ruined, do you?"

"You think I haven't been raped before?" the sister yelled.

Sutherland wasn't sure if she was bluffing or not, but the look in her eyes belied a toughness that said perhaps she had waded through rivers of shit.

"Don't tell them anything, Jaul! They're monsters and we have to protect our home."

"Shut up!" Sutherland smacked the back of his hand across her cheek hard.

She flinched, but never broke eye contact, and managed to hold her yelp inside.

Of course, the boy cracked. "Why do want to know about the Station? Are you going to hurt people there? If there are any," he added, and made himself sound like an idiot.

Sutherland winked at the girl, turned to Horrance and his men with a gesture to stand down for now, then finally turned to the boy with his most pleasant grin. He was ready to break, desperately seeking any excuse to end his sister's suffering.

Just one more nudge. "Of course we won't hurt them. Why would we do that?"

"You're holding us prisoner right now, and threatening to rape me. What kind of *men* are you? You're nothing but bandit scum. All balls, no brains, so eager to inflict the world with your pain. There's no way we're bringing you to the Station."

The girl gritted her teeth and snarled at Sutherland, still so stupidly brave.

"You got us all wrong, darling. You know how it is out here in the Barrens. We can't just go knocking on doors and expecting charity. Sometimes we have to go about things in such uncivilized ways. I don't like the way things are any more than you do, really. But we've already tried to be kind and failed."

Sutherland shook his head, as if truly regretting this. "You've no idea how many times we've traveled, hat in hand, appealing to the kindness of strangers, only to be shut out in the freeze and left to suffer. Some people seem to be scared of us. We don't *want* to hurt anyone, but we do *need* a place to stay. We certainly can't bunk out here with the savages." He laughed. "Yes, we're forcing our way in, but that's only due to necessity. Once inside, you'll see we're always happy to earn our keep. You should see Horrance with a broom."

Sutherland nodded toward the ogre.

The boy yelled, finally finding his balls. "Just leave her alone. Do whatever to me. Just let her go. I'll take you to the Station. I'll help you get inside.

"Stop it, Jaul! Shut your mouth. Don't tell these idiots anything!"

There it was again, her thinking she was smarter than Sutherland. As if he was a common grunt, and not the man who would bring freedom to the entire Barrens and Cities, even if these ingrates were undeserving of his leadership.

He glared at her. He hadn't wanted to rape her before. But now he needed to show her who was boss.

She stared back with a hate and judgment he was used to seeing in those who made the mistake of underestimating him. From the whores who thought he was just some drunken fool to the traitors at Hydrangea who sold him out at their first opportunity. Eventually, he always made them see just who was in charge. Who was the true genius.

Sutherland clucked his tongue. "You know, Jaul. I'm

disappointed in you. After spending all this time out here in the cold, you finally started to warm my heart, knowing how willing you were to protect your friends back at the Station. But now, the way you've given them up … it makes me shiver." He shuddered for effect. "You must *really* love your sister."

He cowered back.

"Well then, I know what to do." Sutherland shrugged. Then, to put awful thoughts into their mind, or worsen the ones that were already there, Sutherland walked over to the huddled men, whispered into their throng, chuckled a few times for effect, then sent Horrance to drag the two scouts to their feet.

They marched back toward where Sutherland had first spotted them, past toward where he'd seen them hunting the deer, heading toward their truck.

They walked in silence for several minutes. The siblings trembled, blue from the freezing air and squirming fear. Horrance opened the truck's rear by shoving the rolling wall to the top.

"Him first," Sutherland ordered, nodding at the boy.

Horrance grabbed him roughly by the arm, hefted him up, and practically threw the boy into the truck.

Wormwood's fingers dug into the girl's arm.

"Her, to me." With great ceremony Sutherland pulled a narrow capsule from one of his coat's interior pockets, then lifted the lid and withdrew a syringe. "Do you know what this is?"

She shook her head, too terrified for bravery or running her smart mouth.

"It's a zombie virus. It's going to kill you." Sutherland chuckled again. "Don't worry, it's quite slow. First it will turn you, through torment and pain, a horrible agony you couldn't possibly imagine. You'll be undead, wishing you could taste the real thing. That is, of course, unless your brother is smart enough to decide that he loves you more than those poor souls who are already lost at the Station."

Sutherland slipped the syringe back into the capsule as if pausing his thought. He peered into the truck's back, and the sobbing coward's eyes. "Do you love them more than your sister? If so, I need details. What is the Station?"

"I don't understand," the boy blubbered as his sister finally started to cry. "Just tell me what you want to know."

"Is it a military base?"

He looked confused. "I don't know."

"Think long and hard," Sutherland said, taking the syringe from the capsule and closing the lid with a loud snap. The girl tried to get away, but Wormwood held her tight as Sutherland stuck the needle into her skin, depressing the plunger. "Because if you don't tell me the truth, your sister will never get the antidote. I want to know how many people are there, what kind of supplies I can expect, and exactly the type of people we'll be dealing with: Peaceful? Bandits? Soldiers? Everything."

It took ten minutes for the boy to spill all that he knew. Unfortunately for everyone, it wasn't much.

"Now can she have the antidote?"

Sutherland chuckled for a final time. "Oh, I'm sorry, Jaul. Of course I was lying. Really, I can't believe that you were foolish enough to … well, you'd think you would have learned better than to trust violent redheads you meet in the snow."

"You fucker!" the girl screamed.

Sutherland grabbed her by the arm, and shoved her over to Horrance. Without needing to be told, the ogre hurled her into the truck on top of her brother.

She tried to jump out, lunging toward the big man.

Horrance swung the butt of his rifle into the girl's

head, sending her sprawling backward with a loud crack. Then he aimed his gun at the boy.

Sutherland approached the truck and met the girl's dizzied gaze, wondering how smart she felt now, how much better than him as she put a hand to her forehead to stop the bleeding.

"We'll leave you two alone. See how much your sister loves you after she turns into a zombie."

"Please," the boy pleaded, "you don't have to do this."

Sutherland met his eyes, then retrieved a blade from his chem suit's pocket. He tossed it into the van for the boy to use on his sister, if he had the balls. "I guess we'll see just how deep your love for your sister goes. Do you love her enough to give up your own life and let her eat you? Or will you do the right thing and put her out of her misery? This is almost as intriguing as the Darwin Games." He grinned. "Have fun, kids."

Then he twirled his finger — a directive for Horrance to close the truck's door.

The siblings screamed as the door descended. Sutherland met the girl's eyes one last time with a wink.

Then the men followed Sutherland toward the Station, ready to claim Ana and kill everyone inside.

THIRTY-NINE

Adam Lovecraft

"Your *dad*?" Adam asked Zelle.

"Zombies attacked, and one of them bit him. I was on my way downstairs to look for some food. Do you guys have anything?"

"Yeah, we've got some stuff." Colton patted his backpack. "Where is he?"

"On the top floor. Is he going to be okay?"

"How long ago was he bitten?" Colton asked.

"It's been eight days."

Adam and Colton's traded looks that more or less said the same thing — *it's only a matter of time before he turns.*

He wondered if Zelle knew. The girl was bright for her age, but that didn't mean she understood how the zombie virus spread, especially if her parents kept her from watching the Games as Adam remembered them doing.

Colton opened his pack. "Let's see if we can help him."

The girl thanked Colton and turned to Adam. "Go get your gun."

He ran back to retrieve his weapon, then followed them

upstairs, watching their lights — Zelle's flashlight and Colton's gun-mounted bulb — bounce off the walls. They'd found the girl, but Adam couldn't shed his sense of doom, weighing heavier with every ascended floor. Adam wondered if Zelle would try to stop them from doing what would have to be done if her father had already turned.

He was a nice, soft-spoken man. Definitely brainier than the average Watcher. Despite (or because) of that, Adam was surprised to learn he was Underground, and wondered if his father and Daniel were also traitors at the time.

He followed Zelle and Colton as they climbed higher into the darkness. At each floor, Adam half-expected to meet Zelle's zombified father. But they reached the top without incident, arriving at a door blocked by two filing cabinets and a chair awkwardly balanced on top.

"I wanted to make sure Daddy was safe. The zombies aren't smart enough to figure out how to unblock doors."

"You're a smart girl." Colton grabbed the first cabinet and dragged it aside.

Adam helped, listening for sounds behind the closed door. Zelle didn't hesitate, pushing the door bar and leading them onto the top floor and another T-shaped hallway. Walls on the left of the first few offices had been blown out, as had the windows in the rooms beyond. Cold wind and snow poured through, chilling the corridor.

"He's down here." Zelle led them to a closed door at the end of the hall with a bookcase and chair stacked in front.

"Daddy, we're here!" Zelle moved the chair away as Colton dragged the bookcase aside.

"Stay here," Colton said before she could open the door.

"Why?"

"He may not be ... the same."

"What do you mean?"

"You said your father was bitten, right?"

"Yes," she said, looking up at Colton, scared. "Why?"

"Do you know what happens to people who get bitten?"

She shook her head. Adam felt his heart breaking, wondering how her father could have failed to warn her. He stared at Zelle's big blue innocent eyes, terrified as she searched Colton's for answers. She was only eight, nowhere near ready to face the world on her own. Maybe Daniel didn't want to scare her, or thought he could outlive the bite.

Colton kneeled and put his hands on her shoulders. "Sometimes when people get bitten they become zombies."

She shook her head. "He's not a zombie."

She tried pushing past Colton, but he held her firm. "Let me check on him, then. Maybe I can help. Better safe than sorry."

"I want to see my dad!" She tried to break free of his grip.

"Please, hold her." Colton looked up at Adam. "Don't let her come in until I give the all-clear." He shoved the girl into Adam's arms and rushed into the room, quickly shutting the door behind him.

Zelle tried to wriggle free, but Adam held her tight.

"It's going to be okay."

"Let me go!"

"Please," Adam whispered, trying to calm her. "It's going to be okay. Colton's just being careful. You remember me, don't you?"

She turned and looked up at Adam. He held his grip on her shoulders just in case. She nodded.

"You know I'd never lie to you. Right?"

She nodded again. "I'm scared."

He let go, holding her eyes with a subliminal, *please don't run.*

"It'll be okay." Adam wondered if Colton was killing her zombie father even as he made this promise. Wind howled as it whipped through the hallway.

Zelle pulled her long black coat tighter around her tiny frame. He noticed that she wasn't wearing the same blue coveralls as the other contestants. Her pants could have passed for his blue in the dark, but her shirt was green.

"What happened to your coveralls?"

"What coveralls?"

"Like mine. The ones they give us when we play the Darwins."

"What are you talking about? I'm not in the Games."

"You're not?" Ice slithered up his spine.

Why did Colton say that Zelle was in the Games, if she wasn't? And why hadn't he mentioned her father? "Was your dad in the Games?"

"No." Her brow furrowed. "Why are you asking if we were in the Games?"

"How did you wind up here?" Adam felt on the verge of knowing what had bothered him since they'd entered the building.

"We left City 6 a month ago. We're on our way to Eden."

"What's Eden?" That must be the Gardens Colton said they were looking for.

"A safe place in the mountains. Daddy and I had to leave when City Watchers found out he was in the Underground. We barely made it out of the City. When we saw that the Games were in the Outback, Daddy said it was too dangerous to leave, and that we had to hide here and wait for them to end. That's when we ran into zombies."

Adam's uneasy mind flashed on several things at once: Colton lying about Zelle, how conveniently he'd had a store of weapons and a device allowing him to tap into the Games' raw feed, and his shooting Hooper when he didn't necessarily need to.

Now he was alone in the room with the girl's father.

Adam grabbed his blaster and threw open the door.

Zelle's father was lying in a pool of blood, sprawled in the corner with a blade through his skull.

Something struck the back of Adam's head and sent him to the floor.

FORTY

Charles Egan

CHARLES STARED at the woman on the other side of the glass. He needed the pane between them, even though it made him feel like the hypocritical coward he was. He should be able to stand by the table without the window creating a divide between them, but he couldn't do it without feeling like a monster.

"You're doing what you have to do," said Father Truth, his own gaze on the glass.

"Did I say I was uncomfortable with it?"

"Your body is saying plenty."

Charles let it go, not wanting a back and forth with anyone, especially Father Truth, who could be exhausting in his delight for verbal sparring. "How is she responding?"

"Better."

"That's good," Charles said, as if he cared about the woman on the table, rather than the small changes in her blood, and what they might mean.

"And is this the latest variation, with Ana's blood?" Father Truth finally turned.

Charles saw the movement in his hazy reflection, but held his stare to the glass. "Yes. This is the last sample from Hydrangea."

"Do you think the new blood will behave differently?"

Father returned his eyes to the window. "We'll see."

So Egan forced himself to keep looking.

The woman was strapped to the table. Her face was an empty sack of sagging flesh, with hollow eyes and an unfortunate (but surely accidental) smile. She looked glazed. Drugged. Gone from her body. The woman lurched up from the table, yanking at her restraints. Her bug-eyes found his and Charles tried not to blink.

Dr. Oswald stood behind her, checking the woman's blood pressure.

"She's somebody's daughter," Charles said.

"Yes, she is. Probably someone's sister as well."

Charles was almost surprised anyone answered him — he hadn't thought he'd said anything out loud. "This isn't right," he muttered, hating what he was doing.

They had started out innocently enough. The Barrens were filled with plenty of people deserving of death. People they could snatch up and inject with the virus. And for a while, that was enough. But winter neared as they circled the cure, and potential subjects became harder to come by. Now here they were.

"What did she do?" Charles nodded at the glass, wanting Father to say something awful, even if they both knew it wasn't true.

"Does it really matter? She's here."

"Yes," Charles agreed. "She is."

Father turned from the window. "Are you looking for someone to ease your conscience, to tell you it's fine to infect people so long as they've committed a worthy crime?"

Charles turned from the glass and looked down at the dwarf. "Something like that."

"You value my opinion, Charles, too much for blowing smoke. Wasn't it *you* who said that morals must sometimes be abandoned in service of the greater good?"

"Put like that, I sound like the State."

"We're all human, doing what we must to protect our interests — whether it's power or family, the aims aren't too different."

"I'd like to think that because it's for family, that makes me less of a monster." Charles pressed into his silence. "Right?"

"*I* think so … for whatever that's worth."

"It means plenty, old friend."

Charles punished himself through another few minutes of staring without words, then finally made the excuse that Father had been waiting for, telling him that he'd be in his office, even though they both knew he'd be looking in on Calla.

"Please keep me informed of Dr. Oswald's findings."

"Of course."

It didn't take long to find Calla. She was in the garden, walking beside Ana, both of them laughing. He pressed his back to a wall and watched his daughter, wondering if she could ever know how often he was a bird in her life's tree, perched high to see what he could.

There had been so few times in Calla's life when she seemed truly happy. Charles wondered how she could be so pure of heart, how her soul could still be sweet after getting shredded so early. The girl was undaunted. Even afraid she would take a step to prove she could. Calla deserved to live, and that's exactly what he kept reminding himself as he pictured the innocent woman strapped to Oswald's table.

Out in the garden, Ana said something he couldn't hear. Calla laughed, then laughed louder. Charles thought back to the time they were wandering the Barrens on her birthday. She was turning five, but had no idea. He had known that her birthday was coming and wanted to tell her so they could celebrate, though he knew it meant little or nothing. He had even wanted to somehow make Calla a cake, despite it being absurd.

She snuggled against his chest that night, lightly snoring, while he whispered happy birthday and softly kissed her head. As happy as he was to have her in his arms, he was angry, the frustration of not being able to note the passing of time in his daughter's life, that such things no longer had meaning in this godforsaken land.

He held his anger in the morning, and stopped counting days from that moment forward, knowing that no matter how much he tried to assign such things importance, they no longer mattered.

His rage boiled under the surface, continuing to seethe until he met Jonah — the man who showed him that life could be lived another way. Now Charles nursed a pair of constant thoughts: he should have wished Calla happy birthday and kept counting the days, and he should have apologized to Jonah for hating him so.

He couldn't wish Calla a happy birthday now — she wouldn't know what he meant — but Charles *could* tell his daughter that he loved her, and pull her closer like he should do more often.

He stepped away from the wall, about to do just that, but a chirp from his comm pulled Charles away. "What is it?"

"Someone has spotted intruders in the east entrance," Father said.

"Any idea who they are?" His heart began to beat faster.

"Men with guns … a lot of them."

FORTY-ONE

Adam Lovecraft

LIGHT BURNED his eyes and chased the fog from Adam's brain.

It was bright enough to be morning, or even late the next day. He woke to see Zelle sleeping beside him on the ground — bound and gagged. He couldn't move his arms, also behind him, and felt numb in the shoulders. His hands were tied, but his mouth wasn't gagged.

Adam bolted upright, turning, searching for Colton, but the man wasn't in the room.

It seemed like they were still in the bank building, but in a different place than where Colton had killed Zelle's father. Light spilled through the filthy window, and lit the city's gray mass. Adam looked back at the girl.

She didn't seem to be hurt, so at least Colton wasn't a total monster. He'd knocked them out and tied them up. At least he hadn't murdered them … yet.

Adam leaned closer and listened, to make sure she was breathing. He would have woken her to ask what had happened, but with a blue rag gagging her mouth, Zelle had nothing to say. He looked around, searching for something to help him break free from the plastic ties binding his wrists, the same ties used by Watchers when they were out of metal cuffs.

He was about to stand when the door opened. Colton stepped in, holding two bottles of water with orange DARWIN GAMES labels in one hand, a blaster aimed at Adam in the other.

"You're awake."

"What the hell is this all about?" Adam glared at Colton.

"Don't be upset. I'm doing this for your own good."

"What are you talking about?"

Zelle woke, yelling into her gag as she lashed out with her limbs.

Colton kicked her feet. "Stop!"

She did, eyes wide and watery as she looked up.

"What's going on, Colton?" Adam asked again.

He squatted across from them and unscrewed one of his bottles, probably from his Opening Rush supplies. He held the bottle to Adam's lips. "Take a drink."

Adam took four gulps before coughing.

Colton turned to Zelle. "I'm gonna remove your gag, so you can have a drink. If you yell, scream, or cry, I'm putting it back on and you won't get any water. Understand?"

She nodded, fear at war with sanity in her stare. Adam was surprised she'd not snapped already.

Colton leaned over, untied her gag from the back, then held the bottle for her to drink.

"What's going on?" Adam repeated for a third time. "What do you mean *for my own good*?"

"No matter what happens next, remember one thing, boy: I saved your life." A solemn nod. "Me and Hooper."

Zelle finished the bottle. Colton pulled it from her lips and she yelled, "You killed my father!"

"He was a zombie darling, otherwise he'd be here with us right now."

"He didn't look like a zombie! And you stabbed him in the head!"

"Trust me, your father had turned. Now keep quiet or it's back to the gag."

Zelle looked down.

"What do you mean you did this *for my own good?*" Adam gritted his teeth, frustrated with Colton's evasion.

"Your father was a good man. I believe you are, too. But there are consequences for breaking the law."

"Breaking the law?" Adam's voice climbed higher than he wanted. Then it dawned on him. "Wait. Are you with the State?"

"I am." He nodded. "I was tasked to find Zelle and her father, then the Gardens."

Zelle stared, too afraid for words.

"So you lied to me? To get my help?"

"I knew she'd be more likely to trust you than me. Especially with Daniel alive. He would've remembered me from City Watch."

"So you killed him?"

"He was turned."

Zelle put her face down, crying. "No he wasn't."

"And Hooper?" Adam asked. "Was he with you?"

"No, he was just another player in the Games."

"And that's why you killed him? Because he would have stopped you from doing this?"

Colton shook his head. "Shit, Adam. Is that how little you think of me? I came back and saved your ass from those bandits after you ran off like a fool! I didn't have to do that. I could've kept going and found Zelle myself."

"You *just* said you needed me to convince her."

"There were other, easier, ways to convince her." Colton shifted his harsh gaze from Adam to Zelle. Tears streaked her face. He reached into his pocket, pulled out an orange cloth, and extended it toward her.

She flinched.

"Just trying to help." Colton brushed her cheeks free of tears, almost as if he wasn't a heartless bastard who had murdered her father before tying them up.

"What are you getting out of all this?" Adam asked.

"I'm doing my job, Adam — I'm getting the order and protection for me and my family provided by the State. Like I said, a number of Underground people have fled to the Gardens. We want to find it and bring those terrorists to justice."

"And what of the people living there? You're just going to attack them?"

"Only if they fight. That's where Zelle comes in. As a show of good faith, we'll bring her to the Gardens and she can stay, assuming they'll have her."

"And what about me?" Adam asked.

Colton turned his head to the side, and was quiet for a moment. "I'm not sure what's going to be done with you."

Adam thought of Ana, and wondered if he'd see her.

"Hold on a moment, will you?" Colton stood, walked over to Zelle and untied her hands, then Adam's. "Don't do anything stupid. I've relayed our location to the State. They've got hunter orbs standing by to escort us out of here."

Colton went to the door and stepped outside.

Adam reached for the second bottle of water and offered it to Zelle. She finished wiping her tears and took it.

"I'm sorry," Adam said. "I had no idea."

"Do you think my father was really—" She couldn't finish.

Adam had been wrong about Colton. He'd been too stupid to see that the man was playing him. And yet, he liked to believe that Colton was bad, not evil, and would have a hard time killing an innocent man.

Tell that to Hooper!

Except that Hooper was about to get us all killed …

Adam argued with himself, weighing his moves. He could attempt to disarm Colton, and might succeed if he could catch him off guard. But Colton (or the orbs) would kill him if he failed.

It also seemed like Colton was arranging to get them out of the Outback. Even if he managed to kill Colton, what then? It wasn't as if he knew how to get out of the Outback. And there was no way he could survive long with the girl. Colton, despite the recent turn of events, might be their only chance of escaping the Outback alive.

But at what cost?

Adam couldn't imagine many things worse than dying in the Outback, and wasn't about to risk the girl's life on a chance that he *might* be able to take the man out. So he would follow along, and look for an opportunity that made more sense in terms of their survival. Still, he wondered why he was being pulled from the Games, and about the purpose of *his* rescue.

Colton stepped into the room holding a comm to his mouth. "Yes, he's right here." Then he handed the comm to Adam. "It's for you."

Adam put the comm to his ear. "Hello?"

"Hello, Adam," said a voice he could never forget.

FORTY-TWO

Keller

KELLER HELD THE COMM, barely able to believe that Adam was on the other end.

It had been so long since he'd heard the boy's voice. He sounded different — hardened by more than a half year in prison and days in the Games.

This is what a ghost sounds like.

"What do you want?" Adam asked, hate dripping from his voice.

Keller couldn't blame him. He'd killed the boy's father. He probably assumed that the former Chief of City 6 was behind his mother's death as well.

"I don't know what I want," Keller said, honestly. "You hurt me, Adam. I thought of you like a son."

"Bullshit! You were using me. You used me to get to Michael and the other Underground. You never cared about me! I've been thinking, and you know what, Keller? I think you only became my friend to hurt my father worse. You knew nothing would make him madder than seeing his son friends with the man responsible for killing the life that he loved."

"I don't know what your Underground friends told you, Adam, but I swear I had nothing to do with what happened to your parents."

Keller wanted to explain that he just found out about the plot from Denton Sinclair, but he no longer trusted his people not to spy on him. There was a divide among the Elders, and Keller had to play his hand or be declared a traitor.

But he couldn't say nothing. It pained him to think the boy may blame the tragedy of losing both his mother and father on him.

Adam was silent. Keller couldn't tell if he believed him or not. "I wanted you to pay, and considered having Colton kill you once you got the girl. But I've changed my mind."

"Changed your mind about Colton killing me?"

"It shouldn't end like this. You don't deserve this. No matter how much you betrayed me."

"You betrayed *us*! You killed my father in front of the world! You can't take that back!"

"I know," Keller said, scotch burning his throat.

"Will you tell Colton to let us go?"

"I can't do that."

"Why not?"

"Because the girl is our key to finding the Gardens and some of the worst Underground traitors."

"You say *I* don't deserve this, yet you're going to go after more people like me. *Innocents*."

"They're not innocent, Adam," he said, anger creeping into his voice at Adam's naiveté. "I know you look up to these people because they brainwashed you into believing their lies, and yes, some may be decent people. But there *are* evil people in the Underground. People who want to create chaos to benefit their interests. You're still young. I wouldn't expect you to understand."

"These people just want to be left alone! They left the Cities; why not let them be?"

"Because the moment we *let them be* is the moment they strike — like your father did at City 1. We can't afford weakness, Adam."

There was only silence.

"Adam?" Keller said.

"What?" the boy snarled over the comm.

"I promise that no harm will come to the girl. Nor you. Go with Colton so we can talk."

"I don't trust you."

"When have I lied to you? Did I hold back the truth sometimes? Yes, of course, but I've never once lied to you. And I'm not lying now."

A long pause, then, "If you hurt Zelle, then I'll slit your goddamned throat myself."

Adam might *mean* it, but Keller also knew that desire and action rarely coalesced. He was more concerned *for* Adam. The boy was angry now, and angry young men had a difficult time hearing reason. Everything was the end of the world in their eyes, but Keller was potentially looking at the real end of the world, and a teenager's threats were nothing compared to what the Underground could do. He could only hope Adam's mood would soften once they were together.

"Please give Colton the comm."

A moment later: "What do you want me to do, boss?"

"Bring them to my house."

"And if they try to escape?"

Keller didn't like the fear and doubt creeping into Colton's voice. "Then kill them. But get the location of the Gardens first. Got it?"

"Understood."

Keller refilled his scotch.

FORTY-THREE

Liam Harrow

LIAM AND KATRINA were about to enter the bank building when she threw her hand out in front of him, pointing into the darkness past the entrance at two lights gliding along the first floor — hunter orbs, searching.

"Shit," Liam said. "What are they looking for?"

"Hell if I know. Come on."

Katrina crept toward a four-story building across the street, an ancient hotel with a weathered sign that read *VACANCY* on a parking lot pole in burned-out neon.

The lobby had no front door. Katrina kept her light off to avoid detection.

The lobby's floor was split open, ancient cracked tile surrendering to vegetation and snow. In the lobby's center, a thick knotted tree had sprouted from the ground and stretched through to the floors above.

"The stairs." She pointed toward a door with a red sign which read *STAIRS* at the other end of the lobby.

Inside the stairwell Katrina clicked on her gun light and led the way. Each step took several seconds as they carefully claimed one, then another, slowly making their way to the second floor where Liam hoped nothing waited.

The second floor was empty. After giving it the all-clear, Katrina crossed the room and stood by the window. She turned back toward Liam, still in the doorway, and waved her beam from him to the glass, suggesting that he join her.

Liam crossed the room and stared out the window, looking out at the bank beside her while waiting for the orbs to leave.

Air was unsettled between them. Too much silence from things unsaid. Liam wanted to break the tension, but didn't know what he could say to make things okay.

"Are you cold?"

Katrina turned from the window with a half-smile. "Am I *cold*?"

"Yeah." Liam shrugged, feeling dumb. "Are you cold?"

"Well, it's freezing outside, and there's no heat in here. I'm wearing the same jacket as you. What do you think, Liam — aren't you cold?"

"Yeah, but you never seem affected by anything."

"I'm affected by plenty." She grunted.

Her words sounded friendly enough to give Liam hope that things could get better between them. Before her sudden surliness and the thing with Chelsea, they had always gotten along well — so well that Liam sometimes felt a spark of envy from Ana. She didn't seem to think there was anything romantic between them, but he and Katrina shared a banter that Ana wasn't really a part of, or invited to join in on.

"Now that you know my general level of warmth, is there anything more interesting you'd rather discuss?" Katrina finally laughed. Small, and slightly raspy, still Liam was glad to hear it.

"Sure." He shrugged. "How did you get so good at killing people?"

"That's more like it." Katrina finished her laugh. "I got good at killing people because I didn't have any choice. I was on my own, after all."

She finished her sentence as if waiting for Liam. He took his cue and asked what he'd never dared to ask her before. "What about your family?"

"I didn't have one. I lost my father when I was small. He was in the Underground; it was only a matter of time before City Watch got him. My mother was taken into custody for conspiracy. I never saw her again." Again, silence, but Liam could hear her wanting him to ask: "Then what happened?"

"I was put into an orphanage, Sweeper Gates, and left to fend for myself. It was awful. The boys all picked on me and the girls were even worse. I hated every second. Until I met a guard named Clancy Harris. He showed me how to hate the Gates less by giving me purpose."

"What was your purpose?"

"He taught me to spy." A smile returned to her lips, as if lit by memory. "I loved it because I was good, and good because I was only eleven. Little girls are easy to ignore, and men tend to say a lot they shouldn't in front of them, things that can be useful to the right people. Clancy was a secrets broker, selling information to the right bidder."

"So, how did that turn into killing?"

"I was caught a few years later, overhearing some things I shouldn't between people of high rank in the City. Watchers grabbed me up and offered immunity if I just told 'em who I worked for. But I couldn't rat out Clancy, or any of the Underground. They'd become like my new family, or the closest I was going to get."

Katrina's voice turned suddenly bitter. "Later, of

course, I found out that Clancy had given *me* up, along with a bunch of others who worked for him. Anything to save his own ass. I learned not to look up to anyone."

She stared out the window, into the snowy night, as if staring into yesterday. "But I didn't know that at the time, and I didn't snitch. I was in prison for three months before Rene came to release me. Rene was hired by Jack Geralt to hunt and gather the kinds of girls that the monster loved most. The quarter year in my cell was to break my spirits so I'd be grateful when Geralt came to *save* me, and so I'd know where I'd return if I disobeyed him."

He swallowed, not wanting to hear the rest of her story.

But Katrina was no longer waiting for prompts. "I was told by the other girls that I should just do as I was told, that life with Geralt wasn't terrible, nice even, so long as I didn't fight, and stayed young enough for his tastes. The oldest girl, Jamara, told me that the best girls graduated from Geralt's most private wing to other parts of his estate. *Just be a good girl and everything will be fine.*"

Katrina steeled herself, bracing against the memory, taking a moment to her breath. It was the closest Liam had ever seen her to tears.

"I'd never even kissed a boy before then. So the first time he took me, I tried to pretend that it wasn't happening to *me*. I told myself it was a character from a flix, and that if I could just pretend long enough, it would be over soon. But my body refused to cooperate with my head. I started crying, kicking, screaming, scratching. But rather than leave me alone, my protests excited the monster."

Another pause, then a crack in her voice. "I became his favorite pet. On the rare occasions when he would use someone else, I'd lie alone in a room full of other girls who could never be my friends, staring at the moon through iron bars in an over-decorated bedroom, somehow colder and lonelier than I'd been in City 2's concrete cell."

She turned to meet his eyes. "I used to imagine myself on the moon — the one thing that almost always helped me fall asleep. I made up stories about a family living there. I'd give them adventures in my mind, then stare out the window and pretend it was all really happening. I thought that maybe if I could believe that my imaginary family was alive on the moon, I could also believe there was a way to escape the horror, and that there was a way I could find my actual family. But when you live in that kind of hell, childish notions are a luxury. I soon saw my dreams for the impossible wishes they were. Then I started wishing for things I *might* be able to do — like kill Rene and Geralt."

"Did you?"

"I tried. I was determined to end them, not just for myself but for every girl that would ever have to follow me. One night I was lucky enough to sneak a knife from Geralt's plate after dinner. I think Jamara might have missed my taking it on purpose when she collected our dishes. I slipped it under my pillow before bed, praying that Geralt wouldn't find it. Lying beside him that night, I worked my courage until I was strong enough to slip my hand under the pillow and curl my fingers around the hilt. I pictured myself pulling it out and sliding the blade across his throat."

Another pause for breath. "But I flinched. I couldn't bring myself to kill another person, no matter how evil he was."

"Wow ..." Liam said, unsure of what else he could say.

"I failed to kill the monster and he made me pay. Beat me until I begged for death, then called a guard and told him to dispose of me. I knew where I was going, had seen it twice with others, both a few years older than me. Argumentative girls were taken to the incinerator. I had no argument left inside me, but he was done with me just the same."

"Oh my God ..."

"The guard took pity on me. I'd seen him around a lot, and could tell the way he looked at me, different than the others, that he had a heart. Most people there regarded us women as trash, repulsive whores whose lives were only good for serving the men in power. But he didn't look at me like that. He led me to the sewers and said I could never come back. We'd both be worse than dead if I did. I'll never forget that part, *worse than dead.* I thought he was exaggerating at the time. Now I understand the incinerator was Geralt showing mercy."

"Did you live in the Barrens by yourself?"

"I spent the first few days alone, then met a family. They took pity on me and nursed me to health, but they told me from the start I'd have to be on my own once I was better. I stayed with them longer than expected, just long enough for me to start hoping they'd keep me around. I thought they were starting to like me. And maybe they were, but I was still an extra mouth. There was one girl, about half my age, and a little boy a couple of years older than her. The dad seemed indifferent, though I don't think he was. The mom was saddest. Even though I try all the time, I can't remember any of their names."

Katrina turned from the window, finished with the view. "I hate Clancy for what he did, but I'd be dead a hundred times if not for all he taught me. Being a good spy means you have to know people, how they behave and why they do what they do. That's what got the guard to take pity on me. I recognized that he wasn't like the others, and gambled that he would spare me, and risk his own life to save mine. Once free, I used my wits to find that first family to take me in and help me. I did what I had to for plenty of years. And things were okay."

Liam knew what she was about to say next.

"That's when I met Sutherland. He gave me the first home I had since I was thrown in a cell in City 2, and made me feel like I deserved it. He was a good man, with the right intentions. And his ideals were arrows through my heart. He wanted to topple the State. He spoke with passion, using words I'd never heard. I saw my hatred for Geralt and all he'd done echoed by Sutherland. He taught me to kill, and I loved my schooling. *Targets must be more than accidents*, he always said, as I learned to kill with purpose. I can't say I was happy, but I was as close as I was likely to get. And then *you* came along."

Katrina's anger suddenly made sense.

Still, her last sentence hurt Liam like he'd fallen from a tree. Sure, Sutherland was a monster, but still a saint when compared to Geralt. And he cared for her, something Katrina had been sorely missing. And things would've kept being okay if Liam and Ana hadn't made her see the despot for what he was. They'd forced her hand, and now that she found herself in almost a maternal role of their odd little family, she was beginning to long for her old life. It might have been hell with Sutherland, but it was familiar.

"I'm sorry," he said, pushing words through guilt. "I didn't mean to be an asshole."

"Don't apologize. I'd become blind. Sutherland wasn't always like you saw him. His change was slow, like boiling water. Warmer, warmer, dead."

"We can all be blind to things sometimes, especially when we allow our hearts to guide us. It's tough to balance our humanity with the need to survive." Even if Katrina's actions weren't right, Liam wanted to know that he understood.

"The orbs are still outside." He nodded toward the window.

"I know. I'm tired. I want to give up for the night."

Liam raised his eyebrows.

"I won't give up on the big stuff, but I think we deserve a nap."

Liam nodded. "I'm tired, too."

"And cold. It's very cold in here."

"Freezing."

"Will you keep me warm? I won't try to seduce you."

"You're too good for that," Liam said.

"So are you." Katrina lay on the floor.

"I'm sorry that you never got to kill Geralt. Maybe someday you will, assuming he isn't already gone." He lay down beside Katrina, put an arm around her and closed his eye, trying not to think of how good it felt to be close to another warm body in the Outback.

He stared out the window, thinking of Ana and hoping that she was thinking of him.

"WAKE UP!"

Liam shoved his way through the fog.

He remembered falling asleep, and the orbs still at the bank.

"Wake up!" Katrina whispered, even more urgently.

"Are the orbs still there?"

She shook her head. "They're gone. But we have something else to deal with."

"What?"

Katrina yanked Liam to his feet and turned him to the window.

Adam was being marched beside a small girl with a large man behind them, holding a gun.

Katrina had her rifle in hand as she looked out the window. "I think I can get a clear shot."

"Do it," Liam said.

But it was too late.

The door exploded open behind them.

The orb flew into the room, cannon spinning with blue arcs of electricity, sizzling like static. It fired a shot, barely missing Katrina, blasting a hole through the wall and clearing glass from the frame behind them.

Liam reached for his blaster, took aim and fired.

He missed and ripped a wide ribbon through the room's west wall as the orb zipped upward to the ceiling.

The cannon crackled louder.

Katrina dropped her rifle, whipped out her sword and swung, forcing the orb to dip.

Momentum shoved her to the floor.

The orb spun, turning its cannon on Katrina.

Time seemed to pause as the orb turned on her.

Liam was directly behind it. Katrina was rising to her feet directly in front of the orb. If Liam did nothing, it would disintegrate her. If he fired from his present angle, he would likely miss the orb and kill Katrina himself.

So he did the only thing he could think of and shouted, "Hey!"

The death machine spun and turned its cannon on Liam. He lunged at it, screaming, arms raised, hoping to further scare it into moving without shooting.

It started to move, but wasn't quick enough.

He seized the white-hot cannon and didn't let go as he

barreled forward, through the hole where a window had been just seconds ago.

Liam and the orb sailed out the second story. He landed hard on the orb and snowy ground. The orb's back was smooth and round, blunting the impact.

Liam sucked wind through his pained lungs, hands and arms burning red against the cold relief of freshly fallen snow lying in a blanket across the lot. The orb whirred to life, rising from the ground, shaky, cannon still crackling as it aimed.

This was it. Nowhere to run.

He failed to save Adam. He'd never see Ana again.

A shadow fell across him. He looked up to see Katrina in a downward arc, sword in hand. She screamed.

The orb turned too late. She drove her sword through its front camera, then raised the blade and thrust it deeper, screaming a war cry as she brought it down hard against the ground.

The orb screeched, trying to flee.

Katrina let go of her sword, and unsheathed the wrist blades beneath her jacket, punching, stabbing, and dismantling the mechanical beast in a frenzied attack, rabid like an animal until the orb was dead.

He stared up at Katrina. She met his gaze, then looked around, fists clenched, blades out and eyes on fire, ready to face whatever was coming.

The murder faded from her face as she looked ahead. "*Shit*. They must've heard the commotion and took off. We need to find him now."

Then she ran back into the hotel to retrieve her rifle, returning with a blaster on her hip, sword on her back, blades on her wrists, and rifle ready to shoot in her hands.

God help the bastard who tried to stand in her way.

FORTY-FOUR

Keller

KELLER ANXIOUSLY LOOKED BACK at the clock.

Jacqueline was late, overdue fourteen minutes to check on him as she'd seemed to do every two hours when she was home. The last thing he wanted to do was discuss why he was in a bad mood — again. Like always, he wanted to finish with her unwanted interruption as quickly as possible.

Her being late only annoyed him further.

The door opened fifteen minutes late. Keller hid the glass at the foot of his desk.

Jacqueline said, "Just checking on you, making sure you have everything you need."

"I'm fine, Jackie."

"You seem preoccupied, sweetheart. Anything wrong?"

"No. Nothing is wrong."

Why couldn't she understand that he didn't feel like talking?

Now she'd give him that sour look full of disapproval and blame, then sigh, slip back behind the door, duck out, and close it just to sigh harder on the other side. Then once she was gone, he'd pour himself a double.

But instead she stayed put. "Don't lie to me."

Keller stared up at his wife, surprised.

"You've been moping, ever since we moved here. I don't want you to stay in here drinking all day … and night. It makes you smell. And I don't like how you're lying, hiding your glasses when I come in the room like I'm an idiot."

"I'm fine." Keller ignored her accusation. "I just have a lot to do, a lot on my mind."

"Yes, a lot on your mind. That's what you always say. But I don't think there's a lot on your mind so much as that one thing that won't go away."

"What do you mean?"

"I mean Jonah's boy, Adam. We've been married for a long time. I know what eats you, even when you wish I didn't. And not just since Joshua — before him too."

"Please. I don't have time for this."

"Then perhaps you don't have time for *us*."

"Come on, Jackie, don't be so melodramatic."

"And don't be dismissive of me." She glared at him, chin quivering, eyes on the verge of tears.

The very real moment unfolding with Jacquelyn sent Keller standing from his chair. All at once, years of guilt settled like a stone in his gut. He stood straighter and walked to his wife, his eyes finding hers. He took her gently and led her through the apartment, into their bedroom in a slightly crooked but hurried line. His eyes flitted around, inspecting the area for hidden listening devices he'd searched for several times before.

He lowered her gently to the bed. She looked up at him, sitting, puzzled as he planted a fingertip firmly to his lips. She blinked, then nodded.

Keller turned the room's music loud, then spun to Jacquelyn, smiled, and sat at the edge of the bed beside her.

She stared into his eyes like she wasn't sure if he was going to try to distract her with lovemaking or about to bare his soul with the conversation they'd been avoiding for much too long.

"What is it?" She bit her bottom lip to keep it from trembling. He didn't think she could possibly be ready for the truth, but he had to tell her now.

He whispered, "It's all a lie. Denton Sinclair and some other Elders unleashed the zombie virus." He tried to keep his voice from cracking, but his whisper only grew louder and more ragged. "They wanted the same thing to happen here, to keep everyone in line. It wasn't … it wasn't Jonah's fault."

Keller started to sob. Jacquelyn pulled him to her chest, and petted the back of his head.

"I think I killed an innocent man." He cried against her, gurgling his confession. She said nothing while rocking him. "I put his family into the Games … *what have I done?*"

His voice split in a deep ravine as he shuddered, "I'm a monster."

Jacquelyn pulled him tighter, then pulled away. "You're not a monster. You're a good man who has had to make some very difficult decisions, under terrible circumstances." She kissed him hard on the cheek. "It does nothing to beat yourself over what you have done. Tell me what you are going to do *now*."

Keller looked at his wife. He didn't feel angry or upset; he didn't want her to go, or wish for her to stop talking. He just wanted something he could be proud of. "I don't know that there's anything *to* do. I can't free Adam. He did betray me, and was working with terrorists. Yes, there's corruption in City 1, initiated by my bosses. And that doesn't excuse the Underground, or the boy's actions."

"So, what's the right answer?" Jacquelyn pressed.

"Maybe there isn't one."

"Shallots," she said, because Jacquelyn never said *bull-shit*. Despite how he felt, a small smile touched his lips, remembering how fiercely he loved this woman. Especially after what she said next. "There's *always* a right thing to do. You're just not willing to see it. You do that: decide what you don't want to see, then build your walls high and hard enough to keep it out. You always have, but it's been worse, so much worse, since Joshua." She held out her hand in offering. "But I know you can see it.

He took her hand, and smiled. His comm chirped and he growled, "What is it?"

"Are you available, sir?"

Kern's voice was at a higher pitch than it should have been, tilting into the *sir* like a child standing on his toes.

"What is it?" Keller repeated.

Kern cleared his throat. "I have something to show you … in person."

No tilting that time. Definite, immediate, and secret.

"What is it?" Jacquelyn asked from behind Keller, just soft enough for him to hear but not loud enough for Kern.

Keller turned to Jacquelyn, shaking his head. Then into the comm: "Come over."

He hung up and wondered. Had they heard him over the music, sobbing the truth to his wife?

"What is it?" Jacquelyn repeated.

"Business." Keller returned to his desk, then opened the bottom drawer and pulled out his blaster. "Whatever you do, keep what I said to yourself, or both our lives are in danger." Keller placed the weapon into her hand. "Use this if anything goes wrong."

"What's happening?" A touch of fear in her voice. "What might go wrong?"

"I don't know. Just keep this as a last resort."

"That's supposed to make me feel better? Tell me *why*."

"I don't know, Jacquelyn." He pulled her into a tight embrace. "Just … *please* … trust me."

She pulled back, but just enough to kiss him. It had been a long time for them both, and it was only the nagging realization that Kern was coming over that pulled him from her arms. Keller left her in the bedroom, closing the door behind him.

He waited by the front door, spending the next five minutes frozen so that Kern wouldn't think he had just finished pacing.

Kern knocked and Keller drew a deep breath as he opened the door. "Come in."

He nodded and stepped through the doorway.

"What is it?" Keller asked.

Kern held out his tablet and nodded at the screen. "We found Dennis Weaver, or Sutherland as he's going by now. He's in Quadrant 11."

"Who else has seen this?"

"Only Jacobson, so far."

"Great! Thank you." Keller gave Kern two taps on the shoulder, then went out to the balcony. Kern followed.

Outside, Keller was grateful for the fresh air, cold as it was. He looked around. Up, down and along the horizon. After seeing nary an orb, he said, "Can I count on you?"

"Of course, sir."

"We have to do this one off the books. No one can know."

"Of course, sir."

Keller smiled. *This*, he would be proud to tell Jacquelyn. "Let's catch this fucker, once and for all."

FORTY-FIVE

Sutherland

SUTHERLAND LOVED the sound of chaos — blasters and death as it echoed around them.

He was making his way through the old train station with his men — all but two who had stayed to guard the entrance — eliminating hallways of startled opposition.

He loved the looks on the residents' faces as these men in City Watch chem suits stormed their castle. A blond man in brown robes attempted to play hero, coming at the men dressed in black with a sword.

Sutherland would have engaged the man in a sword fight, but had no time for whimsy. Not when others in the tunnels might be mounting a more formidable defense. He fired a shot at the man's crotch and laughed as he fell to the floor dying, reaching for the cave of melted flesh where his dick had once sprouted.

Sutherland was scrubbing the Station. Once clean, he could decide what to do with it. For now he went through with workman-like precision. The tunnels seemed to wind for a while, and in enough directions to keep his boredom at bay. The place didn't seem nearly as large or occupied as Hydrangea, but it could make a decent home.

But Sutherland couldn't settle in until he got rid of the rats that currently occupied it.

He pulled the trigger again. Twice. Both blasts slapped a medium-sized brunette — a pretty thing, with a charming little overbite. Sutherland's first shot was sloppy, it kicked her in the stomach and split her nearly in the middle. The second blasted wiped all the pretty off of her face.

The other men were doing their work, though Horrance didn't seem to be finding as much joy in their jobs as the others. Seemed the ogre wasn't just soft in the head.

Something bristled his senses, and sent Sutherland diving to the side. Before the shooter could pop a second shot, he pulled his trigger thrice. One shot made it, enough to take a small chunk of the attacker's upper head, more than enough to drop him dead.

The shooter fell and a small boy — about five years old — ran into the hall, crying for his mommy. Farther down the hall, the child's mother ran toward him as if she could stop the armed men marching toward them.

Sutherland darted toward the child, scooping him up before the mother could reach them, then cradling him in the crook of his arm, he put the blaster to the child's forehead. He turned to the woman. She stopped, eyes wide in terror.

"Please don't hurt him!" She threw her hands together in a prayer her god didn't care about.

"Bring me to your leader, or your pup disappears."

Three men with guns raced up behind the mother with their guns drawn on Sutherland.

"Drop the guns or the kid dies." Sutherland knew he

had won before they placed their guns on the floor. "Who will take me to the leader of this—" He wrinkled his nose. "Does this hole in the ground have a name?"

"I'll take you where you need to go."

At first Sutherland didn't see the voice, but then looked down to find its owner — a dwarf, thirty-something years old as far as he could tell. He had dark brown hair and a neatly trimmed beard. Sutherland had known a few men with trimmed beards. They were always first to die, seeing as they were usually pussies and traitors. But this dwarf seemed like more than a well-coifed toy soldier.

"Please don't kill the child." The dwarf looked at him with kind eyes that — to Sutherland's surprise — almost made him want to say yes.

He set the child down and aimed his gun at the dwarf. "Take me to your leader. You can tell me his name on your way."

"*I* don't have a leader." The dwarf turned and led Sutherland down a corridor. "But Egan is the man you wish to speak with. I suggest you remain as rational with him as you have been with me. He will try you harder, but resist and I believe we'll get through this. He means well, even when he's foolish. Unfortunately, Egan is foolish often, and I am hoping this is not one of those days."

The dwarf paused at a door.

Sutherland spoke to his men. "If anything goes wrong in there, start shooting out here. Everyone. The child first."

He pushed past the dwarf, then ducked inside Egan's office and closed the door behind him.

The man stared at Sutherland open-mouthed from behind his desk. He was halfway to reaching for something, frozen behind the newcomer's blaster.

"So, this all belongs to you?" Sutherland looked around

the room. "The dwarf says your name is Egan. That right?"

"It is."

"Even Jack Geralt has two names. Is Egan your number one or your number two?"

"My full name is Charles Egan. What does it matter? And who the hell are *you*?"

"My name is Sutherland. I'm here for Ana Lovecraft. I know she's here, and I'll leave once I have her. No one needs to die."

"I don't know who you mean."

"*I don't know who you mean.*" Sutherland hoped he got the pitch of idiocy perfect as he narrowed his eyes at Egan. "You are in no position to lie. Tell me the truth or this place will be a memory of what it was this morning."

"Why do you want her?"

"See, you *do* know her." Sutherland shook his head. "As to what I want ... let's just call it unfinished business. Whether she has something that once belonged to me, because she knows the ending to a flix I saw as a child, or because I desperately want the recipe to her world-famous apple pie, it does not matter to you, *Charles Egan*. Now: *where the hell is she?*"

"I don't know."

"You do. And in a moment I'll prove it by shooting your people, one at a time." He leaned toward Egan. "Does this place have an intercom?"

Egan handed Sutherland a comm.

"What do I press?"

Egan pointed to the thinner of two long buttons on the side.

He pressed it. "Ana Lovecraft, this is your old pal, Sutherland. I'm here in Egan's office. Come to me now and you won't be harmed. We'll finish what we started, then you and lover boy can be on your way."

He paused for effect, then continued in his most pleasant voice. "Attention, residents of this shit hole, my name is Sutherland and in case you have yet to notice, me and my friends are making a rather big mess of your humble abode. If you would like us gone and on our merry way, then I've got great news for you. Bring us Ana, and we'll leave you be. Or … you can continue hiding her and force me to make an even bigger mess."

Sutherland paused for effect, then continued. "I've no doubt that you have all heard about the attack on City 1. That was us, and I have two men waiting at your station's air units with enough virus to make City 1 look like a nursery rhyme."

Sutherland paused again, turned to a horrified Egan, and finished his message. "I hope you're listening, Ana. You have exactly ten minutes, starting now."

FORTY-SIX

Liam Harrow

AFTER LOSING THE ORBS, Katrina and Liam followed the three sets of footprints outside the bank until they abruptly ended at the doors outside an old hospital. The building was massive: twenty stories high and wide enough to swallow a city block.

"How the hell are we going to find them in there?" Liam was growing more anxious. They'd lost their lead for good.

He didn't think the man coercing Adam was running from them. He'd probably seen two people in the street fighting an orb and decided to flee before the fight spread to more orbs or people. Adam also probably hadn't recognized Liam with his beard, eye patch, thick dark jacket and pants.

Katrina motioned for Liam to follow her into the lobby. Then they made their way into a restroom.

"Watch the door." Katrina threw her backpack to the ground. She found the box screen and searched the feeds.

Liam focused on the doorway, listening to the building's noises — far off, but still too close, mostly the sound of a building decaying loud enough to hear, and maybe a few humans, living or undead. He didn't want to search more of the hospital to locate the sources. He was down to three blaster clips. They couldn't risk a firefight or face a horde. Katrina was among the baddest of asses, but that didn't mean she could take on a wall of zombies without getting plowed.

"Holy shit," Katrina said.

Liam turned and looked down at the monitor: a view from just above the man with the gun leading Adam, somewhere outside. Oddly, the orb wasn't recording at a distance — this one was right on top of them.

"What the hell?" Katrina said.

"What is it?"

"I don't think this orb is recording for the Games." She cranked the volume and the man spoke.

"How much farther?"

Another man's voice came over a comm held by Adam's keeper: "Just ahead to Carroway Street and into the manhole. Half mile until you reach a ladder with a red arrow. Let us know when you're there. We'll send a truck."

"The orb isn't recording them for the show," Katrina said. "It's escorting them. That bastard's with the State."

"What do you think he wants with Adam and the girl?"

"I don't know." Katrina shook her head. "But we're going to find out."

THEY RACED toward Carroway on a motorcycle stolen from a bandit who'd been stupid enough to stop for a pretty lady. The bandit probably thought he'd be taking advantage, but Katrina and her wrist blades did all the taking.

They reached a manhole which seemed out of place given that there was no snow on the cover and several footprints disappearing into it.

Liam hefted the lid aside with a grin. "Ladies first."

"Being a gentleman or do you just want my ass shot first?"

"Both," Liam said as she descended.

He followed, pulling the lid back over the hole as he joined Katrina.

Then they raced through the darkness, splashing water as her light bobbed. They eventually found a blue orb glowing in the distance, illuminating a path for Adam and company.

Liam hoped they hadn't heard their pursuit. Katrina killed her light, stopped, and aimed her rifle. He wondered if she'd take out the orb or shoot the man first. She might not be able to fell the orb in a shot. That extra time could be all the man needed to put a gun to either Adam or the girl's head and force them into a standoff.

If she shot the man, though, the orb could come at them strong before they could drop it.

She fired into the darkness.

In the distance, Liam watched as the man fell into the water. The orb's blue light turned from Adam and the girl's shocked reactions, toward them.

"Fire!" Katrina dropped to the water and took aim, shooting rapidly at the advancing orb. It fired a bolt — Liam could feel the electricity's heat as it raced overhead.

It wouldn't miss again.

He fired his blaster, one shot after another as Katrina's shots cracked like thunder against the narrow dark walls.

The orb raced toward them, cannon glowing blue as it recharged, readying itself for another shot. Liam stood rooted, firing through his clip as he stared down the glowing death racing toward them. His clip went dry.

The orb fired.

Liam dodged, but not in time. The blast hit him in the left arm, spread like fire through a forest, and left his limb in ashes. He screamed, falling face first into the water.

There was an explosion above him. Katrina must've hit the orb.

Not that it mattered with his world decaying into darkness and pain.

FORTY-SEVEN

Anastasia Lovecraft

"You can't go!" Calla said.

"I have to."

They were in an underground room one floor beneath the main level with Dr. Oswald and Elijah, both ordered to protect them.

"He's going to kill you," Calla insisted.

"No, he won't. I'm the cure, that's why Sutherland wants me. He came here to keep me alive, and if I don't give myself up and meet him, I'll be responsible for the deaths of more innocents. I can't allow that."

"But you can't leave *me*."

Calla sobbed against Ana's chest. The girl was usually so tough. She had a way of making Ana think that she took everything in stride, but she wasn't too proud to let her terror show now. There it was on her face, body, and every tremble.

The wall's speaker crackled with Sutherland's voice. "Tick tock."

The comm hissed as it passed from one hand to the next, then Egan's voice took Sutherland's place. "He's serious, Ana. If you don't come down here, this … man will start shooting more people."

"I have to go," Ana said to Calla and Oswald.

"Please don't go," Calla kept repeating while clinging to her.

Ana couldn't look at the girl. "I have to."

"Then let me go with you. I'm brave. I can do it. I have the virus too. If he won't kill you, then that means he won't kill me."

"He'd take you from the Station with me, leaving your father all alone. No way he, or I, will let that happen. You'll be safe here with Oswald."

"I don't want Oswald! I want you!"

She pulled Calla into a tight hug, then ordered Oswald to open the door.

He did. As Ana stood in the doorway, the doctor set a small pouch into her hand.

"What is this?"

"It's flash powder. They'll almost certainly take your gun, but you should be able to sneak this in."

"Okay." Ana felt hopeful. "Then what?"

"Use it if you need to make a quick escape, or disarm the enemy. Throw it to the ground and you'll get a blinding flash. It will disorientate everyone, including you. Detail your surroundings *before* using it. Know where you're going, because you'll have to run blind the second you throw it."

"Got it." Ana nodded, deliberately turning from a still-sobbing Calla.

"Go quickly."

Ana turned from Oswald and walked down the hall, heartbroken, pretending not to hear the muffled cries of her newest friend behind her. She slipped the pouch into the back of her underwear and stirred her hate for Sutherland as she walked.

She stepped into the common area, where friendly faces, warm discussions, and children at play were replaced with frightened residents, some sobbing over their dead, under the eyes of heavily armed men in black City Watch chem suits.

She passed a crying child. His mother tried to soothe the boy by running a hand over his back. Tightly hugging her son, she stared at Ana from somewhere between fear and accusation, as if to say — *you brought this here.*

Two guards stopped her in the hall just outside Egan's office. The first took her gun as Oswald predicted. She kept herself from flinching as his gloved hands groped her breasts then ran over her backside where the pouch was concealed.

"I believe I'm wanted," she said before he could notice the protrusion.

"I want you," he leered.

Ana turned to the other guard without responding.

"This way," he said, leading her into Egan's office.

The bastard was inside, helmet off of his red hair, smiling like Ana was holding a freshly baked cake. He crossed the room and pulled her into a hug. Full and large, it caught Ana by surprise with no hope of escaping. She forced herself to relax, accept the embrace and maybe surprise him with an upper hand later.

He pulled away. "Why ever did you leave, Ana? You were such an important cog in our community. It never was quite right after you left. The place has truly gone to the zombies."

"I left because you're crazy."

"Oh, I'd hardly say that." Sutherland frowned. "You and I might have different perspectives, but you can't say I'm crazy. Cunning, perhaps, though I'm not sure that's it either. Deadly, definitely, but there's more than that. I rather like *righteous*."

Sutherland stopped. He made his eyes big and cocked his head. Looked around the room, stretching his neck as if trying to see behind Ana. "Where's Liam?" His frown rose into a knowing smile. "Trouble in Paradise?"

"Liam ran off with that whore, Katrina."

Sutherland smile split into friendly laughter, compassionate as he wrapped an arm around Ana. "I'm really sorry, though neither of us should really be surprised. The only shock is that Liam would be so stupid. The world is full of idiots, and he didn't strike me as one. But Katrina is a woman of many charms. I've fallen victim myself. I can see where sweet Liam could have been led astray. Let's not blame him. The poor man will already suffer for having left you."

"What do you want from me?"

"I'm not *exactly* sure." Sutherland shrugged. "I do need you to help with this nasty plague. You're just special enough to help end this virus forever, and bring the other Cities down. I'm not sure about the order …" Sutherland sighed. "I still haven't figured out what I'm going to do about *this* place. Either way, where there are labs, there is work to be done. You can help with all of it."

Egan looked like he was biting his tongue.

Ana said, "I'm not going anywhere with you."

"Great. That's one vote for staying here."

Ana could take his crazy, but she couldn't take it in addition to him being so smug. She was about to tell Sutherland exactly what she thought, but was saved from her fury by a loud knock.

The door opened and Horrance entered, his helmet also off. She'd never really spoken with the man much at Hydrangea. The few times she had seen the big man would have been amid ridicule from Sutherland. Her gears were spinning, wondering if maybe she could use Horrance against his master.

"Yes, Horrance?"

"There's a girl, sir. She's infected."

Good thoughts about Horrance were doused.

"Oh?" Sutherland raised his eyebrows. He looked at Ana and gave her a light, disapproving shake of the head.

"Yes, sir. It's this man's daughter." He nodded at Egan. "Ana's helping them to cure her."

"Is this true?" Sutherland looked at her. Ana felt transparent, like even just standing there doing nothing she was broadcasting the truth about Oswald. He turned to Egan. "Is your daughter infected? That makes you and Ana like family. And any member of Ana's family is welcome to stay with me!"

"Leave my daughter alone!"

Sutherland crossed his arms and stared at the man, as if daring his response.

"Leave her alone!" Egan repeated. "Or you'll be sorry."

"I highly doubt that." Sutherland grabbed the com. "Attention, I'm looking for one Calla Egan. Please report to your father's office within five minutes, or I will turn everyone you know and love into zombies. Thank you, that is all."

Sutherland turned to Egan. "Let's hope your daughter's a good listener."

FORTY-EIGHT

Calla Egan

CALLA STARED at the speaker from where Sutherland had issued his threat. She'd never felt so far away from her father, or Ana.

She turned to Oswald, fists tight, eyes furious.

"I'm not letting you go," Dr. Oswald said, before she could open her mouth to ask him. "Sutherland must want you for his experiments. Believe me, you don't want that."

"He'll kill everyone here!"

"He'll kill them anyway," Oswald sighed. "Your father instructed me to keep you safe — no matter what. I let you out, and Sutherland *will* hurt you."

"Elijah?" Calla pleaded with the boy who was practically her older brother. "Please, let me go."

He looked at the doctor, then back at her. "Sorry, Calla, I agree with Oz. We can't take the chance."

She stomped her feet, staring at the speakers as though Sutherland was inside them. "We have to do something!"

She turned to Oz, meeting his half-human, half-robot gaze. A nice man, and reasonable. Of all the people in the

Station, Oswald and Father Truth were the ones she enjoyed debating most. They didn't let feelings get in the way of an argument. They respected logic, and would cede to a compelling argument. Until recently, they also treated her least like a child.

"What do you think happens if you don't let me out?"

Oz thought for a moment. "I think they'll gas us."

"And what then?"

"Everyone in the Station will become infected, except maybe for you, Ana, and me. We should be immune, though anything is possible."

"And then …?"

"The virus will kill a certain number of people instantly. Those not killed or immune will become infected, alive but mad with rage. They'll start killing one another, trying to feast on whoever's left. Pandemonium."

"How long do you think you can keep me safe from either the infected or Sutherland's men once they start tearing this place apart looking for me?"

Oswald didn't answer.

"Not long, I bet," Calla argued. "And then what? They'll come and take me, maybe kill you and Elijah. Then they'll take me anyway. The exact thing you're trying to prevent. But everyone will have died, and for what?"

"I swore I'd protect you, Calla. And that's what—"

Sutherland's voice returned to the speaker, now like a nursery rhyme. "Oh, Calla? Where are you? Just two minutes to save your father … *and the Station*. You really don't want to be responsible for *everyone's* deaths, *do* you?"

Calla turned to Oswald, begging with tears. "Please!"

"Oh, by the way, could you please bring that traitor Dr. Oswald as well?"

She turned to see his one human eye go wide, his mouth hanging partly open.

Calla looked up at him. "Looks like we don't have a choice."

Oswald nodded and swallowed in acknowledgement. "I know."

FORTY-NINE

Anastasia Lovecraft

ANA STARED at Sutherland as he smiled back.

She had a feeling that he might have put two and two together and figured the only way the Station could be working on the cure was if Oswald was there.

When he asked for the doctor, her shocked expression must've confirmed his suspicions.

"Please," Ana said, "don't hurt him. He's trying to help. You say you want to bring down the State and give power back to the people, we want the same thing here. Dr. Oswald is working on a cure that could give us a tremendous upper hand in this war."

"Yes. That's exactly what he was doing for me until you and your troublemaking lover boy showed up at Hydrangea and turned two of my top people against me."

Something bad must have happened at Hydrangea. Perhaps a revolt. Sutherland didn't usually raid with his men, at least from everything Katrina had told them over the last few months.

He had always seemed so calm and cool at the camp. So perfectly in control. Even when angry, Sutherland was a quiet sort of vicious. Now he seemed on edge, on the verge of snapping. Standing with a sword on his back, blaster in hand, men on standby to release the zombie toxin, the man was capable of anything.

Ana had to be careful not to push him too far, had to wait for the right moment to strike and take him out. She looked surreptitiously around the room, trying to formulate a plan and how she could best use the flash pouch to her benefit.

Sutherland was sitting at Egan's desk.

Egan was sitting on the floor, per Sutherland's request, in front of the desk.

Ana was standing, also per Sutherland's request, in front of the desk, where he could "keep an eye on her."

Horrance stood guard at the door behind her, with a holstered blaster and his left hand on a shock stick. He was her best bet if she were planning to strike first. He was strong, but also dim. But he had also been staring at her like a creep ever since coming into the room. With his eyes on her, she wasn't sure how she could reach the pouch before he saw her. She might be able to get close enough to kick him in the knee and break his leg if she was fast enough. If she grabbed his gun, then she could kill him, throw the pouch, and fire at Sutherland before he could see her.

Assuming he stayed put once the flash exploded. The man was a warrior. He could drop and fire. Or she might accidentally hit Egan, or Calla and Oswald once they arrived — if they were coming.

She reassembled the pieces in her mind, but couldn't put them together before the door opened. Calla and Dr. Oswald were on the other side.

They surrendered their weapons, then Calla ran into the room and leapt into her father's arms. "Daddy!"

Sutherland stepped around the desk, walked past Egan and Calla on the floor, and smiled at Oswald. "So, Doc, how's that research going?"

"What do you want?" Oswald asked, glaring at Sutherland.

"Want? I want for things to be like they used to be. You, me, Ana, Katrina, Liam, my men, all one happy Hydrangea family working to topple the State. That's what I want!"

"Leave these people alone, and I'll come with you," Oswald promised. "I have no quarrel, sir. I only want to find a cure. No reason we can't do that together."

Sutherland folded his hands in front of his waist.

Ana studied every move — waiting for her moment … slowly starting to second guess herself. What if peace could be had? If Sutherland was being honest, and he only wanted things like they were, her actions could trigger a needless massacre.

Heart pounding, she wished Katrina were with her. "I'll go with you, too. If you leave these people alone. It's not like I have a reason to stay after Liam ran off with that whore."

Ana said this both to persuade Sutherland and to let Oswald and Calla in on her lie, in case he started asking questions about Liam. Egan looked up at her, holding Calla tight. Neither spoke, waiting for the enemy's response.

"It's so gratifying to see this sudden change of heart. You were both *so* eager to flee my home. I serve retribution to City 1 and suddenly *I'm* the bad guy!"

Sutherland laughed. Ana glanced back at Horrance, still staring at her as if she were lunch. *Do it now. Do it!*

"I suppose that would be nice, if things could be like they were. You could have your father back. Your brother could still be a good citizen inside City 6, and," Sutherland's voice went from faux buoyant to weighted by hate, "my people wouldn't have overthrown their leader."

Now! Do it now! Before he does something terrible.

Ana began to reach back, but couldn't quite finish her too-obvious move. Horrance would be on top of her before she could reach the pouch.

"Overthrown?" Oswald repeated. "What happened?"

Sutherland yelled, pointing to Oswald and Ana, "You, and you, and that cunt, Katrina! And that pretty boy, Liam! *You* all happened. Undermining my authority and making me look like a damned fool. That weasel Connor Vinson staged a fucking coup — that's what happened!"

He turned, staring at Ana as if reading her mind. Ice flooded her veins as he stepped forward. He was too close, and the pouch too far.

Sutherland shook his head. "So I have no home, thanks to all of you. But ... perhaps all is not lost."

He paused, stepping just inches from Ana, his eyes reaching into her soul, searching to discover her terrible plot. Her leg began to shake uncontrollably. Keller was the last person to intimidate Ana with a gaze, back when he locked her up.

His stare was a hundred times hotter. "Perhaps I've found a new home. Here."

DO IT NOW!

Ana reached back for the pouch, then brought it up to throw at Sutherland's face.

But he was too fast, reaching out and seizing her hand, sending Ana's pouch to the floor. It did its job anyway.

The bright white flash was immediate, and a loud piercing whistle came with it.

She tried to wriggle free of his hand and capitalize on the moment. But even blind, Sutherland was a step ahead.

He punched Ana hard in her chest. She landed on the floor gasping for air.

A loud thump came seconds later, followed by two shots from one of their blasters.

The ringing subsided, replaced by Calla's shrill scream. Ana was still gasping, hand on her chest, trying to stand.

Horrance shoved her down, then put a gun at her head and barked, "Don't move!"

As blindness faded and shapes returned, Ana saw Egan on the ground, his head melted into the floor.

Calla screamed and flung herself at Sutherland.

She stared helplessly as he backhanded the girl, sending her sprawling to the floor, hard enough that Ana heard the thud of Calla's skull.

The girl stopped moving.

Ana cried out between gasps, squirming as she tried to get the beast off of her. The bastard must have weighed 450 pounds.

Sutherland stood with his blaster aimed at Oswald, while shaking his head at Ana. "I want you to take a close look at what you've done, girl." He reached into his pants pocket and retrieved a comm. "Release the gas."

"Release it?" repeated a voice, sounding deeply unsure.

"You heard me."

Ana found her breath. "No!"

She couldn't look at Egan's corpse, so she stared at Calla, lying on the floor, eyes closed, probably dead.

Sutherland went and locked the door. "Once the herd is thinned, we can discuss making this our new home and continuing our research."

Oswald said nothing.

Ana could only cry at what she'd set into motion.

On the other side of the door, she heard the first screams.

FIFTY

Keller

KELLER AND KERN, both in full gray chem suits, approached the truck with blasters drawn.

Kern, a tall man with greased black hair and a body built by six hours in the body ring per day, looked back. "Open it?"

Keller nodded.

They opened the door and saw an infected young woman hunched over a dead man around her age, entrails and gore making a mess on the floor. The zombie looked up, guts dangling from its lips, looking as if she were trying to decide between pursuing the new feast or continuing with her current one.

The girl kept eating.

Kern quietly closed the van door. Best not to expend ammunition or make unnecessary noise.

Keller looked down at his arm band's screen: footage from one of two hunter orbs he called in to find Sutherland.

The orb floated over an entrance to something onscreen. A second later it showed a heat map with two men, in older Watcher chem suits, guarding the entrance. Another view showed a solid structure under snowy ground, what looked to be an old tunnel or network. Moments later, orbs identified the structure as a train station with several underground tunnels stretching for miles.

He pressed a button on the screen and ordered the second orb to join the first, but for both to stay out of view until his arrival.

Keller and Kern positioned themselves atop a hill four hundred yards south of the entrance.

While the two men at the tunnel were wearing the old City Watch gear, the orbs did not recognize either man's ID chips. These men must be part of Sutherland's terrorist "Patriot" group.

The orbs showed no other heat signatures at the entrance or nearby.

Keller pressed a button and ordered the orbs to fire, then watched as their blue blasts instantly snuffed the men to nothing.

"Come on." Keller raced toward the entrance, hoping the rest of their pursuit would go as smoothly.

FIFTY-ONE

Anastasia Lovecraft

ANA CRADLED Calla's head in her lap, watching the girl's pulsing neck, the only sign that she was still alive. Her head had pounded the floor. There was no blood, but Ana couldn't possibly gauge the internal damage.

Oswald sat beside her as Horrance stood in front of them, blaster rifle ready to fire. Sutherland was on his comm trying to reach someone.

Chaos ensued outside the room: screaming, gunshots, and blaster rifles. A few times someone tried to get inside their locked room — she didn't know if it was a sad soul seeking escape or the already damned trying to enter — only to eventually stop or die outside the door. Ana tried not to imagine the people she'd eaten breakfast with that morning now rendered to monsters, massacring one another if not shot down like dogs.

Five minutes in hell already felt like an hour.

"They're not answering," Sutherland said to Horrance. "I don't like this. They had one job — to guard the entrance. How do you fuck that up?"

Horrance shrugged. "I dunno, boss. Maybe they turned into zombies?"

"Are you stupid? We all took the antitoxin, which will keep us safe for a couple of days from the virus."

"Want me to check?"

"No. Stand here and watch them. I'll go." Sutherland slipped on his helmet, checked his blaster rifle, then the energy clips on his belt before looking down at Ana. "Obviously you don't want to go out there. But if you try and escape, Horrance *will* kill you."

Ana said nothing, her eyes on Calla.

"If they move, kill the little one first," Sutherland ordered.

"Yes, boss," Horrance said.

Sutherland left, firing shots into people on the door's other side.

Ana listened to Horrance's heavy breath for a few heaves and bellows before she opened her mouth. "You don't have to do this, you know."

He turned to her, his eyes curious. "Do what?"

"Any of this. You don't have to listen to Sutherland."

"Why *wouldn't* I listen to Sutherland?"

"Because he's not a good person, Horrance. Not like you. And me. *We're* good people, Horrance. Sutherland is bad. He likes to do bad things. Bad things make him happy. Do you understand?"

"Sir likes bad things because they make good things happen later. The end is very good."

"That's what he *says*, Horrance. But it isn't true. The bad makes him feel good, so he wants to keep it around. You can't let him continue. You can stop him. You're stronger than he is."

Horrance shook his head. "I don't like that. My job is doing what Sutherland says, so that's what I do." It looked like he wanted to say more, but didn't know the words, or how to make them come out in order. Then finally: "I do the right things. There is honor in following orders."

"Of course," Ana agreed. "But how do you know you're following the *right* orders?"

Oswald stepped in. "Letting them go is the right thing to do, Horrance. You know that inside. Let Ana take the girl, get the two of them to safety. *You* can do that."

"No." The giant shook his head, slowly.

Oswald continued. "You're not a bad guy, Horrance. We spent time together at Hydrangea. I know who you are. I helped you when you tore your calf in the forest. I was also there when you brought me the little girl in the red dress. Remember her?"

The memory's weight pushed the giant's eyes to the floor.

"*You* brought her to me, Horrance. When those men were drunk, *you* stood up for her. *You* were the one who brought all three of the men to me. You dragged them across the base and down three floors, beaten to pulp, with five broken limbs between them. I remember treating the men. I felt angry because you couldn't just kill them. They were bad guys, but you weren't allowed to do what should have been done. You were following orders. You remember what happened after that, right, Horrance?"

Horrance looked back up at the sound of his name.

"Her body was found mutilated a few days before she was going to testify against them. No one ever found her killers, but I think you and I know who was responsible for that. Don't we, Horrance?"

The giant nodded, slammed his fist into the opposite palm, and snarled, "Fuckers!"

Oswald stood and walked toward him.

The giant lurched forward, his whole body on full alert. "Stay back, sir!"

Oswald raised his hands. "I don't mean any harm, Horrance. I just want to talk."

Horrance looked uncertainly at him. Oswald held his hands higher, and somehow made his scarred robot face seem kind. "Do you ever wish you could do things over, Horrance? Has there ever been a time when someone else has had the last word, and you think of something you wished that you had said *back then*, when you were actually having the conversation? Do you ever wish you could do stuff over, and finally have the last word?"

Ana watched Oswald awaiting his response. The giant nodded and he smiled.

"Don't you wish you could go back and do the right thing with those men? Kill them before they had a chance to kill the girl?"

Horrance nodded again.

"But you couldn't. Because you were following orders. *Sutherland*'s orders. Trying to do the *right thing* even though your inner Horrance knew it was wrong. Now's your chance to do it right the first time. You want to do the right thing, don't you?"

Horrance nodded ... then surprised Ana. "But I can't. I have to follow my orders. That's the most right thing."

"No, Horrance. It isn't." Oswald turned from the giant to Ana. "Get up, Ana, and take Calla out of here now. Horrance is going to do the right thing."

"No!" Horrance was now furiously shaking his head. "Don't do that! You stay."

Oswald spoke calmly. "Leave this room, Ana. And take Calla with you. Horrance doesn't want to regret anything later. He wants to do it right the first time, now. Go."

Horrance looked confused, turning his eyes from the doctor to the girls, then at the door. "No!"

"Go, Ana." The doctor said it so calmly, Ana could only obey. She stood, trembling, hoping the giant wouldn't pound her, then gathered Calla into her arms.

She crossed the room and waited by the door, looking back at Oswald.

The doctor went to the table and picked up a blaster. He held it like it was hot, delicate and high. "I'm giving this to Ana so she doesn't get harmed. It's for outside this room, to protect herself. She'll die without any way to protect herself. You don't want that, Horrance. We want Ana to live. No regrets. No do-overs for later. Let's do the right thing now, the first time."

"No." Horrance was getting angry. Oswald might be pushing him too far.

"Come on, Horrance. You can do better than this. *You are* better than this. Ana is going to carry Calla out of here. You're going to let her because you're not the kind of man who is going to shoot two innocent girls. They never did anything to you, or anyone else. They are nice people who don't deserve to die. Especially because you were following orders that you don't want to take."

"Don't go," Horrance said.

Ana looked down at her, paralyzed by the fear of a wrong move claiming Calla's life like her father's.

"GO!" Oswald cried out.

Ana took the gun, nodded at Oswald, and turned to the door. She slapped her hand on the green button and carried Calla through the doorway, holding the blaster awkwardly, hoping she could aim and fire without dropping the girl.

On the other side of the door Horrance ordered them

to stop. His bark sounded like an energy blast would soon follow.

She froze. But Oswald kept talking.

"You don't want to shoot them. You're doing the right thing, Horrance. You don't want to regret anything later. You don't want to think about it every night. Nothing to keep you from sleeping, Horrance. You can come with us, if you want."

Just keep walking! Oswald is buying us time. Keep walking.

Ana's back was still to Horrance as she put one foot in front of the other, hoping that Oswald was right, and that he'd be following shortly.

"You can come with us," Oswald told him again.

Ana continued forward, looking down the corpse-riddled hall, strewn with dead men, women, and children. No guards, no lurking zombies, no stray fire behind her.

The coast was clear, but Ana didn't know where to go.

She needed Oswald.

"Thank you Horrance, for doing the right thing." Oswald sounded slightly closer.

She took another step.

"You should come with us," Oswald suggested again.

"Come back right now," Horrance pleaded, sounding on the verge of tears.

"No," Oswald said. "*You* can come with us, Horrance. You don't have to stay with Sutherland. You can be free. We'll make the cure. No regrets, Horrance."

"Come back …" His words were now barely a puff.

"Thank you," Oswald called, now right behind Ana.

She jostled Calla in her arms. The girl was starting to feel twice as heavy and three times as awkward.

Oswald was at her back. "Thanks for doing the right thing. You're a good man."

Ana thought she could feel Horrance's anger dying like wind.

But then blaster fire scraped frayed nerves and an otherwise silent tunnel. Ana turned to see Oswald standing behind her, a hole through his chest. His eye was open, startled, as he fell to the floor.

Ana looked past Oswald's empty space, and into Horrance's horrified eyes.

He looked down at the gun as if it had fired on its own, then back at Ana, eyes big and sad, face knotted in confusion.

She tightened her grip on Calla, then turned and ran.

"Come back!" Horrance called behind them, louder each of the three times.

The first blast didn't leave his gun until after she had cleared the hallway.

Ana raced until she found the secret panel which led to the stairwell leading to the room where she had hidden with Oswald, Calla, and Elijah before hell descended.

She hoped Elijah was still inside and hadn't locked her out.

The door opened as she touched the panel to its right. She entered and pressed the red lock button on the inside panel. She turned to find Elijah on the floor, fetal and shaking.

Her heart fell like a stone. "Elijah?"

He looked up with two marbles on fire, face caked with early-forming scabs, saliva drooling from his mouth at the corners. Then he leapt at Ana, almost hissing. She had forgotten that the boy wasn't immune.

She cried out, turning herself around and dropping on top of Calla as a barrier between her and Elijah. The gun clanged to the floor.

He rolled right off her back and fell to the floor.

Ana gently laid Calla down as out of the corner of her eyes she saw Elijah spring up.

The gun was three feet away, Elijah five feet past that.

Whatever human part of him which had yet to surrender to the monster, must have recognized Ana's intent for the blaster. He ran toward her.

Without time to think, she dug her foot into the floor and propelled herself at the zombie. Her body fell back on instincts honed from survival. Seconds from impact with the boy and his wide-open mouth, she raised her hands, grabbed his shoulders, and used his weight against him, spinning the almost-zombie aside as she fell atop the blaster.

Ana grabbed it.

He lunged at her.

She raised the gun and fired, hitting Elijah's gut and slicing it in two.

His torso sailed past Ana, legs falling in a bloody tangled heap.

Ana fell back against the floor, sighing in relief.

Elijah's head and arms twitched, blood gushing from its severed trunk, the hot stench of putrid guts souring the room.

Her stomach spilled onto the floor. She cried out as the vomit left her body.

She turned and crawled over to Calla, pulled the girl's body to her chest, then held her while sobbing.

Sutherland's voice came over the intercom. "Come out, come out, wherever you are."

FIFTY-TWO

Keller

KELLER AND KERN stood frozen at the end of the hallway staring at a massacre of ripped bodies, corpses melted by blaster fire, blood and guts painting walls. Keller fought hard to control the vomit climbing his throat.

Infected men, women, and children maimed, but not yet dead, stared up at them, attempting to reach out for a meal or help.

"My God," Kern said, a rare moment of shock registering through the hardened soldier's shell.

Keller flashed back to carnage from the bombing that had killed his eight-year-old son, Joshua, along with sixteen others at the parade, detonated by Underground cowards. He remembered staring down at his son's dead open eyes after shrapnel had ripped through his skull. No matter how hard Keller stared and swore that his son was alive, he couldn't change the truth that Joshua was never staring back.

He had done more than his fair share of despicable things in service to the State, but Keller had never slaughtered innocents, or women and children.

Sutherland was the worst kind of coward, and had to be stopped.

Keller considered putting these poor people out of their misery, but couldn't waste time, or ammunition, not yet knowing what might be waiting in the station's bowels.

A second hunter orb entered the hallway, and Keller instructed it to go forward and find Sutherland while the first held guard behind them.

The machine floated into the hallway and started to shoot. Keller had instructed it to open fire upon infected, zombies, and any attackers. He hoped that any Station survivors didn't mistake orbs for enemies and mistakenly shoot at it.

Keller and Kern trailed carnage behind the orb. They stepped into a brightly colored area, and more half-disintegrated bodies, but no sign of Sutherland or his men.

A voice crackled throughout the room, from unseen speakers. "Come out, come out, wherever you are."

"This fucker is taunting us?" Kern looked at Sutherland, incredulously. "Let's go——"

An explosion rocked the hallway behind them.

Keller spun to see their guard orb fall to the floor, now a chunk of molten metal. A large man in stolen Watcher gear stood holding a hefty Spinner 1220, the massive coils spinning in bright red as the gun charged, readying forty rapid burst blasts to send their way. The man's eyes were wild behind his helmet's clear glass, his grin manic. In kill mode, eager to add bodies to the count.

Both Kern and Keller fired their blaster rifles as the man unleashed his weapon's fury.

Kern vanished in a cloud of ash as Sutherland's man turned the Spinner toward Keller.

Keller kept firing. His first two shots had missed. Another meant death.

His third and fourth hit blasted the man in the chest and sent him back. He fell and his Spinner fired wildly into walls, the ceiling, and very nearly Keller, who dove to the floor. The Spinner stopped and its red lights faded.

Keller looked over at Kern's remainders scattered in ashes across the charred floor — a man reduced to nothing in a flash.

No time for mourning. Nor would a solider like Kern care for the waste. He would be given a hero's funeral, even if he couldn't tell the man's family, or anyone in City 1, how he died — or have a body to show for it. That's what happened in an unsanctioned battle hunting a terrorist that the State refused to acknowledge.

Keller got up and grabbed the heavy gun. Seconds later, the remaining orb whizzed back into the hallway, eager to show him something. City Watcher Reynolds was onscreen back at City 6 — one of the few people Keller trusted with this off-book mission.

"Sir, there's something you need to know."

"What is it?"

"The orb has picked up a reading nearby."

"What?" Keller wished Reynolds would get to the point before another of Sutherland's men sneaked up on him. If they were all packing Spinners, he wouldn't be so lucky a second time.

"The orb is picking up signs of Ana Lovecraft."

"Where?" Keller asked, heart racing.

The map showed her one level down. It revealed a thermal video of a girl lit red, pacing. Two shapes were on the floor, also red. Actually, three — one looked like a person torn in half. *Did she kill them?*

Keller couldn't be certain it was Ana pacing, but couldn't imagine the girl had found someone to remove her ID chip. "Why is she here?"

"I have no idea, sir. I thought she was dead." Reynolds wasn't among the few who knew of the network's duplicity: faking Ana and Liam's deaths at instruction of the State.

"No. She's very much alive. Are you getting a reading for Liam Harrow or anyone else from City 6?"

"No, sir."

Keller stared at the short video of Ana's frame stalking back and forth. "Is she infected?"

"It's hard to tell. Her movements aren't erratic. But she may not be showing any signs yet."

Or she's immune? Keller wondered.

"What do you want to do, sir?"

"Keep it to yourself for now." Keller then told the orb to follow him as he headed down the hall holding the Spinner with both hands, eager to unleash its lethal blast on Sutherland.

Ana would have to wait.

FIFTY-THREE

Anastasia Lovecraft

ANA PACED while waiting for Sutherland's voice to come back and taunt her.

She looked down at Calla, still on the floor, motionless, but breathing. She couldn't allow that bastard to hurt her.

He'd killed Egan. Was responsible for Oswald's death. He was also to blame for her father's, even if it was Keller who had murdered him in front of the world. It was all she could do not to charge out the door, find the bastard, and take him out herself. But there was no one left to protect Calla.

And there was no way Ana could leave the girl lying on the floor, even if the room was hidden. Someone would find her, either Sutherland's thugs or one of the infected.

Or, if Ana died, nobody would find Calla, and she'd never wake up.

Don't think like that.

She's going to live!

Perhaps not so strangely, her almost maternal instincts toward Calla made her think of her other 'family,' and Ana wondered how Liam and Katrina were doing. Had they found Adam? Or had they been found and slaughtered instead?

So much death in the past two years. First her mother, then nearly everyone she came into contact with. It was so hard to believe that not that long ago her greatest concern was taking another aptitude test so she could finally stop sewing buttons. Ana had loved her family, but took them for granted, assuming they'd always be there.

She used to chase Adam around the house tickling him until he was screaming for help. Then Mom would come and tickle her, and Father would come and tickle Mom, until they were all in a pile, laughing, red-faced and out of breath on the floor.

That was all gone.

And she couldn't continue alone.

Ana was a fugitive from her State, no City would have her. She was enemies with Sutherland, and who knew how far that animosity stretched in the Barrens? How many camps would consider her an enemy?

She could maybe return to Paradise, but she'd been kicked out right after her bite. She was a girl without a home, friends, or family. Alone in hell.

Stop it! You don't know that Adam's dead. He, Liam, and Katrina could come back at any minute. Stop it!

Would Father do this? Or would he suck it up and do what had to be done?

She sank to the floor, putting Calla's head in her lap, running hands through the girl's hair to hopefully coax her awake, and give Ana something to believe in.

Startled by a knock on the door, she reached for her blaster, slipping a finger through its trigger while still holding Calla's head in her lap.

A man's voice spoke, "Ana, open up."

She set Calla's head gently on the ground, and stood,

gripping her blaster with both hands, aiming at the door, not saying a word.

It didn't sound like Sutherland, but it also didn't sound like anyone she knew. But Ana also couldn't think of who knew she might be in here. It didn't sound like Oswald, even if he were somehow alive. *Maybe Father Truth?*

"Ana, I'm here to help." The voice returned, slightly altered through a speaker, likely a chem suit helmet. It was familiar but not enough to place it — too deep for Sutherland, though it could've been one of his men trying to coax her out.

She stood her ground, silent.

"Stand back, Ana, I'm going to open this door. Don't shoot, or you will be killed. Along with your friend."

That voice, so familiar …

Ana backed against the wall, and crept toward the corner, standing at an angle from the entrance. She crouched low, assuming that whoever came in would be looking straight ahead and shooting high.

She might have the advantage. She trained her gun on the door, hands shaking. If she screwed this up, she and Calla would pay.

"I'm coming in, Ana. Three … two … one."

The door clicked — she wasn't sure how the man was able to unlock it from outside — and slid open.

Ana aimed the blaster, ready, hoping she wasn't about to fire on a friend.

A hunter orb hovered into the room, cannon glowing blue, a voice commanding from the speaker, "Put the gun down or you will die."

She'd seen at least two orbs since her arrival, plus the one Elijah had taken when he and his crew saved her, Liam, and Katrina. Its screen was dark as it hovered before her. She could fire, and maybe hit it, but not before the thing killed her. Hunter orbs in close quarters were hard to take advantage of, and Ana didn't know if it was friend or foe.

That same voice from outside the door. "Listen to the orb, Ana."

"Okay." She put her gun down.

"The room is clear," reported the orb.

The man who murdered her father entered the room, and Ana immediately regretted lowering her weapon.

FIFTY-FOUR

Sutherland

Sutherland couldn't believe his peoples' careless stupidity.

The men at the front entrance weren't responding. Nor were any others, except Michaels, who was sweeping the level, searching for Ana and the girl, taking out infected as he went.

Where the fuck is everyone?

Then there was Horrance. The idiot had somehow lost Ana, *and* killed the only person Sutherland could count on to finish the cure. Horrance was a special kind of idiot, the kind that came along only once in a generation, whose mom had been too stupid to drown him in the river.

He glared at the man as he paced, waiting for Ana.

Horrance said, "I don't think she's coming."

"No, really? You don't fucking say!" Sutherland shouted at the ogre, wanting to cleave the head from his moronic shoulders.

As Horrance turned away, looking like he might cry, Sutherland reminded himself to breathe deep, in and out, and relax a little. He couldn't afford to kill Horrance. Nor could he forget that Horrance, as useless and stupid as he was, had helped him escape from Hydrangea when all was lost.

He breathed in, counting to five, then out, again counting to five, wishing he'd had some Crash. Sweet chemical relief. It would be a while before he could indulge.

Sutherland had to function at his peak level, find Ana, then clean these corpses from the Station.

Maybe give the place some fresh paint. Something whimsical, like yellow and pink.

He turned to Horrance, smiling slow and wide with his newest idea.

"What is it, boss?"

"We'll drive her out if she won't come to us."

FIFTY-FIVE

Anastasia Lovecraft

KELLER WAS in a full chemical suit, but Ana would recognize the ugly bastard's crow nose anywhere, she thought as the black glass on his helmet rose to reveal a clearer glass beneath it.

She reached for the blaster.

The orb fired, and melted the weapon. Ana's hand stopped inches from a gooey stew of metal and plastic.

She pulled back.

"Stay put or I will put you down."

Keller aimed the largest gun that Ana had ever seen. There was a circular glass-looking tube winding around the stock with swirling red lights spinning through it.

"You bastard," she scowled. "I'm going to kill you."

"I'm trying to save you, child."

"I don't need your saving. Leave!"

"What about the girl?" Keller looked down at Calla. "I know you hate me right now, and I have plenty to explain, but we must get you both out of here."

Ana swallowed, looking down at Calla.

"How is it that neither of you are infected?" Keller asked.

The truth might jeopardize their freedom, so Ana lied. "We tested immune."

"Both of you? How is that?"

"I don't know." Ana turned back to Keller. "What are you doing here? Why should I trust you?"

"I came to capture Sutherland. He was behind the City 1 attack."

"So, my father was innocent?" Ana spit out.

"Your father was hardly innocent. But I'm not here to argue his guilt. As I said, we have much to discuss. Believe me, Ana, I am not your enemy."

Sutherland's voice came over the intercom. "Attention residents of this godforsaken hellhole. I've decided that I no longer want your precious train station after all. Blood is so hard to scrub from the walls. So I'll be leaving, but I should warn you that my men have set bombs around the station's perimeter, and those bombs will detonate in ten minutes. If you want to live — I'm talking to you, Ana and Calla — if you wish for amnesty, then all will be forgiven. You can come with me. But hurry, the clock *is* ticking. Quite literally. Meet me outside the Station and we'll put all this nastiness behind us."

Then, following a long pause: "Or you can stay here and die. Your choice, but I'm tired of playing nice. Good day, Ana."

"Does he really have bombs?"

Keller's voice was more nervous than Ana had ever heard it. She wondered what he'd gone through in getting this far into the Station.

"I have no idea," Ana answered. "Do you think he's lying? Do you think it's a trap?"

"Almost certainly. But we can't take the chance he's

lying about the bombs. He had a weaponized virus, so he can clearly take this place down."

"What are we going to do?" Ana hated the *we* that didn't belong, and herself for slipping it into the sentence. She was not on Keller's side. But, at the same time, she had to figure the best play for her hand. Just as her father would advise.

He turned to the orb and its now onscreen Watcher. "How long would it take for more orbs to back us up?"

"Twenty minutes, sir. Maybe more. That would include the risk of someone at City Watch discovering the request. Would you like me to order more, sir?"

Keller shook his head. "We don't have time. We'll play this by hand." He looked at Ana. "You two coming with me?"

"I'll have to carry her," Ana said. "She hit her head."

"Okay, then you stay behind me. The orb will take the lead. Here ..." Keller reached down and stripped a blaster pistol from his belt.

As her hand closed around the gun's handle, Keller pulled it back until she met his eyes. "Don't shoot me in the back. The orb will kill you both. Understood?"

"Yes." Ana yanked the pistol away. He smiled ruefully. "You can always try to kill me after we get out of here alive."

"You better have a good plan," she said, ignoring his efforts at ... whatever he was trying to do. She knelt down and gathered Calla in both hands.

"I'm sure it's better than hiding in here and waiting to die." Then Keller ordered his pet orb into the hallway.

They followed one corridor after another. Their route didn't seem familiar, but Ana felt too defeated to map it. She stepped over bodies, horrified. A small girl, Ana thought her name was Lora, had shared her mom's home-made cookie with Ana yesterday. Now she was staring up at Ana with eyes that couldn't blink. Her throat was gouged, eaten or torn from the rest of her.

My fault. Ana swallowed and longed for it all to be over, following the orb and telling herself with every step that soon enough she wouldn't be forced to ever make another awful decision. She tried to think ahead, to what Keller would do with her and Calla once they got free, but she couldn't fall into that trap of wishful thinking.

There were enough possible traps ahead.

One step at a time, until they were clear of this terror.

After several turns through many halls, she finally realized where they were — just outside the exit tunnel. However, there was a fire at the entrance. Black smoke clouded her eyes, stinging as it rolled toward them. Ana wondered if the fire had been set intentionally, or was a bloom from the stem of chaos.

She wanted to stop and turn around. She called out for Keller, but he kept moving forward, into the smoke. She had no choice but to follow him into the darkness. Sudden rain from the sprinklers did little to smother the smoke.

She coughed, struggling to both hold Calla and navigate the darkness. The heat was intense, covering her face and body with a second skin of sweat, blending with the water. She blinked, trying to peer through a haze too thick to see through.

Calla started coughing and slipped from Ana's wet hands.

Ana stopped, grabbed her body in the dark, and lifted the girl again, choking on smoke as she picked Calla up.

She was lost in the inky darkness, blind, not sure which way to go. Ana tried to cry out for Keller, but could only cough. She turned, trying to decipher direction, but everything was black.

Keller stepped in front of Ana, his lights on her and Calla. "I have a thermal view in my helmet." She was struck by the ever-increasing softness in his voice. Almost kind. "Stay close and I'll get us through."

Keller charged deeper into the wall of smoke. Ana carried Calla, stumbling after him.

Calla began to choke again, the smoke likely burning her lungs as they burned Ana's.

"It's okay," she whispered to Calla.

Ana looked up, blinking into the smoke. She saw daylight ahead, clean like a promise. The sight gave her strength. She tightened her grip around Calla and rushed forward, passing Keller, hope fueling her flight to fresh air.

"Come back!" Keller called behind her. "Be careful!"

Calla was heavy in her arms, but Ana couldn't bring herself to care. Keller wasn't shouting, or shooting as he fell farther behind.

She fled the tunnel, into the daylight, and fell with Calla in the snow, both of them breathing in deep gasps of air and coughing the smoke from their lungs.

The joy was short-lived. The hunter orb raced past her and Calla and fired into the woods.

Someone fired back, a blast of energy tearing through a tree to Ana's left.

She glanced up and saw more shots coming.

Keller put himself between Ana and the gunmen in the woods, and opened fire with the giant gun. "Stay down!"

Snow and rock kicked up around Ana as she lay on top of Calla, pressing the girl into the snow, hoping to make a low-and-flat, barely-there target.

Keller blasted the tree line, screaming as if it somehow helped scare the men away.

The gun was deafening, but Ana could still hear Calla's

bellow in her ears, crying loudly for her father, and trying to push Ana off of her.

"Daddy! Where are you?"

Ana hugged her tight, keeping them both on the ground.

Keller ceased fire long enough to investigate the perimeter. "Wait here. I'm going to make sure it's safe."

Ana's ears were ringing as she turned, still on the ground, and watched her father's killer walk into the woods, the hunter orb just ahead of him, firing off shots at either Sutherland's troops or zombies.

The ringing began to fade in Ana's ears. She was about to get up and off of Calla when she felt a blade at her throat.

Her hand tightened on her blaster, then the blade pressed into her skin and softened her grip.

Someone pulled the blaster from her hands, then yanked her to standing, peeling her from Calla.

She turned to see Sutherland.

Calla cried out.

"Shut up or I'll kill her!"

Calla looked up at Sutherland, terrified, then toward the tree line, searching for a Keller who was no longer there, gone along with the orb.

Ana wondered if Sutherland was fast enough to have ended both the orb and Keller before she could notice.

"Now, now, little Calla," said Sutherland in a syrupy voice. "There's nothing to be afraid of. If I wanted you dead, you'd already be dead. But look, you're both still alive! Now, I'm going to remove this knife from Ana's neck and you are both going to follow me. Do you understand? Nod if you do, Ana."

She nodded, the knife still sharp and cold against her throat.

"Calla? Do you understand?"

The girl was clearly frightened, and could barely look back at Ana. Ana gave her a small nod, and Calla nodded in return.

"Good." Sutherland removed the knife, then trained his blaster on Ana. "Now let's go. You lead the way, Ana, so I can keep an eye on you."

"Where are we going?" she asked as they marched forward, in the opposite direction that Keller had gone.

"To find my truck, so we can get the hell out of here."

They walked for a few minutes, the cold wind picking up and bringing snow with it. Ana shivered in her soaking clothes. If Sutherland didn't kill her, hypothermia might.

"What happened to my father?" Calla asked, confused, walking in between their captor and Ana.

Sutherland stopped clomping. He looked at the girls, brushed snow from his jacket, then focused on Calla. "I'm very sorry, dear, but your father won't be coming with us. Unfortunately, he's dead. Now, this wasn't my fault. Your father was an enemy, and made the silly mistake of staying in my way. Nothing personal."

Calla clearly disagreed. Something broke inside her.

She rushed Sutherland, blindly flailing on her way to attack. Ana watched in slow motion as the girl pinwheeled toward him. He made a fist, reeled back, and punched Calla hard in the face.

Calla cried out. Ana wasn't sure if she imagined the sound of something snapping before seeing the very real fountain of blood spraying from the girl's broken nose.

Calla dropped to the ground. Sutherland arrogantly turned his back to Ana, kneeling over the girl. Ana was through with hesitating today.

She charged toward his back.

Sutherland, as if awaiting her stupidity, turned toward Ana before she could reach him, sword drawn.

He swung his blade in a wide arc that cut the air in front of Ana, forcing her to hurl herself backward.

She slipped and fell forward as Sutherland took another swipe.

He stabbed through her leg. She screamed, and fell to the ground, soaking wet and freezing, blood spilling from a leg on fire. Sutherland stood over her, holding his sword as if deciding whether to end Ana.

She heard something like a dog growling and looked over to see Calla. She gritted her teeth, shook her head, and rushed Sutherland a second time. She launched her body, landed on his back, grabbed on, and used her weight to knock him down to the ground.

His sword fell just a couple of feet from Ana.

Calla punched Sutherland in the back of the head furiously, getting in as many hits as she could before he screamed out, loud enough to rattle her core.

Seconds later, he shook Calla off of him, grabbed and threw her nearly four feet ahead of him, where she landed in a gasp.

Sutherland walked over to Ana, balling his fists as she tried crawling away. He dropped on top of her, straddling Ana, and punched her twice in the stomach.

She cried out, trying to stand, but her leg betrayed her and she fell to the ground.

Sutherland turned back, to make sure she wasn't a threat, then laughed at her helplessness, wrapping his hands around Calla's throat to choke her.

"Look what you did, Ana! Just LOOK what you've made me do!"

She slithered toward his sword, but the pain was intense, and moving her leg made it feel like the limb was exploding. Her heart hammered in her frozen chest as she kept pulling herself forward, knowing she'd never reach Calla before Sutherland murdered her.

"You coward!"

Sutherland kept choking the girl, ignoring her taunts.

"You fucking coward, you're really gonna kill a child?"

Sutherland ignored her, laughing as he leaned closer to Calla, perhaps to better look into her eyes and whisper something terrible while snuffing her life.

Ana reached out, despite the pain, fingers clawing cold, wet snow, searching for purchase to pull herself forward.

But the sword, like Calla, felt a million miles away.

Ana could do nothing to save her.

Calla was going to die.

And so was she.

Ana heard the footfalls of someone running up from behind. Probably zombies.

But when she looked back, it wasn't the shuffling undead. Instead, it was a tiny shape racing toward them. It took a moment before Ana registered the figure as Father Truth.

The dwarf grabbed the blade — almost as tall as him — and yelled out an incoherent scream of syllables, still racing forward, barely slowing as he picked up the sword.

Sutherland had exactly enough time to turn and see the dwarf before a swinging blade cleaved the head from his body.

FIFTY-SIX

Calla Egan

CALLA GASPED for air and kicked the headless corpse from her body.

It fell back, neck spurting hot blood into the snow as Calla scrambled toward Ana, lying still, eyes closed, with her arms outstretched.

"Ana!" Calla's scream was drowned by the howling wind and brewing storm.

Father Truth dropped to the snow beside Ana. He ripped the blood-drenched pants along her left calf and looked at the wound.

He said to Calla, "She's lost a lot of blood. Put pressure on the cut. Keep holding it, even if she wakes and screams."

Calla looked at the wound, blood gushing, and turned away before pressing her hand down, afraid she would wake Ana or hurt her even worse.

Branches snapped in the surrounding woods as the storm grew violent. Calla's heart beat harder. She'd seen enough blizzards to know that they needed to get inside quickly, before they were blinded and unable to find the Station.

Father Truth ripped off his shirt, tore long strips from the bottom, and made Ana a makeshift tourniquet.

"Keep pressure on it." He reached under her leg with a length of cloth, then folded a second strip and handed it to Calla. "Put this on her wound, press down."

Calla saw movement from the corner of her eyes and looked up to see dark shapes approaching. As the wind dimmed and flurries whirled softer, she recognized them, Trina and Harris, a couple who'd come to the Station last year.

At first, Calla was happy to see them. More help. Then her stomach ate itself as she realized they were no longer Harris and Trina.

She turned to warn Father Truth, but snow swept in faster and she saw several more dark shapes moving within the white — zombies spilling out from the woods, about to converge on her, Father Truth, and Ana.

"Father! Look!"

He glanced up, then back down. "We have to stop her bleeding first!"

Moaning grew louder, just audible over the screaming wind, as if the zombies' anticipation swelled with their approach.

Her heart pounded. The world blurred as Calla tried to focus on Ana's leg rather than the approaching zombies. She kept her eyes on her hands holding the cloth, not daring to look up at the undead on their way. She'd lose her will and let go, then Ana could die.

Moaning grew louder. Something moved from somewhere behind her. The wind picked up and brought more blinding snow, chilling her wet body to the marrow.

A tree crashed somewhere in the storm.

Father Truth spoke fast. "Almost there …"

He tied the tourniquet loosely above Ana's wound, then he reached back and grabbed another strip of cloth. He quickly folded it and brushed Calla's hands away, and laid it over the first cloth. He slid down the tourniquet and tightened it.

The zombies closed in, arms reaching for them.

Father Truth scrambled, reaching for his sword as a zombie behind Calla grabbed her.

She squirmed free, and fell back.

The zombie, a tall, spindly dark man with white eyes, clawed at Calla's leg and grabbed hold of her ankle. He dropped down, mouth wide open, ready to bite.

Calla screamed as she spun, kicking the zombie hard in the jaw. It fell back, but got up too quickly.

Calla was the only thing standing between him and Ana. She didn't dare turn to see how Father Truth was faring. She could hear him grunting and the sound of metal slicing limbs, but she might lose hope herself if she saw him conquered.

Calla glanced back to search for Sutherland's blaster, but the snow was too thick to see it, or anything.

The zombie threw itself at her.

She dropped to the ground and it flew past her, landing on top of Ana.

Calla yelled, launching herself at the zombie, and pulled it off of Ana.

They rolled down the hill several times until they came to a hard stop as her back slammed into a tree.

The zombie was on all fours, practically growling just a few feet in front of her.

Beyond it, through thick swirling blankets of snow, she saw Father Truth surrounded, barely fending off another three zombies. Beyond that, two more — Harris and Trina, no less — approaching Ana.

Calla cried out, trying to draw their attention.

Father Truth turned instead, perhaps thinking Calla was hurt.

One of the zombies jumped him.

No! Calla stared helplessly, wanting to intervene, but could do nothing as the closest zombie barreled toward her.

She pivoted, trying to dodge and send it straight into the tree, but her foot slipped on the wet snow and she went down face first onto the ground.

The zombie was on her back.

Calla then heard the most welcome sound of her life: *a hunter orb firing its cannon.*

The zombies on top of Father Truth fell away. A second shot from the orb hit those closest to him.

Calla managed to squirm free, but just as quickly as she slipped, the monster pulled her back.

She flailed, squirmed, and tried to kick it away. But all she managed to do was land on her back. The zombie pounced on her, mouth open, hissing.

She threw her hands up, pressing them hard against its wet flesh, pushing back against its forehead and neck, trying to keep it from winning inches. She stared up into the zombie's white eyes, and its chomping, rotting mouth as it came closer.

From the corner of her eyes, Calla saw the orb firing blue blasts into the zombies closest to Ana.

She realized with horror that the orb didn't see her. She'd rolled too far away. Calla cried out, trying to keep the zombie's face away from hers. It was rotting flesh and muscles, and stronger than it had any right to be.

Her fingers were slipping on its wet skin.

Its mouth was getting closer.

Its weight was too much for her to push off.

Please! Someone see me!

Suddenly, movement behind the tree. Another zombie, a fat giant the size of Sutherland's large man, lurched forward, just five feet away.

One zombie would pin her down. The other would eat her. There was nothing she could do.

Calla cried out again as the second zombie dropped to the ground, inches away, scooting its mouth toward her stomach, pulling her shirt up, its black teeth opening and closing as she was pinned beneath the first zombie.

She squirmed, trying to move, but the zombie on top of her was too heavy. She continued, grunting under the pressure as she tried to move away.

But she couldn't even make it an inch as her arms were about to give way above her. It was as if the two zombies were competing to see who would get the first bite of her flesh. She looked down just as the second zombie opened its mouth, teeth inching toward her belly.

Another blast — this one red — obliterated the fat zombie's lower half, then a blade sliced through the first zombie's head and a man wearing a full black chemical suit yanked the zombie away and kicked in its skull.

He turned, firing on more approaching zombies, as Calla sat stunned. She wanted to thank him, but could only suck in air, thankful to be in one piece.

The man held out a gloved hand and helped her off the ground.

"Come on," he said, walking toward Ana and Father Truth.

Father Truth was struggling to gather Ana as he called out to the man in the suit. "Can you help me get her inside the Station?"

"Yes." The man bent to scoop Ana from the snow.

"Are you sure you want to go back in there? They unleashed a virus."

"There's a second part of the Station, walled off and running on a different system than the first. I'll show you the way until we can clear out the main station."

"So you all were prepared for this?" the man asked.

"Not quite, considering how many we lost. Who are you?" Father Truth looked up at him. "City Watch?"

"In a fashion." The man smiled. "The name is Keller. Provisional Leader of the State."

FIFTY-SEVEN

Anastasia Lovecraft

ANA WOKE UP FEELING BLURRY. The world agreed.

"Don't move too fast."

The man's voice was unfamiliar, beside her bed. Well, not completely unfamiliar. There was something about it ...

He came into focus. She couldn't believe her eyes.

"Adam?"

Her brother smiled and gave her a timid nod. "Yeah ..."

Tears burst from Ana's eyes as she ignored his advice, and bolted up, throwing her arms around him and pulling Adam into an embrace.

She pulled away, looking him over. He looked so much different than she remembered. Leaner. No baby fat. Scruffy hair and a light stubble.

Her baby brother looked like a man.

"Oh my God, you're okay!"

Tears continued to pour forth, then she realized two things at once. They were still in the Station, even though the last thing she remembered was fleeing the place as it was being overrun with the infected.

"Where's Liam?" She felt suddenly certain he was dead.

"I need to tell you something," Adam said.

"No." Her chin quivered as bad news darkened Adam's eyes. "No, no, no."

The door behind him slid open. Most of Liam appeared in the doorway, wearing pants and no shirt. His left arm was missing, the nub bandaged in thick white. She tried to stand, but pain shot through her leg and shoved her back down to the bed.

"You were stabbed in the leg," Adam said. "Stay put."

Liam came to her, tears in his eyes as he smiled. "I told you we'd get your brother back."

"You better never leave me again!" She reached around Liam, careful not to brush against his bandaged stump, and embraced him. "Are you okay? What happened?"

"Father Truth says I'll be okay, barring infection or anything else."

Ana pulled Liam and her brother into hugs, not wanting to let either man go — ever again.

The door opened again, this time bringing Katrina, joined by Calla, Father Truth, and a small girl that looked familiar, but Ana couldn't remember where she'd seen her.

"Ana!" Calla called, running over and jumping onto the bed, hugging her.

As Ana held her tight, she looked up at Katrina. She could've sworn the tough woman's eyes were welling up.

"Thank you," Ana said. "For keeping Liam from losing more of himself."

"It wasn't easy, and you owe me ... but you're welcome."

The familiar-looking girl stared oddly at Ana.

"Who is she?" Ana whispered to Adam.

"It's Zelle, our old neighbor."

"Oh …" Ana said, slowly remembering. "How did you wind up here?"

"Your brother found me. Then he saved me, with Katrina and Liam, after my father died. He turned after he was bitten."

"I'm sorry." Ana tried to smile.

"There's something else you need to know," Katrina said.

"What's that?" Ana asked.

"Zelle will tell you."

Ana looked at the girl. "Okay."

"There's a safe place we can go where the State can't find us. My dad called it Eden, but most people call it the Gardens."

Ana looked around, confused. "Where are the Gardens? Are we leaving here, then?"

Father Truth said, "The State will be coming here. No way to avoid it with everything that went down."

Ana remembered something from before she'd passed out — Keller.

She looked at her brother, wondering how to break the news that the killer was here.

As if on cue, the door opened. Keller stepped into the room. Her heart raced, certain that Adam would strangle him. Instead her brother looked over as if Keller were another well-wisher.

"Hello, Miss Lovecraft." Keller was wearing his uniform, but not the chemical suit or mask he'd had on when she'd last seen him.

"He saved us, all of us." Calla squeezed her hand.

"Why?" Ana asked, refusing to believe that he'd suddenly turned over a new leaf.

Men like Keller didn't change — not for the better. They got worse. Entrenched in corruption, enslaved to the system, forever invested in clinging to power, no matter what they had to do to maintain the status quo. Everything she'd seen from such men — Oli, Sutherland ... even Egan, in his own way — had been trapped into the roles they had created for themselves. To believe that Keller was any different ...

"I owe your father an apology," Keller said. "I owe you all an apology."

Ana tried not to cry at the thought of her parents' deaths, and Keller's involvement.

"I was lied to by the people I serve. And only recently have I seen what that meant."

"But you killed my father, on stage, in front of the world. He did it in front of you, Adam!" She turned to her brother, pissed that he wasn't grabbing a gun and shooting their father's killer in the face. But her brother only looked back at her, something — *sympathy?* — in his eyes.

"I can't begin to ask you to understand, change the past, or bring your family back. Your father was a good man. But the State doesn't reward men like your father, it rewards and promotes men like me — men who are so allegiant to the lie that they become blind to the truth."

Adam looked at Ana. "Keller sent someone into the Outback to get Zelle, so the State could find the Gardens and get people they're looking for."

"But I'm pretending I never saw you, instead. Go to the Gardens. I'll tell the Elders they're only a lie. I'll say that this station was home to the traitors. They're dead now, thanks to the Patriot scum, Sutherland, or rather Dennis Weaver."

"You're letting us go?" Ana asked in disbelief. "All of us?"

"Yes," Keller said. "Once Father Truth here says you're ready, you can take whatever you need and go find the lives you deserve."

"Why are you doing this? And how do we know you won't change your mind and come looking for us later?"

"I want to fight *my* enemies, not the State's. I'm not saying the Underground, or these so-called Patriots, have it right. They're terrorists … well, a lot of them are. You can't change the world by bombing innocents and attacking Cities. You can only make it worse. Things must change from within. I'll find others who are also tired of fighting, who can help me change the leadership, find something in between what we have and the anarchy craved by the Underground. Something closer to the Old Nation's foundation."

Ana stared at Keller, trying to reconcile the man she'd come to hate — the man who'd shoved her family into the Games, and murdered her father in front of an audience — with the man speaking now.

Could he possibly be telling the truth? Am I the only one who thinks he's lying?

She couldn't just sit here and listen to this. "Is anyone else buying this? Am I the only one who isn't ready to forgive this bastard for what he did to our father?"

Her brother said, "Nobody wanted to kill Keller more than me. But he *did* save us. And he got me out of the Games. From what these people have said, he saved you, too. We could kill him, but it won't bring Father back. Or change the world. And the State would never stop searching for us. And he'd never have a chance to atone for his sins."

"No one understands what you're feeling more than I

do, Ana," Keller told her. "The Underground bombed a parade and killed my son. It's hard to see you all as anything but monsters. But yesterday and tomorrow aren't the same thing."

Keller offered his hand.

Ana looked from Adam to Liam, into Calla's eyes, then finally Zelle's.

Adam was right. If they killed Keller, this would never end and their future would be worthless.

Yet, she couldn't forget all that Keller had done. As she stared at his hand, she remembered that very hand taking her father's life. It was all she could do not to rip his arm off and beat him to death with it.

Yet, she thought of all the people she'd had to kill, both in the Games, and as they fought to survive the Barrens. Most deserved it, but not all. How many people were the "good guys" in their own stories, and she the villain?

Still, she couldn't bring herself to shake his hand. Not now. Perhaps not ever.

She met Keller's eyes and shook her head. "I can't forgive you. I'd like to believe you, and maybe you are working toward some kind of atonement. I'll do whatever the majority wants, and accept your help in getting us out of here, but you can't expect me to just forgive and forget."

Keller lowered his hand and nodded. "Perhaps someday."

"Perhaps," Ana said.

THE END

A Quick Favor

Thank you for reading *Z2136*.

If you enjoyed this book would you please consider writing a review of it on your favorite bookselling site so other readers might enjoy it too. Just a couple of sentences. That would mean a lot to me.

Thank you!

Sean and Dave

Sean Platt is an entrepreneur and founder of Sterling & Stone, where he makes stories with his partners, Johnny B. Truant, and David W. Wright, and a family of storytellers.

Sean is the bestselling author of over 10 million words' worth of books, including the Yesterday's Gone and Invasion series. Sean is also co-author of the indie publishing cornerstone, Write. Publish. Repeat. and co-host of the Story Studio Podcast.

Originally from Long Beach, California, Sean now lives in Austin, Texas with his wife and two children. He has more than his share of nose.

David W. Wright is the co-author of edge-of-your seat thrillers including the best-selling post-apocalyptic series *Yesterday's Gone*, the paranoid sci-fi *WhiteSpace* series, and the vigilante series, *No Justice*, as well as standalone thrillers *12*, and *Crash* which was recently optioned for a movie.

David is an accomplished, though intermittent, cartoonist who lives in [LOCATION REDACTED] with his wife and son [NAMES REDACTED.]

He is not at all paranoid.

He is "the grumpy one" on the *The Story Studio Podcast* with fellow Sterling and Stone founders, Sean Platt and Johnny B. Truant.

David writes about books, TV shows, movies, and

video games he enjoys; his struggles with anxiety and OCD; writing; and posts the occasional drawing at his personal blog at davidwwright.com

You can email him at david@sterlingandstone.net

We swear, he almost never bites. Unless you feed him after midnight.

For a full list of his most recent books visit sterlingand-stone.net.

The Tomorrow Gene Series

Null Identity

The Tomorrow Gene

The Tomorrow Clone

The Eden Experiment

Karma Police Series

Jumper

Karma Police

The Collectors

Deviant

The Fall

Homecoming

Yesterday's Gone

October's Gone

Yesterday's Gone Season One

Yesterday's Gone Season Two

Yesterday's Gone Season Three

Yesterday's Gone Season Four

Yesterday's Gone Season Five

Yesterday's Gone Season Six

Tomorrow's Gone

Tomorrow's Gone Season One

Tomorrow's Gone Season Two

Tomorrow's Gone Season Three

Available Darkness

Darkness Itself

Available Darkness Book One

Available Darkness Book Two

Available Darkness Book Three

WhiteSpace

WhiteSpace Season One

WhiteSpace Season Two

WhiteSpace Season Three

Stand Alone Novels

Burnout

The Island

Crash

Emily's List

Pattern Black

Devil May Care

The Secret Within

Also By David W. Wright

Z2134

Z2134

Z2135

Z2136

Cold Vengeance

Cold Vengeance

Cold Reckoning

Hidden Justice

Hidden Justice

Hidden Honor

Hidden Shame

Hidden Virtue

No Justice

No Justice

No Escape

No Hope

No Return

No Stopping

No Fear

Karma Police

Jumper

Karma Police

The Collectors

Deviant

The Fall

Homecoming

Yesterday's Gone

October's Gone

Yesterday's Gone Season One

Yesterday's Gone Season Two

Yesterday's Gone Season Three

Yesterday's Gone Season Four

Yesterday's Gone Season Five

Yesterday's Gone Season Six

Tomorrow's Gone

Tomorrow's Gone Season One

Tomorrow's Gone Season Two

Tomorrow's Gone Season Three

Available Darkness

Darkness Itself

Available Darkness Book One

Available Darkness Book Two

Available Darkness Book Three

WhiteSpace

WhiteSpace Season One

WhiteSpace Season Two

WhiteSpace Season Three

Forevermore

ForNevermore Season One

ForNevermore Season Two

ForNevermore Season Three

Stand Alone Novels

12

Crash

Emily's List

Threshold

The Secret Within